GREYPATH

Marie Loerzel

Greypath
© 2018 Marie Loerzel

Printed and bound in the United States of America.
Elemental Press. All rights reserved.

ISBN: 978-0-9912036-2-8 (Paperback)
ISBN: 978-0-9912036-3-5 (eBook)

Cover design by Lisa Perzentka

For my kids,
elements carve their own paths

CHAPTER 1

This wasn't how it was supposed to happen. Not that I devoted any time to researching how it was supposed to go. I've always been far more of a delusion of grandeur kind of girl than a brainy, academic superstar. It didn't matter anyway. All I wanted was the nothingness that was waiting for me at the other end. The particulars of how I got there weren't important. They say the devil is in the details. But, I think we all know the devil was made up by humans, just like god was. Fooling us into believing there's some kind of order to the universe backed by a clandestine logic for why things happen the way they do. Simply, have faith in god, an invisible, omniscient being who can tell the billions of people on the planet apart and love us all individually and unconditionally. If you believe in him and worship him, of course. Unless you fuck up. In which case, you'd better find Jesus fast and repent or you're going straight to hell. That's what I learned from three years of Catholic Sunday school anyway. Guilt and fear. I hadn't thought about St. Christopher's in years. I suppose it's no coincidence under the circumstances. Now that I was going nowhere fast.

At least that was my plan; to fade into oblivion. But, you know what they say about plans: "The best-laid schemes o'mice an' men Gang aft agley." I only remember the quote because I had to memorize it for my high school Lit class a month ago. It loosely translates from the original sleep-inducing poem by Robert Burns into modern day English as, "plans get fucked up a lot." Like now. It should've happened already. I should be dead. Or at least actively in the process of dying. Unless dying is more of a passive kind of thing, which it just might be. I can't really say because I haven't tried to kill myself before, so I don't have any prior experience to draw from. I did take a whole bottle of pills though. Well, the bottle wasn't exactly full. There was about a third of a bottle of prescription sleeping pills that had been sitting in my dad's medicine cabinet for at least ten years. I took what was left of them, but who knows maybe they were expired or something.

What the fuck is wrong with me? Why didn't I go buy the extra large bottle of extra strength Unisom? Right...because I'm a minor and I can't buy sleeping pills over the counter, that's why. There's something about the name Unisom that sounds so peaceful. Like there'd be doves flying and I'd have this whole epiphany of how the universe all really does make sense and you really do get what you deserve and all that new age-y bullshit. Although that would probably have just made me feel like even more of a loser, if that's even possible, and right before I die too. Making the fact that I'm a serial screw-up my last dying thought. Can an overdose of melatonin kill you? I could've gotten some at the health food store. No one would've suspected my malicious intentions with an herbal supplement. Not in the GNC, especially if I bought it with a carob protein shake to build muscle mass. On second thought, that is suspicious. No teenage girl wants to build muscle mass, because muscles add bulk. I should know, I'm seventeen with the body of a thirty-something year old woman who's popped out a few kids already. My stomach is doughy complete with stretch marks, my thighs need their own zip codes and my ass is the complete opposite of anything anyone would call perky. That's why I have some Adderall I bought off of a kid with ADD at school hidden under the holey socks in my dresser to act as a diet aid. In an attempt to create a new reality, one that's much better than what I see when I look at myself in the mirror. Losing weight would change everything, I was sure of it. But, when I took the pills, they didn't seem to suppress my appetite at all. In fact, somehow I seemed to manage to eat even more.

I stood at the sink, took the childproof cap off of the sleeping pills and dumped them on the mauve colored formica vanity in the bathroom. Then downed them one by one with the remnants of a warm, flat Diet Coke I'd picked up at the corner store after school the day before and left on my nightstand overnight. It was easy at first. You'd think swallowing the pills would be the hardest part, but it was getting past the lack of carbonation in the soda that was the most difficult. Everyone knows it's the sensation of the fizz in your mouth and the slight burn on its way down your throat that makes soda so gratifying. But after downing about seven tablets, it started to feel like they were scraping my throat when I swallowed, making it increasingly hard not to gag them back up. Personally, I've never been a fan of pain. If I was going to ingest all these pills, I was going to need some help. I found it on the shelf next to the bottomless jar of Vaseline that lasted my entire childhood; the Chloraseptic spray. All the better, it was even mint flavored, allowing me to pretend my toxic cocktail was peppermint schnapps mixed with Diet Coke.

I'd only had peppermint schnapps at a party once in my sophomore year of high school, which was two years ago now. A whole slew of liquors were sprawled out on the kitchen table of Steve Gibson's house (a senior from my school that I barely knew) with two-liter bottles of soda for mixing. The schnapps seemed the least intimidating, probably because the peppermint reminded me of candy canes. I'd never made myself a drink before, so mixing a tall water glass with half liquor and half Diet Coke seemed reasonable. When all the schnapps was gone, that's when I started doing shots of tequila. I got shit-faced fast and left the party stumbling home drunk, having left my virginity there. But, that's a whole other story for another time.

When I'd taken all the pills, I popped the top back on the empty pill bottle and returned it to it's original spot in the medicine cabinet. Then I walked across the hallway to my bedroom, flopped myself on my bed and covered myself with several layers of scratchy old wool blankets passed down from my grandmother, required amenities for living in an old drafty house. Laying on my back, I stared at the fleur-de-lis design on the wallpaper. Behind my dresser I noticed a tear in the paper that I'd never noticed before, revealing the previous, older wallpaper adorned with pink roses underneath. Why would someone put new wallpaper up over the old paper instead of tearing it down and starting fresh to get a nice smooth finish? It didn't make sense. And how many layers of paper were there underneath that I couldn't see? I lay in bed wondering while waiting to drift off into oblivion.

Time is deceptive, slowing down to a near standstill at times and then spontaneously sprinting forward at others. My heart began beating a bit more rapidly like it did when I took Adderall, except without the hand shakes and inability to focus. No, this was completely different. My body felt heavy as I sunk into the mattress, while my heart pounded wildly in my chest pulsing blood through my body, the sound of it whooshing and reverberating in my ears. This wasn't what I expected at all. My heart should gradually slow down, almost unnoticeably until it finally stops. Not that I'd researched what actually does happen to your body when you take sleeping pills. That seemed like too much work. I wanted a bloodless, uneventful, peaceful death. That's the way I imagined it anyway.

I stopped believing in god when my mom died. What kind of sick, cruel, bastard of a god would take a mother away from her young kids? It just didn't make sense to me. I started to panic. What if all that Catholic bullshit was right after all? What if there is a god? And I've committed suicide, one of the worst sins there is and I was condemned to hell. I'd never see my mother again, who I was positive went to heaven if there is such a place. Who am I kidding? I've always been destined for hell anyway. I've lied, stolen make-up and a pregnancy test from the drug store. The second offense really wasn't my fault because the test wasn't for me, it was for a friend, making it more of an act of charity. So, I think I'd be forgiven for that. Unless I just brought all of this onto myself, which I'm sure I did. Because I just didn't believe enough in anything, most of all, myself.

Think. Think. Think. Isn't there some Catholic loophole where I can just absolve myself of all my sins by repenting or something. No one mentioned it at my First Communion. There's got to be something I can do. Some kind of insurance policy that assures I won't go to hell. Like a life insurance policy, but for death. So no matter if there is or isn't a god, I'm not going to live in eternal damnation. I've been living in temporary part-time damnation for a while now and the whole point of killing myself is to get rid of the suffering, not to live in it for eternity.

"Holy Mary, full of grace........the lord is with thee....."

God dammit! What the hell? What comes next? How does it go? I knew it by heart when I was eight years old just like all the other second graders whose parents had forced them to miss cartoons and spend their Sunday mornings at church instead. All to wear a white dress, eat a horrible stale wafer that stuck to the roof of my mouth at communion and confess all my sins to some stranger I couldn't even see through the confessional window. It could've been Darth Vader on the other side for all I knew. Only I've seen the priests exiting the confessional and they're just mere mortal men wearing dresses. Not that there's anything wrong with that, but what entitles them to front row seating to listen to my litany of sins? In protest of my First Communion and being forced to wear a very itchy tulle dress, I committed a lie of omission. I didn't mention that I wasn't sure I actually believed in god. Not to anyone. Being agnostic wasn't one of the seven deadly sins as far as I know, but I was sure it'd still keep me out of going to heaven. What's the appropriate act of contrition for wavering faith? It was probably a day's worth of Hail Marys. Prayers seemed to be the answer for everything at St. Christopher's church. Which even when I was eight seemed over simplistic in a convoluted and unfair world. But, back then, my lies meant something. That's when things still mattered enough for me to try to protect my family from them even if they weren't true. Back when I still had a mother.

Things were different now. The lies and sins were more menacing than benign. I haven't stepped foot in a church since my mom's funeral. And since I'm not Catholic, I can't absolve myself of them anyway. They'd accumulated into an agglomeration that I allowed to define me. I was a collection of fuck ups that everyone would be better off without. It started with petty theft from drugstores, culminating from my desire to be someone else. I stole all kinds of things I wanted but couldn't afford, but mostly, things no one would even want. Like teal eye liner. I know...what was I thinking? Teal doesn't look good on anyone. Looking back now, I should have pocketed some timeless black eyeliner, which is my staple nowadays. But, I didn't know any better back then. I just happened to be good at it, I offer up the fact that I never got caught as evidence. I don't steal things anymore. Unless you count taking things from my sister, but no one counts that. That's just the price of sisterhood. The progression of where things went from there was far worse. I don't want to get into the details, but I considered it paybacks for my sister's constant intrusion in my life. I still do, but I can see now that some of it was unwarranted, although I'd never tell her that.

At the least, I'm a disappointment and if I'm being completely honest I'm closer to a disaster. Leveling everything in my proximity. I excel at failure. It's what I'm best at. In fact, I'm doing it right now; failing at killing myself. I mean, everybody dies and most people don't even have to try, it's that fucking easy. A lot of people fight valiant battles against death to stay alive. I, on the other hand, invited death in, plodded and waited for the right time when my dad was out of the house for most of the day photographing a wedding to execute my plan. My sister had gotten married and moved out a couple years earlier. It was only after I took the pills that I started overthinking everything. That's how much of a devout loser I am.

I tried to lift my arm, but it felt so heavy I had to lift it from my shoulder, forcing my elbow up, like I did when it fell asleep from me tucking it under my pillow with my heavy head resting on top. I left my dead arm to dangle, using my other arm to bat the covers off the rest of my body. Forcing my weary body out of bed. My legs were too weak to carry me, so I got down on all fours and army crawled to the bathroom like a wounded soldier in battle. The difference being, I chose to do this to myself. What if I didn't die and the pills did something irreparable to my body? Like brain damage and I lived the rest of my life as a vegetable. Or worse, my body was paralyzed, but I was left with an overactive mind. That would be even worse than being dead.

I knew what had to be done. I'd done it before, but only like three times. Ok, ten if I'm being really honest. Maybe even more than that. If you keep a secret from everyone, the numbers don't matter anymore and the truth becomes kinda elastic bending to whatever you want it to be. Nothing matters when you stuff it down far enough anyway. Unless that stuff is too much food. Then, obviously, you need to get rid of it because nothing defines a girl more than her weight. With the obvious exception of the size of her boobs. Being that I'm small breasted with thunder thighs only makes this another lose-lose situation for me. My face isn't doing me any favors either. My prominent, straight beakish nose dominates the rest of my features, overshadowing my green eyes, the only feature I like about myself. And they're not even mine, I acquired them from my mother. She was classically beautiful and bore a striking resemblance to the actress, Gene Tierney, who I saw in the movie Razor's Edge a few years after my mom died and instantly became obsessed with her. I imagined her eyes to be as olive as my mom's, but I don't know if they were because all her movies were in black and white. Turning on the TV and obsessively watching the classic movie channel fueled my fantasies of seeing my mom again even if it was only her doppelganger. Unfortunately, I don't look anything like my mother. My older sister, Lara, was gifted with her genetics, while I take after my dad's side of the family: I'm entirely a Greypath. At six feet tall, my stature makes it impossible for me to go unnoticed. I was constantly asked if I played basketball or volleyball, but I never liked sports and was naturally cumbersome and gawky. Yet another failing on my part.

Resting my head on the cool rim of the porcelain toilet bowl was oddly soothing. That was until I inhaled the putrid stench of the filthy bowl I was supposed to clean but forgot to. When Lara lived at home, I knew that if I left it long enough, she'd become so disgusted and frustrated that eventually, after a long lecture on how gross and lazy I am, she'd do it for me. But, now that she didn't live here anymore, I lived in my own filth. However, this was the first time my apathy turned out to be advantageous. I didn't even need to lift a finger to ram it down my throat in order to empty the contents of my stomach. The foul stench alone was enough to make me puke. Today must be my lucky day.

Once I started I couldn't stop. The retching came in waves until I was empty and left dry heaving with my throat raw from the acid in my stomach. I wanted to be sure the pills were out of my system. Then I cast judgement on everything that I'd spewed out: the pills, the two pieces of white toast I'd slathered with thick slices of cold butter and then the king size Snickers bar I'd eaten for breakfast. Although eating the first meal of the day after 11am probably technically made it brunch, but I wasn't rich or pretentious enough to have brunch.

I'd aborted my suicide attempt. I was clean, absolved, virginal even. I'd redeemed myself. Without the help of anyone and the judgement that would've come with others knowing about it.

I fell asleep on the linoleum floor between the old corroded metal scale used at health clinics and the toilet that was running because I didn't take the top off the tank and reach my hand to jiggle the valve with the balloon thing on it after I'd flushed it. I was awoken by pounding on the bathroom door with a dust bunny stuck to my cheek.

"Henny, are you in there?" Lara's voice yelled while she pounded on the door.

Henny is my nickname. My parents couldn't decide on a name for me, so my dad suggested combining their names Henry and Essie (short for Esther), which is where my name Hennessy, spelled just like the Cognac of the same name, came from. Having a unique name prevented me from finding souvenir coffee mugs and keychains with my name printed on them in tourist traps with gift shops, which is kind of a big deal when you're in middle school. It also made me gender ambiguous on paper. I figure that's the reason why when I got my driver's license it declared I was male even though I clearly checked the female box.

"No." I shouted back, relieved I had locked the door out of habit even though no one else was home, though I couldn't remember having done it. What was she doing here anyway?

Lara had a deceptively loud and threatening knock for someone with the waifish body of a ballet dancer. It was only befitting she was named after a ballerina that my mother, who was very cultured, admired, while I was given a fancy name for brandy. My sister is beautiful, delicate and refined. And I'm androgynous, brutish and slovenly, with a propensity to burn your throat and induce poor decisions. It was my destiny to be this way I guess.

"What are you doing? You're supposed to be at work." She asked accusingly through the door.

"I'm dead." I said only half joking.

"You wish!" She said like she knew what I'd done.

"You know my work schedule now? Are you keeping tabs on my period now too? By the way, we need more super tampons. Can you put that on your shopping list?"

"Your sarcasm won't protect you. And your boss has been calling my cell phone looking for you, that's how I know. I tried calling you several times and when you didn't answer, I dropped what I was doing to come check on your sorry ass. Seriously, I don't know how you even have a job, much less keep it. God, you're so irresponsible!"

"Can you call her back and tell her I have the flu?"

"Really Henny? You overslept again didn't you? If you didn't stay up so late doing god knows what you do, you could get up in time for work at noon."

"I didn't oversleep this time. I'm sick. Really. Call her and tell her I have the flu. It's the last time I'll ask you for anything. I promise!"

I couldn't dispute that I was completely irresponsible and didn't deserve my job. I wasn't even looking for a job, it just fell in my lap. I was at the mall, which was simply a convenient meeting point for my friend Tonya and me, as it was about halfway between our houses. A lot of the stores at the mall had closed down a few years ago when the Ford plant that employed most of the population left the city of Lostport because they started outsourcing their jobs overseas. As usual, I had arrived at our predesignated meeting place predictably early. Waiting for Tonya, who was habitually late to show, across from the defunct pay phone located down a dimly lit and unfrequented hallway of the East restrooms. I don't know what it is about public pay phones that pacifies me. Maybe it's knowing it will never ring again; a useless abandoned artifact that no one has any expectations of. I sat slumped against the wall, retrieving my sketch pad and pencil out of my messenger bag I bought at the army surplus store and carried with me everywhere. My dirty blonde hair, too dark to make me look entitled, too light for me to be taken seriously, cropped into a short edgy cut with longer pieces framing my face and falling into my eyes. I was wearing my usual uniform of a men's baggy, shapeless t-shirt and abused jeans with black engineer boots completing my lesbian-ish vibe. I sat etching the outline of the public phone, intricately shading the receiver and the buttons. No matter how many times I drew it, it never looked right.

"You sixteen?" A woman's voice startled me as I sat lost in my drawing.

"Look I'm not bothering anyone, ok?" I said with my head still buried in my sketch pad.

"Didn't accuse you of anything. Looks like you have some time on your hands." She said with a gravely voice.

I looked up to see a thin woman, who appeared to be in her 60's with wavy grey hair in a disheveled bob with friendly blue eyes and fine pucker lines around her mouth from years of smoking.

"I'm waiting for someone." I said dismissively.

"Aren't we all? See that T-shirt cart over there called The Sweatshop? That's mine. Had an employee who didn't show up for work today. If you're sixteen the job is yours."

"Ok...I guess." I said after a long pause.

That's how I met Amitty and got my first job selling graphic T-shirts and sweatshirts from a small cart in the middle of the mall. Working at The Sweatshop afforded me lots of free time to doodle and sketch. I drew the empty store fronts, but my favorite thing to sketch was the barren circular racks locked inside of them. Sometimes I'd get ambitious and try my hand at drawing the people I saw around mall. The shopkeepers hoisting the garage style gates to their stores open, teenagers hanging out at the food court after school, mothers coaxing their kids to go to 'just one more store' and then, the old people walking laps around everyone else. I was a voyeur watching life pass me by from the middle of the Lostport Mall.

CHAPTER 2

My father used to be a vibrant force. You could feel his energy when he walked into a room. No one could help but notice him and it was more than his commanding six foot four frame. It was a humble confidence and the way he made everyone around him instantly comfortable with his timid, but knowing smile. He'd always been soft spoken, frequently lost in thought and usually at a loss for words, as if they were too constrictive for him.

My mother, on the other hand, surrounded herself with words. Although she was shy like my father, she found solace in words. The walls of my parent's bedroom were lined with a fortress of my mother's books meticulously organized by genre on the shelves. When the shelves became overburdened, the newest acquisitions were haphazardly stuffed sideways to lay on top of the other books, filling every inch of allowable space on the bowing bookcases. Most of her book collection was comprised of books from the library where she worked that she had rescued when they were slated to be discarded because of missing pages and/or broken bindings. The old books and the dust they accumulated contributed to the musty library smell of our decrepit turn of the century house, which in hindsight might be why I was chronically congested and had a lot of respiratory infections a kid. Even with the smell and a bit of shortness of breath now and again, there was something comforting about my mother's stacks of books. I think part of what made them so soothing was that I always knew where to find her. In the corner of her bedroom her legs tucked up on the seat of the armchair with her head stuck in a book a world away. Her light brown hair twisted into a makeshift bun and fastened with a pencil. Sometimes she'd hastily pull the pencil out of her hair to underline a passage or make a note in the margins of a book, her hair cascading down into loose waves falling just below her shoulders. That's when I thought she looked the most beautiful, when she was contemplative and thought no one was looking. But, I was always looking. Sneaking around corners to catch glimpses of my mother whom I idolized.

My feelings toward my sister, Lara, who was four years older than me, were completely the opposite; she was my archenemy. Mostly, because I didn't exist in her world except when I was irritating her. If I was going to stay relevant to her, my role was pretty obvious. I was in the third grade when I decided it was my calling in life to torment her. Turns out, tormenting a girl who's in middle school is a really low commitment operation and only takes a minute or two a day, which is a good thing because I'm nothing if not lazy. When I saw her type in her Facebook password, I filed it away in my memory to use at a later time. Later that week, I logged in to her account and posted "I love Brad Givens" as her status update. Which in my defense, was completely true. It wasn't, however, common knowledge, especially to Brad's girlfriend Jenny. That's when Jenny started rumors that Lara had a STD. Because that's how girls settle things like this, by systematically destroying the reputation of their competitor. Of course, I didn't plan on things going that far. And back then, I didn't even know what a STD was, so I didn't even know the extent of the emotional damage I'd caused. All that mattered was that Lara was paying attention to me.

There were no conversations between Lara and me. Only disagreements, spats, arguments and full-on fights. It was impossible for us to get along; we were complete opposites after all. She was the perfect daughter: beautiful, studious, athletic and kind. Lara made everything she did look easy, which made me think it was. I, on the other hand, overthought everything. From my inadequate, boyish looks and lack of academic discipline to my disinterest in sports and incurable mischievous curiosity. I was the let down of the family. No one ever said that I was, but they didn't have to. I knew it. Truth doesn't need words the way lies do. As a chronic liar, I can attest to that. My lies weren't malicious or anything like that and they didn't hurt anyone. That's what I told myself anyway. I did it to boost my self esteem. With just a bit of deceit, I was a much better, more acceptable version of myself. One who did her homework and chores. The liar in me never skipped early morning swim lessons in a frigid outdoor pool, choosing instead to ride her bike to the nearby park, but only after stopping at the corner store to buy candy with money stolen from my mother's wallet. Although I'd also steal from my dad or Lara, I wasn't really too picky on who was funding my junk food addiction. The thing was, I was really good at deception and rarely got caught; maybe at a ratio of one in ten offenses, which are really good odds when you think about it. With such a great success rate, there was no motivation on my part to change my ways. Not only did it work for me, lying and stealing also gave me a sense of independence, even though I knew I was completely dependent on sponging off my family.

Everyone in my family was simply too busy to notice any inconsistencies with me. My sister's life was cheerleading and all the social obligations that go along with being popular and in demand. My mother worked full-time and my dad was gone a lot for his job. He was a photographer for the small time Lostport News up until a few years ago when he got a job at the Niagara Falls Gazette which has a much larger circulation. He'd take photos of the falls frozen over in the winter and the daredevils who wanted their shot at fifteen minutes of fame by trying to go over the falls in a barrel, canoe or trying to tightrope over it during the balmy summer months. Then his big break came. He took a photo during a brutal snow storm that stretched across the Northeast last winter of a homeless woman sitting on a park bench wrapped in layers of blankets, covered in snow and the photo went viral. After that, new and decidedly bizarre opportunities opened up for him and he started flying to New York City a few times a month to so photoshoots for Vogue magazine.

It was an especially odd turn of events because my father had no fashion sense himself whatsoever. He'd worn a white button down shirt, Levi's jeans with a brown belt in the same matching shade of brown to match his oxford boots. His silver Timex watch on his wrist ticking away every second rather emphatically ever since I can remember. In winter he'd wear a gray wool v-neck sweater and in summer, a short sleeve button down shirt in a subdued black and gray plaid. He could have been wearing the same exact clothes for years. Or maybe when he found something that fit his substantial frame at the Big and Tall store he just bought multiples of the same thing. Either way, I liked the consistency of it and that I could easily pick him out of a crowd, made even easier by the fact that he towered over everyone else. Not that we went out anywhere where there were crowds with any regularity because we didn't. There were no amusement parks, movies, parades or other special occasions where we'd go out as a family because my dad wasn't a fan of these kind of frivolities and even less of a fan of crowds.

Funny thing is, people are drawn to reserved individuals like my dad. Something about their restrained demeanor has a soothing effect that mimics a zen-like enlightenment kind of feel. Which wasn't my dad at all. He was a conventional, old-fashioned guy. The only crowd he'd make an exception for was weekly mass Saturday nights at St. Christopher's. Choosing to go on Saturday evenings because Sunday morning mass drew an even bigger crowd. And even then, we'd arrive late and leave early to avoid idle chit chat from other parishioners and getting stuck in traffic in the parking lot. I never paid much attention at church, but I did spend a lot of time studying the statue of Jesus on the alter and being really impressed by his abs. Even though I was distracted, I knew exactly when it was time to sit, kneel or stand and I could do the sign of the cross faster than anyone else at church. I'd pick a person at random and then race them in my head providing a welcome diversion from my boredom. Church seemed like a total waste of my time. Time that I could be wasting doing absolutely anything else. One of my favorite ways to spend time was looking through my mom and dad's old pictures. It fascinated me to think that they had lives before Lara and I came along.

Flipping through the pages of my parents' wedding album was like looking at two completely different people. My mom wore an ivory wedding dress the day she married my dad. She said her mother disapproved of it because it was off-white and she was embarrassed and ashamed that everyone would think her daughter had a reputation. The satin bodice had a scoop neckline with slight cap sleeves and a full tulle tea-length skirt, her flaxen hair tucked into chignon adorned with one gardenia like Billie Holiday in lieu of a veil and small drop pearl earrings that highlighted her long, elegant neck and uncomplicated beauty. Ballet flats completed her transformation into the ballerina she'd always longed to be. My dad anchoring her next to him with his arm wearing a single breasted black suit with a slender gray tie. There was nothing complicated or fussy to distract from their combined beauty. They looked so young, confident and unfettered in the photos taken that day. I'd never seen them look that way. The last photo in the album is of my dad scooping my mom in his arms leaving the reception hall. She was clutching her small bouquet of gardenias in her hands with her bare feet dangling haphazardly over my dad's arm. His suit jacket was off exposing his white buttoned down shirt with his collar and tie loosened looking adoringly at my mother while she coyly averted his gaze.

***

My parents were always a mystery to me. Never more than the day that changed everything. I wasn't home when it happened. After I stole some money from the change jar kept in the kitchen next to the phone, I took off on my bike; it was the ultimate freedom. Eventually, I rode to the corner store to score some junk food where I was such a regular, that the old man Joe who owned the place always felt compelled to make small talk with me. "Here's Henny with her pennies", he'd always say. Adults were always commenting that I was a sullen kid and then they'd go out of their way to try to make me smile. Throwing an unconvincing smirk his way was just the price of doing business with him. But, I was irritated that I had to play this little game with him and that he always called me by a nickname I hate. I'm sure he overheard me being called Henny from the other kids at school who frequented the place because of it's close proximity to the elementary school, because I sure never offered it up. I'd try to sneak in quickly and go undetected, avoiding eye contact and heading straight to my target.

Usually a king size Twix and some potato chips; sometimes plain, sometimes salt and vinegar, depending on my mood. There was just something about candy that left me craving something salty afterward; something to cancel out the sweetness. The combination left me satisfied with a belly full of empty calories. Sometimes I'd take my stash to the park with me to savor it. And sometimes on particularly brisk days, I'd devour it on my way out of the store, standing between the set of double doors at the entrance trying to soak in the warmth, like I did that day.

I sped off on my bike, pedaling as fast as my legs would allow, headed for the neighborhood park, specifically the big tractor tire anchored into the sand that I considered to be my own private hideout. It was a bitter January day, the air was especially dry and unsettled. The wind whipped between the houses and across the open field at the park, blowing directly into my face, preventing me from catching my breath, leaving me gasping for air between gusts. Even huddled up inside of my refuge sheltered from the elements, it was too frigid to be outside, so I headed for home. A combination of a thin layer of ice on the sidewalk and riding directly into the wind, forced me to walk my bike home. It was only about a half mile, but with the brutal, wintry conditions, I could barely feel my fingers and toes and not much of anything between them either. I thought I was numb, but that would mean I didn't feel anything and I was feeling sharp excruciating pin pricks in my extremities. Right before I got stabbed in the heart.

There were fresh tire tracks in the snow and my dad's car was parked hastily in the center of the driveway in the middle of the day. I took off my jacket and sneakers leaving them in a damp heap in the entry way headed for the kitchen to put the kettle on for some hot chocolate to help warm me up. Lara was slumped at the kitchen table with her head down resting on top of her folded arms. Her baggy sweater leaving just enough of a gap to easily stick my icy hand in and rub it up her back to make her scream. But this time, she didn't react to my attempt at torturing her. Instead, she raised her head slowly and deliberately. Revealing her swollen, bloodshot eyes.

"Where've you been?" She asked in a motherly tone.

"What do you care?" I asked indignantly.

"Henny, you've been gone for hours." She said softly with a concern in her voice that I'd never heard before.

"Since when do you care if I'm gone for hours?" Before I'd gone to the store, I was over playing at a classmate's house a few streets over. I knew I wasn't allowed to be over at her house, which is why I didn't tell anyone where I was going. I didn't know the reason at the time. It was several years later that I learned her stepfather was accused of sexual abuse.

"Look, it doesn't matter right now. Come here, I need to tell you something." She said with an outstretched arm urging me closer to her.

"Since when do you tell me things?" I asked suspiciously.

"Mom's gone."

"To the store?" I asked confused.

"No. She's dead. She died."

Everything moved in slow motion. Lara's lips and the fluttering of her eyelashes when she blinked. The room seemed to spin around making me dizzy. My feet felt as though they were anchored in concrete and my arms were dangling weightless.

I was ten when my mom died suddenly and unexpectedly from a brain aneurism. My dad died that day too. Not literally, but figuratively; slowly retreating into himself. My sister was fourteen when she almost immediately assumed the role of my evil stepmother, like she was born to play the part. My dad stopped traveling and pursuing fashion photography or much else. He took up residence in the solitude of the darkroom he'd built to develop his photographs in the basement. Surrounded by the chemicals that transformed brown film into beautiful portraits of all of life's happy events: weddings, graduations, newborn babies and expanding families while he was consumed with his misery. In his darkroom he could observe life from a safe distance. Even the lives of his daughters.

After a few years of grieving, we came to terms with the fact that she was never coming back. At least Lara and I did. My dad never seemed to move past the denial stage. Her clothes hung in the closet next to his, her voice was still on the greeting of the answering machine and he faithfully slept only on his side of the bed, as if her ghost were lying next to him every night. But the truth was, her spirit lingered in the house because he was determined not to let her go. Because then she'd be gone forever. He was Catholic, so he believed in heaven and hell and all that. He just believed she was going to heaven and he wasn't. I guess the apple doesn't fall far from the tree. Since he couldn't be with her in life or death, he seemed to settle for occupying the same space that she once did. After a few years, Lara and I thought maybe he'd find someone to fill the void, even if that wasn't us. But, he made it clear that no one compared to the memories of our mother.

Of course, early on, I did everything to prevent him from moving on. Because I was angry and what the fuck did I know? I was just a little kid without a mom. Sure this kind of thing happens every day somewhere in the world, but not to me. Leaving my dad with a teenaged daughter overcompensating for the tragedy of her mother's death, Lara, and an angst-filled tween consumed with questions, moi. I read the outdated encyclopedias and antiquated dictionaries that were in my mom's stockpile of books searching for answers. But, all I found was the definition for pusillanimous, \pyoo-suh-LAN- uh-mus\ adjective; 1. lacking courage or resolution; cowardly; faint-hearted; timid. 2. proceeding from or indicating a cowardly spirit. It defined me. Hennessy\ proper noun Pusillanimous Hennessy "Henny" Greypath.

I turned eleven years old unceremoniously three months after my mother passed away. There was something so lonely looking about the number eleven. A one standing next to another identical number one, but with what seemed like a huge gap between them. At least I scored an i-pod out of the whole birthday deal, even if it was a guilt gift from my dad, something to help make up for my loss. Putting my earbuds in meant I could disengage from the world and be alone even when I was in a room full of people. I found myself drawn to mournful songs about the meaningless and urgency of life like "Indifference" by Pearl Jam and "Fly on the Windscreen" by Depeche Mode, sinking deeper into my own grief and subsequent depression.

It was a warm day in May when I came home from school early because we had a half day for some reason or another. I had my ear buds in and walked through the back door directly into the kitchen. That's where I saw them. My dad was kissing Mrs. Everet, our neighbor from two doors over who had two nerdy teenage boys, not to mention a husband.

I dropped my backpack, it thumped on the linoleum floor with the weight of my text books.

"What THE hell?" I shouted. Eyeing Mrs. Everet with her over-processed blonde hair and gaudy pink lipstick wearing a blue flower print Land's End sundress and Teva sandals.

I'd obviously startled them.

"I just dropped off a casserole for your family, sweetie. My you've grown into a beautiful woman! What are you sixteen now?" She said, making an obvious attempt to suck up to me.

That's when I reached down into my backpack and pulled out the first thing my hand could grasp. An old worn paperback copy of *Deenie* by Judy Blume with the pages curled up. I'd traded my friend Jodi a green bikini top of Lara's for it in a thing we called the Dirty Deeds Exchange. And I threw the book right in Beatrice's face. Beatrice was Mrs. Everet's first name, although everyone called her Bea.

"Henny, don't do this to yourself." My dad said.

What? I wasn't doing anything to myself.

"I'm doing it to that slut." I said pointing to Beatrice.

I'd overheard Lara's friends call someone a slut, although I didn't know what it meant, I knew it was really bad. And I loved how such a short, uncomplicated word rolled off my tongue and packed such a punch. I knew it had a lot of power and it made me feel powerful to say it. It didn't matter what it meant or if it was true or not. This is when I started to refer to her as Beatrix, which gave her a much more villainous sound. In later years, I shortened it to "Trixie", which made her sound like she was either a sorority girl or a prostitute and neither connotation was good as far as I was concerned.

I boycotted the tuna casserole she'd made for us for dinner and went on a hunger strike. It only lasted a night, but I still think I made my point.

CHAPTER 3

er face had a reddish tinge like she either had one long continuous sunburn or she was an aged alcoholic. She tried to cover up the pock marks left by cystic acne on her cheeks with a thick layer of foundation. Her long straight dark brown hair had scant fringy bangs she was always brushing away from her secretive brown eyes accentuated with black eyeliner. That was her signature look. Tonya had a badass Chrissie Hynde kinda vibe and she was my best friend.

"You can go back and see her now," the heavyset nurse said.

I couldn't think of anything I wanted to do less in that moment than see her, because I didn't know what I was going to say. It was one of those extremely awkward occasions I wish there was a line of hilarious socially inappropriate greeting cards for so I could let it do the talking for me. But, I don't think you can make abortion funny.

"She's in exam room #3, it's down the hall to the right all the way at the end," the nurse said in a soft buttery, soothing voice.

Tonya was lying on the exam table on her side, fully dressed facing the wall. I could hear her sobbing quietly when I entered the room. When she heard my footsteps she wiped her eyes and turned over onto her other side to face me. The paper liner on the exam table crunching as she propped her elbow on the table and rested her head in her hand. Her face was even more blotchy and red than usual. Her black eyeliner smeared from wiping the tears from her eyes, making her look like a strung out heroin addict.

"How was it?" I asked. It was a stupid thing to say, but they were the only words that came to my head.

She sat up slowly allowing her legs to dangle over the edge while her hands gripped the side of the table next to her knees before second guessing herself and then folding her arms in front of her.

"There's this machine that's like a vacuum and they suck it out. Had I known that, I probably could've done it myself with a Dyson. What if the doctor didn't get it? What if I'm still pregnant?" Her voice wavered with emotion.

"I don't know. Do they sell prom dresses in the maternity section?" I regretted saying it as soon as it came out of my mouth and held my breath waiting for her response.

I was relieved when she laughed.

"You could get a white dress and a scarlet 'A' on it and go to prom stag all Hester Prynne-esque. Bonus, no one else will be wearing the same dress to prom. So there won't be any drama about that. You'd be memorable. You might even get your picture in the yearbook. Think about it, maybe you'd even be popular enough to win prom queen!" I deadpanned.

When she snort laughed I knew it was just the comic relief she needed to break the somber mood.

Truth was, Tonya was already pretty popular. But not the enviable kind of popular my sister Lara was back in high school. Tonya was popular for all of the wrong reasons with all the wrong people: the stoners, misfits, dropouts, outcasts and me. She was the queen of the losers and I was her sidekick, making me the ultimate loser.

"Let's go grab some pizza", she said.

"Let me just take you home. Post abortion protocol calls for rest and I dunno... eating chicken noodle soup with saltines and ginger ale or something like that."

"God Hennessy, I'm not sick with the flu! I need to celebrate that this is over and move on with my life. Plus, I'm starving."

I hadn't expected an impromptu post abortion pizza party downtown at Pie Town, the best New York style pizza joint in all of Lostport. My expectations were more along the lines of soap opera style drama, existential questions and regret. Definitely a lot of regret. But, it wasn't my abortion, so who was I to judge her indifference or how she seemed to compartmentalize and rationalize the whole thing. It was like she didn't feel anything. And that's when I realized she wasn't as fierce as I thought she was. In fact, she was just like me. Avoiding her feelings and fearing rejection the way I did. Only she was much better at it than me. And more tragic, as it would turn out later.

———————

Amitty had arranged everything. Not only was she born and raised in Lostport, but she also owned a business and was married to a drug addict. No one knew the city or it's seedy undercurrent quite the way she did. The Sweatshop, her T-shirt cart business, helped supplement her income after her husband went on disability after a motorcycle accident a few years earlier, which left him with an addiction to the prescription painkiller, OxyContin. I knew her frequent visits to The Sweatshop during my shift to restock and do inventory were just a ploy to get away from her husband. That the mall and the usual (and unusual) characters who frequented it acted as a diversion from her failing marriage. It was an interactive soap opera of sorts for her. It was when Tonya stopped to talk to me at work after she took the pregnancy test I'd stolen for her from CVS. I was the only friend Tonya had that she trusted enough to confide in. That's when Amitty figured out Tonya was pregnant and when she told us her story and offered her help.

"It was the late 60s", she said. "Everything was changing and yet everything was exactly the same as it had always been. Supposedly, it was a time of freedom and rebellion, but the same patriarchal standards still applied to women. Janis Joplin was our hero. But we all knew, society's gold standard for women was Jackie Kennedy, who ironically was married to the most powerful philanderer in the world. Which was sad and pathetic. But, what was even more goddamn pathetic was that we all wanted to be her. And our mothers wanted that for us even more than we did. Mothers always want their daughters to achieve the things they couldn't. I never took a test, never went to the doctor. I didn't need to, I already knew. So did most of my high school. The girlfriend I'd confided in told another friend. The way all gossip starts I suppose. Dean was a college boy and back then when I was 16, he was a man as far as I was concerned. I didn't know that some boys never become men no matter how old they are. And I thought that since he was a college boy that that was some kind of guarantee that he'd do the right thing for some reason. But, he just ran scared when I told him. Disappeared into thin air. My god I was so stupid. Heard years later he became a lawyer.

My mother took charge of the situation. She sent me away to her distant cousin Abby's house in Virginia to provide a cover for my pregnancy so she could keep up appearances for the neighbors. She told them I was going to a private finishing school there. She told me my 'Aunt' Abby was a nurse so she'd be better prepared to care for me in my condition than she could. When I got there my 'Aunt' was older than the dirt floor in her basement. She could barely care for herself, let alone me. I begged my mom to let me come back home crying to her over the phone, but she insisted this is what was best for me and the baby I'd be forced to give up for adoption. I think my mother half believed the fabrication that I was in finishing school over the truth. She never acknowledged I was pregnant. Denial is the strongest drug there is.

Those were the worst five months of my life. Caring for an old, ungrateful woman I wasn't even sure how I was related to. All while carrying a baby I had grown to love inside me that I was being forced to give away to strangers. I never met the adoptive parents, didn't even know their names. I just heard through Vera, at the adoption agency that they were a young couple that couldn't have children of their own. Which left me plenty of room to fill in the gaps of the story with all the childish fantasy I needed to believe. That my baby would be better with them. That they could love her more than I could because there were two of them and only one of me. My mother said I was too young to know what love was. And since there was nothing and no one to tell me otherwise, I believed her.

My daughter was born on my own birthday, May 25th. The only birthday gift I got when I turned seventeen was being her mother for an hour. I nestled her into my chest while she suckled. It wasn't popular to breast feed back then, but it came natural to me and it was the only thing I had to give her. I named her Hope. I knew her adoptive parents would give her another name, but seeing as though I didn't know who they were, it didn't matter much to me what they'd call her. That's how adoptions worked back then, the records were sealed. My mother said giving up Hope was my second chance, but it didn't feel like that when I handed my baby back to the nurse who gave her to her new family. Funny thing about second chances, sometimes you just make the same mistakes over again because the lesson wasn't done with you yet."

———

The only thing I was sure about was that I didn't want to be a mother. You're either a nurturer or you're not. And I was nothing short of a cold-blooded killer. At the age of seven, I murdered my guinea pig, Fluffernutter (Fluffy for short). I snuck him out of the house and took him on a field trip to the playground, sending him down the big slide. I was probably just bored, but I convinced myself it would be fun for him. He didn't die right away, he lay there at the end of the slide on the dirt packed down by years of pounding by the treads of kids' sneakers, twitching. I didn't know what to do. I was too disgusted to pick him up in his condition. And I further rationalized that moving him in any way would probably just injure him more. But really, that was just a way to make myself feel better about walking away and doing nothing. Leaving me feeling guilty and ashamed. Meet denial: my new coping mechanism.

That's why I never questioned Tonya. I never asked her anything about her pregnancy or abortion, including who the father was. It didn't occur to me she felt anything. One time I found a picture of my sister Lara at about the age of four on the deck of the Maid of the Mist with Niagara Falls in the background. My sister was dressed in a yellow raincoat, her eyes squinted from the dew in the air. Her blonde hair in soft damp ringlets, one hand outstretched above her head into the mist and the other one reaching for the pinky finger of my dad's huge hand. Since my dad was a photographer, he was usually behind the camera taking the picture, but this was one of the few photos taken by my mom who was pregnant with me at the time. I'd only realized that the photo was stolen from our family photo album when I discovered it under Tonya's bed.

It wasn't the only time she'd stolen things from my house. There was a $2 bill that she'd also pocketed. I'd gotten it in a birthday card from mother's sister, my Aunt Evelyn, who passed away from breast cancer a couple months after she sent it to me. The next time I saw a $2 bill, Tonya and I were at a gas station and she was reaching into her wallet to buy a pack of Marlboros with a fake ID. The cashier who'd never seen $2 bill before called the manager over to see if it was a real acceptable form of payment. That's not all, there were other things over the years; odd things. A plaid collapsible umbrella and a paperweight I made for my dad in grade school. And those are just things I'd found at her house. Who knew if she'd taken other items and had them stashed away somewhere. Her reaction to me finding stolen mementos of my childhood was always the same. Nothing. She didn't offer up any explanations or excuses. She'd simply say, "take it".

She saved her breath for more valiant pursuits; namely boys. Particularly the boys of particular interest to other girls. Why I told her about my crush on Owen, the twenty-something year old guy with wavy blond hair and light eyes donning a mysterious limp, who worked at the same library my mom had before she died. There was just something about him. I'd stand at the row of computers in front of the circulation desk pretending to look up a book in the database while stealing sideways glances at him to see if he was watching me. He never was. Which made me crush on him even harder. I needed to get closer to him. To confirm definitively whether his eyes were blue or grey. I needed to know if he had a girlfriend. Did he go for sophisticated brunettes or snarky, depressed dirty blondes? Also, did he like mustard or mayonnaise on his sandwich. I wanted to know everything about him. Including where he lived because fourteen year old girls are stalky like that.

Tonya beat me to it.

"Henny, he's a loser, I don't know what you even see in that man-boy gimp. He works at the library and still lives with his mother." She said.

"He has a job. And a mom. Not everyone does you know? That doesn't make him a loser." I said defending him.

"That's not how I meant it and you know it."

"How did you mean it then?"

"He's not worth you fawning over him and making a spectacle of yourself."

"It's gotta be the quietest spectacle in history then, because I don't even talk to him. And if I did I'd whisper because he works at the library!"

"Ok, (exhale) I didn't want to tell you this, but I saw him in a parked car on Main street on Friday night. He pulled up to the corner and a guy got in the passenger's seat of the car and then Owen leaned over and kissed him. Turns out, he plays for the home team. You never stood a chance. I'm telling you this for your own good."

Whenever someone says they're telling you something for your own good, it's a lie. Also, the entire story was a lie she'd made up because she'd developed a crush on Owen herself.

CHAPTER 4

"You're listed in her will as the guardian for the kids." My dad announced in the same way he'd deliver the weekly weather forecast or any other random, inconsequential fact.

I was twenty-two and I could barely care for myself, let alone three little kids. Where was their father anyway? As if he was even there for them from the start. My sister's marriage was shaky from the beginning. In high school they were the "it" couple. The only requirement to achieve the honor of being the "it couple" is winning the genetic lottery, which they both did. Everyone in high school wants a couple to pin their hopes and dreams on, living vicariously through them. Before they come to despise them and their coveted "it" status secretly hoping they'll break up. At Lostport High School that couple was Lara and Rick. They dated their junior and senior years and after they graduated, when everyone else was packing up to head off to college, they got married at the courthouse downtown, just the two of them. They got divorced at the same courthouse eight years, three kids, and one stage IV breast cancer diagnosis later.

It was after Rick left Lara for another woman he'd been having an affair with that their marriage ended. That's when I started referring to him as Dickhead and also, when I started to get to know Lara, my sister, who I'd spent years both envying for her beauty and despising for her role as my evil stepmother. It began innocently enough as pure pity on my part. Like a Lifetime movie where one tragedy is compounded by the next and just when the heroine can't take anymore, she gets this newfound spirituality and turns her life around becoming a famous yoga instructor who inspires others to live their best life by becoming more bendy and going vegan or something along those lines. Except my sister didn't have an inspirational happy ending, she died. I always thought she lived a charmed life; that everything came easy to her. It turns out, she had a train wreck of a life. Then she died suddenly at the tragically young age of twenty-six from the brutally belligerent cancer that claimed her. She was twelve years younger than my mother was when she died. But, instead of leaving two kids behind, Lara left three. And her incapable, immature, serial screw-up of a sister to care for them.

"I can't do it, Dad! I'm not like her. I don't even like kids." I said.

"You're right, you're not anything like your sister. You two were always completely different from each other. She always did the right thing and tried to make everyone else happy. But you...you're more independent and stubborn. That's what they need right now. They need you. They're your nephews and niece and I know you love them."

"Of course I love them. But, I've only ever babysat them for a few hours at a time when Lara was going through chemo. I couldn't even fill two or three hours, I mostly sat them in front of the TV and they still drove me insane. I've never been so happy to go back to my apartment alone. I don't know how to raise kids. And if they lived with me, I'd have no apartment to go back to. No escape. I can't take care of them. Not the way someone else could."

"I know what it's like to feel like you aren't qualified to be raising kids. My biggest regret is that I wasn't a good father. You can't go back and make it up. I'm not much help now either at almost sixty years old with a heart condition that slows me down. I can't keep up with three young kids. Rick is MIA and we both know he's unstable and unreliable. I don't know if he has family to take them, but I know Lara wouldn't want Rick or his family to have custody of the kids. That's why she named you as their guardian Henny."

They were the most revealing and confessional words my dad had ever spoken about his own parenting or lack thereof, wedged between his honest plea for me to take my sister's kids in and keep the little family we had left together.

"Maxwell, for the love of god, stop opening and closing the freakin' car door already! Somebody's gonna get their fingers stuck in there. Right about now, I hope it's you and not your brother or your sister because maybe you need to learn this lesson the hard way." I scolded my oldest nephew.

It was only my third day of being a guardian and I'd already resorted to calling Max by his full name when he pissed me off. Which was constantly. Kindergarten had clearly gone to his head. That kid thought he was the CEO of the house, asserting control over Jackson, his brother who was only one year younger than him. They both had the same dark unruly wavy hair, mischievous eyes and face full of freckles. But, their relationship with each other was antagonistic bordering on co-dependent. Not only was Max bossy, he was also assertive to a fault. When Jack was too lazy to make a truck out of Legos, he'd whine to manipulate Max into doing it for him. Thank god for the school bus that picked Max up in the morning giving the rest of us a seven and a half hour reprieve from his tyrannical tendencies. With Max gone, Jack got free reign on exploiting his two and a half year old sister, Casey. She was beautiful, like her mother with wavy blonde hair and brazen green eyes. Born with looks that gave her the biological advantage to coerce people into taking care of her. Some girls make it through their entire lives using nothing more than their good looks as currency to carry them through. Not Casey though. Even as a toddler she was tenacious and fiercely independent. She was a lot like me in that way.

"Where the fuck did I put my art stuff?" I asked while searching the apartment for cardboard boxes I'd stored my random sketches in over the years.

"Watch your mouth, there are children present!" Jay, my roommate reprimanded me.

I met him in a bar a couple of years before, having just been ditched by my girlfriend, Nicole, for a guy she just met and left with, leaving me stranded. Jay was standing at the bar. A bit over six feet tall with sandy brown hair, green eyes and thick brooding, bad boy eyebrows and lips that moved deliberately around his words, "Molson Dry" when he ordered from the bartender. His choice of beer was my first clue that he was Canadian. His arms rested on the bar while he waited, forcing him to stoop a bit, giving me a great view of his perfectly round ass in the American Eagle jeans he was wearing with a gray T-shirt and a bit of a pretentious attitude. I had "slutted up" at Nicole's insistence before we left the apartment we shared together to head out for the night. I reluctantly agreed to let her choose my outfit for the occasion, reasoning that she had far more experience with guys than me and I suspected dressing trashy had more than a little to do with her success. She insisted I borrow her leather skirt, and somehow I managed to squeeze my fat ass into it, even though it was much shorter and more revealing on my six foot frame than her average sized five foot five one. I accessorized it with a Jimi Hendrix T-shirt and my engineer boots, which by this point were battered from years of wear. But, even all slutted up, I still felt insecure and transparent.

I was nineteen which was the legal drinking age in Canada and only a convenient five minute drive from where I lived in Niagara Falls over the bridge to the other side of the border. There wasn't enough liquor to make me outgoing and flirtatious, but it didn't stop me from trying. "Hennessy", I said shouting to be heard over the music. I'd never had cognac before, I was just ordering it to get his attention. Which it did. Before the night was over, he took me back to his place. Where I found myself in his bed. Passed out after I'd puked on his rug next to the night stand. Jay chose to sleep alone on the couch. Not only because he's a gentlemen and I was repulsively drunk off my ass, which I was, but also because he's gay. Of course, I didn't know that at the time.

Somehow the fact that he wasn't even remotely attracted to women didn't stop me from lusting after him. It might have even fueled it. Maybe, he'd never been with a girl before and wanted to try it. He had. Maybe she wasn't the right girl and I am. He doesn't like girls you idiot. Despite my ulterior motives to make him switch teams and fall in love with me, we became friends. I must be a great actress because Jay was oblivious to the fact that I was completely obsessed with him. Then, when he gave up on his dream to move to Toronto to open his own restaurant and I gave up on my delusion to move to New York City to pursue who the hell knows what, he got a job as a sous chef on the American side of the border. Nicole had just moved out of the apartment we shared in Niagara Falls and moved in with some guy named Troy she'd met the week before. I needed a roommate to make rent and Jay needed an apartment. Not only was the timing perfect, but it was practical and mutually beneficial for both of us. Or so I thought, until he moved in. And I listened to the man of my dreams bang the man of his dreams (more like the the man of the night) through the shared wall that separated our bedrooms. This wasn't how things were supposed to turn out when we started living together.

"They're in the other room, they can't even hear me, Jay." I said defensively.

"Kids hear and see everything. Especially when you think they don't. They're sponges. Whiny, needy, germ infested little bastard sponges."

"Shhhh...they can hear you Jay!" I teased. "Spare me your stories of how your mom ran a daycare and you know everything there is to know about kids, ok? I'm very aware that I have absolutely no fucking clue what I'm doing, thank you very much."

"You're gonna be great, Hennessy. If nothing else, you can be an example to them of what not to do."

Truer words had never been spoken.

"I can't even cook. I made them mac & cheese three nights in a row already."

"So what? That doesn't make you a bad mother." He said supportively.

"I'm their aunt and legal guardian. I'm nobody's mother!" I reminded him.

"You're moving into your dead sister's apartment to raise her kids and you're driving her station wagon. A fucking STATION WAGON! You'll probably even get a cat. Maybe join a book club or carpool. Who knows? Give it a year and you might be PTA president. You can call yourself whatever you want, but it doesn't change what you are."

He had a point.

"Completely screwed, that's what I am. And forced to quit the life that I've made for myself here in Niagara Falls to move back to Lostport."

"Since when do you have a life?"

He was right again. I was the assistant manager at Doodles, an art supply store. I barely had any friends. I rarely went out, preferring to stay home to hang out with my gay roommate, who I was in love with. And now I was moving out, heart broken feeling like we'd just broken up when we were never even a couple to begin with. I was crushed.

"Just help me find the damn boxes so I can pack it up in the car with the rest of my stuff will you?"

"Thank you for meeting with me today Miss Greypath. First of all, my condolences on your sister's passing. I remember meeting her at kindergarten orientation." Said Mrs. Doone, Max's kindergarten teacher.

I'd heard a month's worth of similar sentiments. So many "sorries", "condolences" and head tilts filled with pity. I never knew how to respond. I tried "thanks" at first, but it just sounded fake and obligatory, which was how I meant it, but it was far too honest for social exchanges like these. No one could possibly be as sorry as me that my sister was gone because I was left playing the lead role of her in the real life docu-dramedy. I decided silence coupled with a blank stare was the best way to accurately convey my feelings to strangers on the subject.

I was sitting in the same elementary school where I'd been a student. Only now, individual desks were replaced with tables students shared. They also shared the markers, crayons and other school supplies that were placed in bins in the middle of the tables, making it look more like a hippie art commune than a school.

"Well, the reason I asked you to come in today, is because I'm concerned about Maxwell's behavior at school." Mrs. Doone said.

I'd never had the misfortune of having Mrs. Doone for a teacher when I was a kid. But, I didn't have to be her student to know her reputation for being a hard-ass. All the students at Haven Hills Elementary talked about her and how mean she was even back then, earning her the nickname "Mrs. Doom". She was old back when I was a kid, but now she looked like a walking corpse. A diminutive, gaunt woman with thin short gray hair she'd colored over with an unconvincing and unflattering flat dark brown color. She wore lipstick in a shade of barbie-doll pink that she must've bought in bulk back in 1982. Her make-up accentuated the feathery pucker lines around her lips from years of smoking. I never imagined when I left elementary school that I'd be sitting in a really small uncomfortable chair across from Mrs. Doom. Or that I'd move back to Lostport to raise my dead sister's kids. And I'd never realized that there was a repeating pattern in my family of mothers dying and sisters raising the kids they left behind. Deja fucking vu.

"Well, let's just get straight to it then. Maxwell, is extremely overbearing in class. He doesn't allow his classmates to participate in discussions and frequently interrupts during my lessons and diverts attention from the subject at hand to his own shenanigans." She explained.

"That sounds like Max." I said in agreement.

"I'm forced to move his Good Neighbor Card from the green zone to the red zone for his poor behavior at least four or five times a week, but usually more. It's not fair to the other students who have come to learn only to have Maxwell distract them. Also, he seldom completes his homework."

"I bet he was devastated that you moved his Good Neighbor Card." I said.

She seemed oblivious to my sarcasm.

"It certainly doesn't seem that way to me. I constantly have to reign him in and regain control of a class that's erupted in laughter because of his antics."

"I'm glad to hear he's at least funny. Especially since it doesn't seem like he's good at standing in line, sharing and taking turns. And really, homework in kindergarten is a bit ridiculous isn't it? Shouldn't they just be having fun since the rest of their life is basically gonna suck?"

"Fun has no place in kindergarten anymore, Miss Greypath. Children go to preschool to learn social skills now. The academic expectations are significantly more ambitious than when you were a student here. We turn out more educated kindergarteners here nowadays. Now that we've established that kindergarten is important, let's get back to Maxwell. He's consistently had problems with staying on task since the beginning of the year. His disruptive behaviors are consistent with ADHD. Most kids are diagnosed in First grade, but I'm a proponent of early intervention whenever possible. He needs to see a doctor and some counseling would help too. Considering."

"Considering what? That I don't have enough going on right now? Maybe you should consider that he's in his first year of school and his mom just died. And I'm in my first month as his guardian and I have no fucking clue how to do any of this. Maybe you should consider that he's doing his best and so am I. Did you ever think that maybe you're too strict and perhaps it's time to retire and give the job to someone who actually likes kids?"

"Due to your verbal abuse, I'm going to end this conference right now. If I need to schedule another meeting to discuss Max's behavior in the future and I'm sure I will, I'll request that the school counselor and principal be present. And just to be clear, the counseling I mentioned was for you."

In one way, getting fired from my job at Doodles, the art supply store where I was working, was one of the nicest things anyone had ever done for me. After I got Max off to school, I still had Jack and Casey at home and then I had to get to work in Niagara Falls which was a twenty-five minute drive away now that I'd moved back to Lostport. All Lara's friends had kids of their own and were burned out from babysitting The Three Stooges (my new nickname for the unit that was Max, Jack & Casey) when she was doing chemotherapy.

My dad had even helped out for a couple hours at a time, which was all he was capable of after having been diagnosed with a heart condition a couple years ago and being put on medication that slowed him down and left him lethargic. The free babysitting well had run dry and I'd taken all the time off from work I could. I get that Doodles really had no choice but to let me go, but that didn't make me feel any better about the situation. Plus, now I had to spend all day every day with The Stooges.

I had no job, no life and no plans for what I was going to do about any of it. I knew I needed help, I just didn't want it and I didn't have a clue about where to get it even if I did want it. I'd always figured things out for myself and despised people who told me what to do. Before this happened, I always knew what to do. Although knowing what I should do, doesn't mean I did anything about it. And I might have sabotaged myself more than a few times in the process. Like when I fell in love with my gay roommate and when I refused to even consider going to college, just to name a couple off the top of my head. I didn't have any lofty dreams of being a lawyer or anything like that. My high school guidance counselor, Mrs. Neals, suggested I read *What Color is Your Parachute?* to help me find a career path. I never found out what color it is because I never read it. Accepting mediocrity early on was my path. I'd be delusional to waste time and money investing in myself believing I'd be the exception and find success doing something I was good at, never mind something I loved. Because I was sure I wasn't good at anything. Perhaps my biggest mindfuck was deluding myself into believing I wasn't deluding myself.

I wanted The Stooges to live the delusional life too. Not delusional enough that they expected to go to Disney World on spring break because we couldn't afford that, but optimistic enough to believe that there will occasionally be cake and ice cream when and if I got another job. A more realistic, scaled-down semi-delusion really. Most importantly, I wanted them to have someone to share the cake and ice cream with. Someone who loved them despite being a self-absorbed, unemployed, serial screwup. I wanted to be there for The Stooges, even if I didn't have any idea how to do that. Even if that feeling was a fleeting thought in little daydreams between the yelling, fighting, frustration and exhaustion.

CHAPTER 5

Ifound them in the night stand one of the first nights I slept in my dead sister's house. The mattress on her bed dipped on the left side with the imprint of her body. After she divorced Dickhead, she had the bed all to herself. Conceivably, she could've stretched out in the middle of the queen size mattress, but I knew from sleeping on it that the crater sized indent wouldn't allow her to, sucking her right back to the same place because that's precisely what kept happening to me. It was an inescapable cocoon that was both soothing, but yet uncomfortably binding at the same time. I opened the drawer of her night stand looking for a hair tie to keep my shoulder length hair from falling in my face while I tossed and turned in my sleep. But, I didn't find one. Instead, underneath the Mother's Day cards and scribbled drawings The Stooges had made for my sister, that's where I found an old dark green journal and a bright pink vibrator.

Why do we keep our secrets close to us when we sleep? Our fears and our desires commingling with the mundane in an ordinary drawer. Words both tender and terrifying jumbled together with lip balms, kleenex and medications. And why would anyone think a nightstand is a safe place to hide things they don't want to be found?

I kept my secrets locked inside me, buried so deep, even I don't acknowledge them. Let alone share them with anyone else. Until something as disturbing as discovering your sister's sex toy dredges them to the surface.

It repulsed me to think she had carnal desires. I know everyone has them and that they're natural, but it's still disgusting. Since she played the role of my mom longer than my mom had, it was like finding my mom's vibrator. I didn't want to think of either Lara or my mom as a woman with needs. In my mind, I'd elevated both of them to a level of martyrdom akin to that of Mother Theresa, pure of heart and free of any impure sexual thoughts. I was sure Lara was the patron saint of abandoned children. First raising me when I was little and then her own kids. And doing it all on her own because The Stooges were deserted by their dad. How could she abandon me with these kids now? Why does a martyr have to die to be canonized anyway? It wasn't fair. I figured that out at ten years old when my mom died. I just didn't realize how much more unfair life could get. It was compounding with interest, along with my debt and my despair about the situation. I felt like I was being slow roasted on a spit. The vibrator was just a symbol of how fucked I was, serving as a reminder that life wasn't done with me yet.

Sex tasted like tequila and burned like I was taking a piss with a severe vaginal yeast infection. At least that's how I remembered it. My legs were cramping hoisted over the broad shoulders of Tony Marino, a linebacker on the football team at Lostport High. He was a senior and I was a sophomore. Before Lara got married to Dickhead and moved out she told me that tenth grade was the best year of high school. You weren't a nervous freshman trying to figure where you fit in to the whole high school scene or a junior prepping to take the SAT, but you didn't have the pressure of being a senior on the verge of becoming a legal adult and having to figure out your place in the real world yet either. Sophomore year held no expectations. Least of all that I'd lose my virginity and only be left with a vague and confused recollection of how it happened. It wasn't how I'd expected to lose something so important, but it was memorable in that there were parts of it I'd never forget, even though I desperately wanted to.

I wasn't attracted to him. In fact, I'd always found him completely repulsive when I saw him at school. Where he could usually be found standing in a doorway of the halls surveying the social scene and verbally harassing underclassmen. With his signature buzz cut and cheap sunglasses he wore every day regardless of the weather or wether he was outdoors or inside. His face was riddled with acne and his neck was so thick it looked more like an extension of his head resting on top of his bulky upper body, dwarfing his scrawny chicken legs. He was an upside down triangle with poor grammar and even worse hygiene; his hair and skin always had an oily sheen. There was a rumor that he slept with the music teacher, Ms. Wilcox, last year. Though no one ever confirmed it, he did visit her classroom a lot for someone who didn't take a music class. But, the rumor alone was enough to cement his status as one of the cool kids.

I remember his face as a blurry montage while he was thrusting his penis into my vagina. His brown eyes were squinty, distant, cold, ugly and one drooped. His breath smelled of Doritos and beer mixed with vomit. I don't know how I got in bed with him or why. How could I be naked from the waist down having sex with someone who repulsed me? I couldn't have agreed to this. I wouldn't have. But, I don't remember how it happened no matter how many times I went over it in my head. I couldn't recall because I was passed out drunk and when I woke up, he was on top of me missionary style.

When he finished, after what seemed like an eternity, but in actuality was probably only a couple of minutes of utter torment and terror for me, he headed to the adjoining master bathroom to piss. While I searched the matted carpeted floor for my panties, jeans and boots hurrying to put them on and get out of there as quickly as possible. When I walked out of the bedroom utterly distressed, I walked straight into a raging party in the living room, filled with students from my high school looking at me knowingly. The next week at school I was the hot topic of gossip. Not only was it humiliating, it was beyond bizarre that people ranging from mere acquaintances to complete strangers knew more about my first sexual encounter than I did. Was it date rape? Can you call it date rape if you never dated the guy? Maybe it was a normal, regular everyday rape. I was too ashamed to ask anyone those questions though, so I didn't do anything and then I was ashamed about that too. I just tried to pretend it didn't happen. Shockingly, denial didn't do anything to make the memories go away. And over the years, not only did the shame stay with me, it metastasized.

Rationalizing someone else's abuse against you is easier than you think. We're humans; searching for patterns and predictors after a traumatic event is something we do instinctively. If my abuser was a stranger I didn't know forcing me to have sex in an alley, it obviously wouldn't have been my fault. But, since I was drunk at a party on a bed at someone's house I barely knew, with someone I did know (if only barely) with his dick inside me, I clearly shared some of the blame. I'm sure that's the way everyone would see it. Especially Sister Helen from St. Christopher's. Maybe even my own mother if she'd been alive, but I honestly wasn't really sure what she'd think, she died before I had the chance to know her as a woman. I only knew her as my mom.

———

It was covered in a faded green tightly woven fabric that was rough to the touch when I ran my fingers over it. All the entries were scripted in a cursive that I'd never seen before. Notably absent of dates with rushed, curt entries in direct contradiction to the languid, graceful handwriting.

"Your dress is too short!" He took scissors, put them between my legs starting at the hem of my skirt cut lengthwise up to the

bodice of my favorite dress. I was scared and shaking. When I looked up I saw my little Essie, peering into the kitchen from the hallway, sullen and looking scared too.

He gave Evie a thorough beating after she stole money from the change jar for candy at the corner store. Her arm was hurt so bad, we thought he'd broke it. The welts he left took upwards of a week to turn from black to green.

"I saw how you were looking at my boss at the Christmas party, Mary. You were looking at him like a lusty tramp. If I find out you slept with anyone, let alone my boss, so help me god, I'll dig you a ditch so deep no one will ever find your body.." His hands pressed down on my shoulders near my neck before he shoved me pushing me backwards into a heap on the floor, then he kicked me in the gut.

"You get those bruises from having rough sex while I was at work again?"

I can endure this. For Evie and Essie.

"No one else would put up with you. You're lucky I married you."

He came home from work in a mood and slapped me in the face. I don't know why.

Frank came to bed after I was asleep, pulled up my nightgown and forced himself on me.

The journal entries ended as abruptly as they had begun. I'd deduced from the content that the author was my grandmother, Mary. And her abuser Frank, was my mother's father. Both had been deceased for years. I don't know what they died from or when, my mother never talked much about her family. Only her sister Evelyn (Evie) from time to time, who was not only a witness to my grandfather's abuse, but also a recipient of it. I wondered if he ever hit my mom, as if it even mattered. The emotional abuse he inflicted on his family was probably worse than the physical abuse anyway. I was about four or five the last time I saw my grandfather. Ironically, he was wearing a white wife beater T-shirt and dark blue pants with suspenders that stretched over his generous belly. I'd always remembered him as being charming. He'd always joke with me and Lara trying to make us smile. Which made me favor him over my quiet, demure grandmother who was always busying herself with something or other who never seemed to have time for us. But now I saw my grandfather as sinister. And my grandmother as long-suffering.

Of course it was pink, aesthetics were always important to her. Lara had the innate superpower of noticing the smallest of details and knowing how to cultivate and nurture them. She was feminine in a way that I never was. I tended to have a more masculine personality. I was oblivious of the details and I had no idea how to cultivate or nurture anything. I was a tomboy trapped in a woman's body and I was sure Tony Marino had broken it irreparably.

Silicone is a many splendored thing. It doesn't conform to anatomical correctness, it doesn't have the musty smell of genitals and it doesn't require the forethought of birth control. So, it couldn't get me pregnant or give me a STD. And I didn't have to think about what silicone wanted from me. Or that things will go further than I want them to. I don't have to see it out in public and cower pretending I don't know it intimately. No one will ever call me a slut for my self-silicone love, because no one will ever know. Unless it woke the kids up with it's loud buzzing when I turned it on. Although that could be the sound of a blender or an electric toothbrush for all they knew. But, I should probably buy those two appliances in case I needed a cover story if The Stooges should happen to hear it. Making it at least a semi-probable, feasible lie. Except kids don't live in the probable world, they live in a world of fantasy and believe in cute fluffy bunnies that deliver candy on Easter and anonymous benevolent fairies who buy teeth for cash, so I'm sure I overthought the whole thing. If my current, harsh, unemployed reality needed anything, it was a little more fantasy.

I buried myself under all the covers on the bed to buffer the sound of the hum when I turned it on. Still fully clothed from the day, I unbuttoned the top of my jeans, unzipped them and shimmied my Levi's down to my knees. My cold fingers unintentionally grazing my thigh as I did, creating a shudder of anticipation. Although I didn't know quite what to expect. I pressed the hot pink button turning it on to it's lowest setting, holding it loosely in my hand feeling the tingle from the vibrations with my hand. I tested the water by touching it to the front of my thigh before slowly moving it toward my inner thigh. The sensation felt good, so I repositioned the vibrator over my panties (and the panty liner I was wearing) to massage my mound. I'd never felt anything so sensual. Pleasure I greedily wanted more of.

I put the shaft between my generous thighs, clamping it between them before I started moving it back and forth barely grazing the outside cotton of my underwear. Then a warm wave of euphoria started at my crotch and pulsed through my entire body. It was my first orgasm. The first of three that night. Though, my biggest joy was realizing that Tony Marino hadn't broken me.

CHAPTER 6

I covertly checked the liquor cabinet when my father went downstairs to get his reading glasses he'd left in the darkroom. The Beefeaters was a fourth of the bottle full, the same as the last time I checked it a few weeks ago. When I was little, seeing my dad bring out the bottle after dinner with the strong sentry carrying a spear on the label made me feel safe and protected. Maybe because I knew it comforted him and made him feel less lonely after my mom died. It was only when I got older that I noticed that the bottle started to appear before dinner. Sometimes he skipped dinner entirely and Lara and I ate alone while he was in the darkroom processing photos with a gin and tonic made with the slightest splash of Schweppes. It was only when I went down to the darkroom to say goodnight to him, after he'd had countless cocktails, that he'd have anything to say to me. That's when he told me stories about my mom, asked about my drawings and remembered he'd forgotten to make a dentist appointment for me again. Though he never could muster the words to tell me he loved me, that's when I felt it. I didn't need to hear the words, even though I desperately wanted to.

People say alcoholics drink to numb the pain, but I think it's the opposite. I think it was the only time he had the courage to feel. Or maybe it was the only time I felt like I had a dad. Either way, I always inherently understood him. Not only did I look like him with my intimidating height and strong masculine features, I was also just as inhibited as he was. Preferring to be alone with my tortured thoughts rather than burden anyone else with them. There was no escaping it, I was my father's daughter.

He'd been sober for two years now and by sober I mean he gave up drinking gin every night and switched to beer. Ever since he went on medication for a heart condition and his doctor stressed that alcohol would interact with the medication. And everyone knows alcohol is hard liquor and beer is just piss water, so it doesn't count. While my dad didn't seem to be real keen on living, I guess he wasn't ready to die either, which was a good thing. Sure, he didn't give up alcohol altogether, but he did significantly reduce the alcohol percentage in each drink even if he was consuming more to compensate for that. I accepted his stubborn rationale figuring he was still coming out ahead in the long run.

He didn't book many photo sessions anymore or go down to the darkroom every day like he used to because his heart left him weak and listless much of the time. But, he did take pictures of Maxwell, Jackson and Casey when I dropped them off to go to a job interview at a department store downtown that I didn't end up getting. Not that I wanted the job, because I didn't, but I was desperate for an income. I just didn't know how I was going to make everything work when I did finally go back to work. I knew I needed to get a job in Lostport, there just weren't many opportunities.

Funny thing about pictures. They capture a moment that only exists for a fraction of a second. Photos allow you not only to see the things that you didn't notice before, but with the frame frozen for eternity, it encourages you to dissect it. In real time you can second guess having seen something or anything at all. But, when the frame is still, you can't help but see what was right there in front of you the whole time. Like the way the pictures my dad took of The Three Stooges made them look innocent. Saintly even. The flip side of seizing a moment is that the image can be completely deceptive too.

"The other day I found an old journal at Lara's house." I said. My dad returned to the living room out of breath from walking back up the stairs, sitting down in his favorite arm chair.

"She did like to hold on to things like your mother did. They were both sentimental, especially when it came to books." He said.

"It wasn't even hers though. It looked like it was Grandma Mary's." I said probing to see if he knew anything about the journal or it's contents.

"Oh?"

"Did you know about it?"

"Yeah, I knew about them." He said, his eyes avoiding mine.

"There was more than one?"

"Yes. I don't recall how many there were, but we found them hidden in different rooms all over your grandparent's house when we had to move her from her house into a nursing home years ago."

"Did you know she was being abused by Grandpa?"

"He wasn't a good man, Henny. Your mom tried to help her leave for many years, but she wouldn't. Essie didn't want you and Lara to know."

"Why would she keep that from us?"

"You were young. Besides, what good would it do? She wanted to protect you and give you a normal childhood where you didn't have to worry about the things that she had to growing up."

"Why the hell wouldn't she leave him? Did he stop?"

"She did leave him lots of times when she was younger with your mom and Aunt Evelyn. But, it never stuck and she always went back. Things would get better for a while before they got worse, but they were always bad. Sometimes the more you try to help, the more it hurts the person you're trying to help in the first place."

"So where are all the other journals?"

"You girls were never supposed to see any of them. I thought I'd gotten rid of all of them after the water damage from the old, leaky roof several years ago and your mom's books started to mold."

———

I was robbed of knowing who my mother truly was and how much she endured to become the woman she did. She was a mystery to me. When did Lara find the journal? How long did she know? Why didn't she tell me? Was she trying to protect me too? Or was it because she thought it wouldn't matter to me? Looking back now I can see why she'd think that. I acted like I didn't care about anything. Why did I store up all that childhood resentment for Lara all those years? And why didn't I bother to get to know her? Because I thought I knew her and that she was perfect, that's why. Before I inherited her life and realized that just like with my mom, I didn't know her at all.

I'm unemployed with three kids to feed, perhaps the only people in my life who don't know what a complete failure I am. It's only a matter of time before they figure it out; that I was their Plan C. That it was either me or foster care because there was no one else left to care for them. And maybe foster care was the better choice. First of all, foster parents actually apply for the job. Then they get training on how to do the job...for free even. Then, when they're deemed competent at taking care of kids (and after a complete and thorough criminal background check to make sure they're not drug dealers or child molesters) and only then, does the state place kids in the home and the foster parent earns a paycheck to help care for the kids. God, all I have to do is be a complete stranger to these kids and we'd probably all be better off. It seemed logical enough at the time. I'm sure if I just explained my situation to someone they could help me out and make this work.

The Office of Children and Family Services' automated phone system triaged my call through the same set of choices:

Thank you for calling the New York State Parent and Child Connection Help Line. If this is a life threatening emergency, please hang up and dial 911 for emergency assistance. Message repeats in Spanish. To continue in English, please dial "1". Please listen closely as our menu options have changed.

Dial 1 To report child abuse and neglect.

Dial 2 For the abandoned infant hotline.

Dial 3 For the domestic violence hotline.

Dial 4 For information on child abuse clearance.

Dial 5 For child care or to make a child care complaint.

Dial 6 If you're interested in a child or sibling group photo listed in the New York State adoption album on our website.

Dial 7 For information on criminal history fingerprint checks. Or for family court, surrogate court or attorney information.

Dial 8 For child support issues.

Dial 9 For general information regarding foster care, adoption, adoption subsidies, and authorized adoption agencies.

For all other calls please dial 10 or remain on the line.

After dialing ten because there was no "how do I relinquish my guardianship to become a foster parent option", then waiting on hold for thirty-five minutes until someone finally picked up the phone, they promptly disconnected me. I was so frustrated that I packed up Jack and Casey to haul them down to the Child and Family Services office so I could communicate with a real live human. Not that I wanted to talk to a real live human, especially with two little kids in tow. But then again, I didn't want any of this, I just didn't know what else to do.

The only thing that's worse than going to a government office for anything, is going there with kids after lunch. Not that Jack and Casey ate their egg sandwiches. They wanted grilled cheese, but you can't make that without cheese. And since we had eggs and bread it was either egg sandwiches or french toast and french toast was a much bigger commitment. Requiring that I mix the eggs with milk, then dredge the bread in the egg mixture before frying it, but not on high heat because then I'd burn it like I burned everything else I tried to cook on the stove. Even after it was cooked, french toast still requires more choices like cinnamon or butter. Then there's the matter of syrup, which we didn't have. So, clearly french toast wasn't an option. Even though I explained that several times to two-thirds of The Three Stooges, I couldn't opt out of their whining about not liking egg sandwiches. Complaining was the only time they agreed on anything. And often, it was as good as my day got.

We just sat down in the crowded waiting room when Jack started making demands.

"I need a snack." He ordered.

"No, you don't. You just ate. You don't need anything." I replied.

"My tummy is growling. It says it needs fruit roll-ups." Jack made his appeal.

"If you ate more of your lunch you and your stomach would be quiet and probably napping right now."

"I don't like egg sammiches, they're gross." He grumbled.

"Fruit rollups are grosser. Plus, you know we don't have fruit roll-ups. You've asked me a hundred times already. Which reminds me, after this we need to stop at the grocery store."

"To Wegmans?"

"Look, we can't go to Wegmans anymore if you're going to steal gummy bears from the bulk bin like you did last time. Nothing in the big bins is free. Can you promise me you won't go all kleptomaniac on me again?"

"I don't even know what a creepomaniac is."

"I have some pencils and a sketch pad in my bag. Maybe you could draw me a picture of what you think a creepomaniac looks like."

"Awwwwwwww.....he's so cute, how old is he?" One of the worst things about going anywhere with kids is how it makes it easy for overeager strangers to strike up a conversation with you. She looked to be about thirty-five years old with a petite frame and a light brown bob with large brown bulgy eyes.

"Four." He was closer to five, but I thought it best to keep my answer brief as to not encourage her further.

"That's a great age." Obviously she must be childless. Because no one is that delusional unless they're a grandparent and she didn't look quite old enough for that.

"I'm adopting a three year old boy myself. His mother had him when she was in prison. She lost the rights to all seven of her kids because of drugs. Who goes and has all these kids when they can't even take care of themselves? It's criminal how so many minorities can't take care of their own." She said.

"Minorities?" I regretted asking the question before it even came out of my mouth.

"The majority of kids in the system are minorities and of course a lot of their parents are in prison. These kids don't stand a chance without people like us."

"People like us?" I couldn't stop myself from asking.

"You know, responsible mothers who stay at home with their kids and raise them in a stable environment." The being white part was just implied.

Why did this woman assume that we were bonded by motherhood and a racist white superiority complex? I wasn't a mother or a racist. I didn't choose to have kids or stay home with them and the last thing I was doing was providing them with a consistently stable environment. And I just happened to have pale white skin, it wasn't a state of mind or anything.

I was considering the most kid friendly way to tell her and her skinny, pretentious white ass to fuck off when I noticed Casey. Crouched under a black plastic waiting room chair two rows back, sitting in a puddle of her own pee. I'd been so distracted by being forced into an unwanted conversation with someone who I instantaneously disliked that I'd lost sight of her. It's not that I didn't try to get her to wear a diaper, a pull-up or at least really thick absorbent fleece pants. It's that she wouldn't do any of those things and insisted on wearing big girl panties. Lesson number 462 of parenting, bring an extra set of pants, panties, wipes, bandaids, snacks and patience with you wherever you go.

"Miss Greypath?"

I coaxed Casey out from her hiding spot and made Jack pick up his creepomanic drawing and pen (reminding him to pick up the pen several times) and hurried to the counter. A fifty-something year old African American woman waited for us. Her name tag read *Cassandra Wilkinson*.

"What can I do for you?" She asked.

"I'm the legal guardian of my sister's three kids." I said pointing at Jack and Casey. "The other one is in school right now. And I'd like to become their foster parent."

"Your sister has relinquished her rights and you have legal guardianship of all three of them then?" She asked.

"She didn't relinquish it so much as she died and named me as her kids' guardian in her will."

"Sweetie, I'm sorry about your sister." She said sympathetically. "What about the father? Is he deceased as well?"

"He's not in the picture, he abandoned them years ago. We don't know where he is right now. And I'm currently unemployed, so I thought if I was their foster parent, the income would help me take care of them."

She bent in closer to my face so that I could smell the tuna from her lunch on her breath and started talking in a whisper. "Honey, I've been working in foster care for 10 years. We do have some really good folks that are foster parents, but the last place you want to put a kid that you love is in here. Because doing that makes them a ward of the state. And trust me, you don't want that. Besides, the first thing we'd do if you wanted to pursue foster care is to make contact with the father and see if his relatives could care for the children outside the system." She explained.

"I don't know what I'm supposed to do! I just need some help." I pleaded on the verge of tears.

"Are you on unemployment? Cause that's where you should start." She said trying to be helpful.

"Ok, how do I get on unemployment?"

"We don't have anything to do with unemployment in this office. We only handle foster care. Hang on, maybe I can find the phone number for unemployment around here somewhere for you."

She headed to the back room where all classified information like the super secret phone numbers to other government service offices with automated phone systems are kept. Oh good more bureaucratic bullshit to wade through. I looked down at Casey who'd pressed her butt up against the counter and slid herself down to the floor, leaving a trail of wet urine behind her. Jack, held the sketch pad loosely in his hand almost grazing the floor.

"How's your creepomanic? Can I see it?" I asked.

"Not done yet." He said.

"You don't have to show me. It's good to keep things to yourself sometimes and then share them when you're ready."

"Ok, I'm ready now."

There was an oversized lizard in the middle of the page, with a long tail and an even longer split tongue sticking out. He'd drawn a fairly detailed creature in a matter of minutes.

"Wow! I didn't realize you could draw this well. That is a fantastic lizard Jack!"

"Not a lizard, a creepomanic." He corrected me.

"Oh, of course. That's what I meant. Does he have a name?"

"Cancer."

My eyes welled up until the tears streamed down my face and I tasted the salt of them on my lips.

"My mom was going to be here, but I didn't have time." he said pointing at a spot next to the lizard with a pen.

"I know buddy."

Cassandra returned to the counter with a phone number for the unemployment office scrawled haphazardly across the top of a plain yellow post-it note.

"Here you go, sweetheart. Take care of those kids now. And good luck!"

The only thing I knew for sure was that I needed all the luck I could get.

CHAPTER 7

I didn't choose it, so much as it chose me. My hair hadn't been cut in months, the split ends grazed my shoulders now. At least it was long enough to put it up in a ponytail every day and avoid the whole what-to-do-with-my-hair conundrum, just like almost every other mom raising young children does. Not that I was a mom, I just had all the challenges of being one, but without the gross, way-too-much-information birth story to share at potlucks when all the other moms gathered in the kitchen to complain about their husbands. Not that I had a husband to bitch about either. I didn't have a significant other to criticize about how they load the dishwasher, the shaving stubble left in the bathroom sink or forgetting to take the garbage out again. I imagine that's why people get married, so they have someone to share the blame with.

We made an urgent, impromptu trip to get new shoes for Max after he wore a hole clean through the bottom of his sneakers. We tried duct taping them, but it proved not to be a watertight solution and his sock got drenched when he walked through the snow in them, making his foot prune like he had trench foot. And I didn't have health insurance to take him to a doctor if it turned into gangrene or needed to be amputated. The situation necessitated yet another trip to Walmart. That's where I saw the box of hair color. The sultry brunette model on the packaging looked like Mila Kunis, which coincidentally was pretty much what I wished I looked like. It's not like I intentionally made a decision to buy it, color my hair and become her. I blame the beauty industry for manipulating my insecurities and cuing my spontaneous impulse to trade in being a boring dishwater blonde to become a smoldering brunette. Surely, this would change how I felt about myself. No longer would I be a dowdy, exhausted, pseudo mom trying to conceal her thunder thighs under baggy sweatpants. As a brunette I'd be fashionable, sexy, put together, more patient and instantly twenty pounds thinner.

Even though I felt desperate to make a change, I couldn't go through with dying my hair when I got home. I'd say that I thought everything through and realized I was deluding myself that coloring my hair would make me more confident or solve any of my problems, but that wasn't the case at all. I was just too lazy to do it. The universe has a way of bringing you the things you desire, but in a totally screwed up way though. Because that's when I met Leslie, who looked curiously similar to the model on the box of hair dye I bought.

———————

"No, Ma. This is the guilt trip thing again. Look, you're old I get it. But, if the thirty years of smoking haven't killed you yet, you're not going to die if you don't see your grandkids this weekend." Leslie said.

She was sitting on a park bench next to the playground having a loud and engrossing conversation on her cell phone. She had thick wavy shiny espresso brown hair with almond shaped eyes with an enviable athletic body she showed off in black leggings and a slim fitting emerald green jacket. Her two boys were shimmying their way up the slide when the one lower one grabbed for the leg of his brother getting a firm grip on his brother's shoe and pulled it right into his own face, busting his lip open.

"Mama! Luca kicked me in the face!" The instigator lied.

"Look Ma, I gotta go, Enzo's bleeding.....He's a boy. Blood just means he's still alive.....You had six kids and we could've started our own blood bank with all the fights we had growing up. But, now that it's your grandson you're concerned? I gotta go. I'll see you Monday. Love you." She said before she hung up.

"Can't I talk to your grandma for five minutes without things going all MMA with you two? Come here and let me inspect the damage." She said addressing her boys.

One of the boys, an exact replica of his brother, stepped forward holding his mouth working his big innocent puppy dog eyes for his mother.

"But he did it! He made me hit him!" Shouted the twin.

"Save it. This is not about you right now Luca." She said with her index finger in his face to shush him.

"Open your mouth." She instructed. "You got all your teeth. No need for stitches or a trip to the ER. So, tell me what happened."

"Luca kicked me really hard in the face!" He pleaded.

"No! He pulled me down the slide." His twin retorted.

"Enzo. What happened right before you got kicked in the face?"

"Nothing." He said after looking down and clasping his hands together.

"Don't lie to your mother. Whatever happened to you, you started it and you deserved what you had coming to you. Now, go sit over there next to that tree until I tell you you can get up."

"But, he kicked me!"

"But...go to the tree already." She annunciated and exaggerated the words in a slow, deep mocking voice moms use when they're pissed off.

He stood in front of his mom with his arms crossed giving her the death glare.

She stood up slowly, intentionally towering over him with all five foot ten inches of her frame to intimidate him. He finally relented, turned and walked to the young maple tree strapped to a post to keep it from being knocked over by the wind at the edge of the park.

I was impressed by her no nonsense parenting style.

"And he would be my little liar." She said turning to me.

"Mine is over there." I said pointing at Jack spinning the tire swing with no one on it while Casey climbed up the stairs of the baby slide to slide down over and over again as if she was on a continuous video loop.

"Your son looks about the same age as my boys. Five?" She asked.

The term 'son' startled me. And it took me a minute to recover while considering my options. Do I correct her? Or not? I decided not to, even though it felt like a lie.

"He's four actually, I have a kindergartener who's five, but he's at school right now."

"My boys are in kindergarten too, I'm just letting them blow off steam after their dentist appointments before I take them back to school."

"I'm Hennessy." I said reaching out my hand, trying to play the role of a mom convincingly, purposely gripping her hand firmly attempting to exude confidence.

"What a cool name. I'm Leslie. Named after Leslie Stahl. You know, the journalist on 60 Minutes. My mom has this weird admiration that borders on an obsession for white working women. Not what you'd expect from a traditional Italian stay at home mom with a slew of kids. My generic white girl name is probably why I gave my boys traditional Italian names. What you do in adulthood is kind of a reaction to your childhood, you know?" Then she paused and said, "I think you need to go deeper."

"I'm sorry? I make it a point not to talk about my childhood at the park...with people I just met and kids around." I said awkwardly.

"I meant your hair. You've got this mousey thing going on. You need some color. You need some highlights to brighten it up, but you also need some low lights to give it depth. Trust me, it'll look great with your pale skin and bring attention to your pretty green eyes."

I know I'm not supposed to trust a complete stranger dispensing free advice at the park, but somehow, I did. Probably because it was the exact opposite of what I instinctually wanted to do with my hair. And since my judgement on things was usually wrong, I figured she must be right.

"And attention is good?" I asked.

"Sorry, I used to be a hair stylist. So when I look at people, I see possibilities. Funny enough, it's pretty similar to what I do for work now."

"And what's that?" I asked.

"I would say I'm a dancer, but I don't want to give you the wrong impression. I'm a stripper. I work over at the Booby Trap. I did hair up until a couple of years ago when I figured I could make more money taking my clothes off. Plus, I have more time at home with my boys now than I did when I was a hairstylist. Turns out, drunk, horny men are much better tippers than sober, suburban women. Maybe because they have to work harder for less pay than a man, so they're tighter with their money. That's my theory anyway. What about you? What do you do?"

"Right now, I'm pretty successful at being unemployed." I said.

"The club where I work has an opening for a cocktail waitress. Unless, you're a lawyer by trade or the Gloria Steinem type."

"I'm more of a broke, degree-less, desperate, post-modern feminist with 3 mouths to feed type."

"Great. Then I can hook you up with Barbara who runs the place. She'll like your snarky attitude."

"But, I don't have any experience waiting tables. And I'm not sure I'd be a really good fit for a strip club. For starters, I think me carrying a tray full of drinks would only end in disaster. Then there's this..." *I pointed to my hair "...and this" *pointing at my body.

"The one and only qualification for any woman to work at a strip club is low self esteem. It's how we all start out. From the sounds of things you're actually overqualified for the job. You can learn the rest. For the record, you're prettier than you think you are. You've got this natural, wholesome farm girl look going on that a lot of guys are into."

I wasn't sure about the farm girl comment, but I knew she meant it as a genuine compliment. I also knew I didn't have any other prospects for employment and after having gotten a taste of the what Child and Family Services had to offer, which was nothing, I didn't expect that the Unemployment office would be much help to me either.

———

Even if I didn't desperately need a job, I still would've wanted one just to get away from The Three Stooges and their incessant needs for a while. I hadn't even learned how to meet my own needs and now I was responsible for the health and safety of tempestuous and malleable little minds. The whining and fighting were constant. Both theirs and mine. Even though I was twenty-two years old and therefore legally an adult, the truth was, I was just a child myself. I liked to watch cartoons, ignore responsibility, leave my bed unmade, throw temper tantrums, doodle and eat junk food. Canned spray cheese? Nerf gun wars? Wearing the same unwashed clothes for three days straight? Yes, please! The question is how does a grown ass woman-child find a babysitter to watch the young children in her care at night while she goes to serve drinks to men leering at naked women dancing in a strip club so she can feed said children? It didn't go unnoticed that I was going to be playing the supporting role instead of the lead in my own life yet again. Guys go to strip clubs to see strippers take their clothes off. They want lap dances, not a blundering cocktail waitress spilling drinks in their laps. Not that I wanted to be the center of attention, on stage taking my clothes off in front of a room full of horny men. I didn't even like to go into the dressing room in a department store and accidentally catch a glimpse of myself half naked when I was trying on bras. All of my flaws: my small asymmetric breasts, fat dimply thighs, paunchy gut and my masculine face illuminated by the unflattering fluorescent lights. Why do they always have fluorescent lights in dressing rooms? And more importantly, what the hell was I going to wear on my first day at work anyway?

––––––––––––

Bethany came over promptly at 4:00pm. She was probably a year or two younger than me, but I felt much older than my twenty-two years now that I had The Stooges to care for. She arrived in sweat pants with "PINK" written across her perky ass. Her light brown hair pulled back into a sloppy, looped ponytail wearing thick blue eyeliner around her big brown eyes and carrying a huge sling of a green bohemian print purse. She looked like a sorority girl the morning after a frat party. Wholesomely hungover and yet perhaps marginally smart enough to write a fairly competent term paper that was due the next morning. Although, I heard from her mom, my neighbor three doors down, that she wasn't going to college because she'd recently started her own business. I learned this after psuedo-stalking Bethany who looked like a good babysitter from my living room window where I watched her as she pulled in and out of the driveway frequently in her old, practical blue Nissan Sentra. Whatever her business was, she seemed like a hard-worker. Most importantly, she looked the part of a babysitter and I desperately needed one. When I finally got the courage to go over and talk to her the day before my first shift at work (because I'm a procrastinator), I was happily surprised to find out that she was interested in watching The Stooges. But, what made her the most qualified to fill the position, was that she was available and willing to work for an unreasonably low sum of money for some unreasonably rambunctious kids.

Jack answered the door, throwing it open and exposing Max who was sitting on the toilet in the bathroom with the door open investigating his boner with his hand. Casey at the tender young age of two had also dabbled in self love from time to time. She experimented with her body in the bathtub, the way girls do, by rubbing the fishing pole bath toy between her legs. I didn't know if Jack knew his penis could do anything other than squirt pee out like a firehose. A practice he relished, which was absolutely fine by me as long as his stream actually made it into the toilet (which it rarely did). I already knew more than I wanted to about the body exploration practices of the other two. What I didn't know before The Stooges came into my life is that these kind of sexual instincts are natural in everyone, even little kids. I just had to remind them that it's best done when they have privacy, with the bathroom door closed. Not in front of the babysitter.

No one in my family ever sat me down and had the talk with me when I was approaching adolescence. When I heard friends talking about sex in fifth grade, I just instinctively knew that I wasn't supposed to do it because we were Catholic. And if I did have to have sex when I was married because I was trying to get pregnant, I knew I wasn't supposed to enjoy it, because that's what Jesus would want. Unless it was what god or the holy spirit wanted. That whole trinity thing confused the hell out of me. Thank god it was going to be a long time before The Stooges were ready for "the talk". I didn't want to pass my sexual inhibitions on to my sister's kids. Lucky for me The Stooges were already on their way to being sexually liberated at a young age. Not that

I wanted the babysitter to know that within the first few seconds of meeting them. Maybe it's good for her to see what she signed up for before I left so she had the chance to run. But, she didn't. Which is a good thing, because if anyone was going to run away, I wanted it to be me. I fantasized about it all the time. The cars I drive away in, the places I'd go by myself without the whining of three little kids. And since I'm fantasizing here, I'd also be strikingly beautiful just like Lara.

After apologizing to Bethany for the brief potty porn incident with Max, making awkward small talk (as if there's any other kind), and playing bounty hunter to coax Casey out of hiding (which she loved to do at the most inappropriate moments), I kissed The Stooges on the top of their tangled mops of unbrushed hair. They were starting to take on a slightly sour stench. I tried to remember how many days it had been since I'd last made them bathe and felt guilty when I couldn't remember. Mental note: force the sour Stooges to shower tomorrow before one of them develops impetigo. Then, I drove my dead sister's beat up station wagon, the interior coated with a layer of cracker crumbs off into the sunset bound for the strip club. It was nothing like my fantasies, reality never is. Even so, I was still free of kids for the next six hours. Not realizing I was just trading little masturbaters in for bigger ones.

It was the first night at work in the middle of my shift when I met him. He had the look of an HOA President: short dark hair greying at the temples with piercing blue eyes wearing a pressed white button down shirt with dark wash jeans and loafers. He was sitting at the edge of the stage and when I bent down to serve him his third Amstel Light of the night nearly dropping the tray full of drinks in his lap. It's a miracle that I managed to navigate the dark crowded club in the five inch black leather boots Leslie lent me. "Until you earn enough money to buy some super slutty shoes of your very own", Leslie told me. She purposely let me borrow the first pair of boots she'd bought to strip in because they aren't as high as the seven inch heels she wears to dance in now. Even in her "low" heels, I stood at six foot and five inches. My freakishly tall height, combined with the heavy handed makeup Leslie insisted I wear, made me look like a drag queen. "Buy some cheap sexy skirts and tops at the thrift store, but never skimp on shoes. You'll see." I was getting all my career advice from a stripper. A couple days earlier she'd also given me an edgy jagged bob haircut and those highlights and lowlights she'd mentioned the day we met.

"Want to earn $50?" He whisper-shouted into my ear over the thumping bass of the music.

"I'm just a waitress, I don't do lap dances." I shouted back into his ear with a mist of accidental spittle from my mouth. I don't know how he could've mistaken me for a dancer, even with the club being so dimly light.

"I don't want a lap dance. You don't have to do anything. Just meet me by the men's room."

"I'm not going to give you a blow job in the bathroom."

"I told you, you don't have to do anything. Just meet me by the men's room." He insisted.

"You want me to meet you by the bathroom and you'll give me $50?"

"Yes."

It wasn't the money, as much as it was the curiosity of how I could make $50 without doing anything. But, the money didn't hurt either. It was the white pressed shirt that somehow helped convince me that I could take him at his word. I know it was stupid, but after I'd finished serving a round of drinks to another table, I met him at the back of the club in the hallway next to the men's room anyway. Where he was standing waiting, with his hands clasped and his head tilted down slightly, looking sheepish. Looking up at me briefly before he shifted his gaze to my boots.

"Take one of them off." He instructed.

"That's what you want? You want me to take off my boots for $50?"

"Just one of them actually. But, yes."

"Well....um.....they're not even mine. What are you going to do with it? I mean, I borrowed these and have to return them in the same condition."

"I'll return it unharmed, I promise."

"I've been on my feet sweating in them all night and I'm sure they're pretty rank."

"Take off the boot." He said in a surprisingly commanding way.

Could it be any easier to make a quick $50? I did need the money. Leaning back against the wall, I bent down and unzipped my right boot. Peeling it off my sweaty calf and all the way down to my ankle, before attempting to pull it off standing on one foot to no avail. I gingerly lowered my body down to sit on the floor, twisting to get my right boot off before handing it over to a complete stranger who took it into the men's room with him. I sat there waiting for approximately five minutes while a guy with a foot fetish jacked off to my borrowed, foul smelling slutty boots. It felt so good for my foot to be out of those hot, unbreathable, unbearably, uncomfortable shoes though. I sat on the disgustingly dirty industrial grade carpet before pulling my foot in and caressing it with my hands. Massaging my foot felt so good I didn't want to stop. Bringing my thoughts back to the fact that there was a pervert in the bathroom giving himself a massage with the aid of my boot. What kind of freak pays a stranger to masturbate to a putrid smelling, scuffed up boot? And what kind of person allows a freak to do that with her friend's boot she graciously loaned to her? It was the easiest, but most repulsive, $50 I'd ever made. His face was flushed when he walked out of the men's room and returned the boot in the same battered condition he'd gotten it in, handing me a crisp $50 bill, just like he said.

CHAPTER 8

"Devon. His name is Devon. And you're welcome." Leslie said.

"You knew?" I asked in shock.

"I loaned you the boots he loves. Thought you could use a jump start on your tips. A little something for your shoe fund until you can buy your own. Plus, he gets what he wants and you get what you need. Everyone gets something out of the deal and it's a win-win."

"You're sick and twisted, you know." I said.

"Those are my two best qualities."

She was right about everything, except for the shoe fund. The shoe fund wasn't for me at all, it was for The Stooges. Max had destroyed another pair of sneakers and I'd sent him to school with duct tape on them again. What's even worse is the only color duct tape I could find around the house was fluorescent pink.

"Adversity makes you strong." My mom used to say that all the time, but I was little, so I didn't have a clue what adversity meant. And I didn't care about being strong because having muscles was the last thing on my mind. My strength had always lay in my cunning deception. But, my self-deprecation was a close second. I used both of them to my advantage against Lara. I didn't care much for brute force. Guerrilla warfare was how boys handled things. Quick, dirty and to the point. Girls inflict emotional carnage. Slowly, deceptively and without end. We can't help it that we notice everything, dissect it and then seek to destroy anything we perceive to be a threat. And Lara was a clear and present danger to my self confidence, leaving me no choice.

It was innocent enough. That's a lie; I intended it. All of it. I just didn't really think it through like I don't with most things. Bleach is both extremely accessible and really cheap. It seems benign with all that cleaning, disinfecting and whitening it does. Much the way people probably saw me as just an innocent kid from the outside looking in. But, on the inside I was a dark, sullen kid consumed with fear that I wasn't good enough. Constantly comparing myself to my sister Lara, who I saw as perfect in every way. Not only was she beautiful and voted homecoming queen for two years in a row when she was in high school, she was humble enough not to care because she was way too smart to buy into popularity contests and that winning one meant anything. It's always the popular people who have the luxury of being ambivalent about their heightened status of being in the in-crowd, because they never knew what it's like to be an outsider the way I did. I feigned indifference about my social standing or lack thereof, but I was anything but ambivalent about it. I wanted to be seen for all the good things about me...I just wasn't sure there were any. Which is why I wanted to be Lara.

Yet, I hated her at the same time. Because obviously, I knew I couldn't actually become her and in the end I'd be stuck being me. It all made perfect logical sense in my head. And in my defense, I was in eighth grade at the time and the currency of middle school girls is hating other girls.

Not everyone has their older sister transition into being their mother overnight. Not that Lara replaced my mother; no one could do that. I lived off the memories I had of my mom, but as I got older those memories became more scarce. They seemed more like dreams; blurry, fuzzy and bleeding together into a video montage of my life before I turned ten when she died and everything changed. You think when someone dies there's nothing left to lose of them, but that's not true. There's always more to lose, you just don't know that until it happens and then it's too late.

"Henny, you're so disgusting! How can you live like this? Look at it!" Lara lectured.

There were blobs of blue toothpaste on the counter where I'd set the toothpaste tube cinched at the middle with the top off and it continued to ooze. There were also globs of it in the sink and flecks of it on the mirror.

"Towels don't dry when you leave them in a heap on the floor. And smell it. Do you reuse these?" She asked picking it up to sniff it, then making gagging sounds before dropping it back on the linoleum floor. "Seriously, it's vile! I don't feel clean when I have to use a bathroom that's disgusting. You've gotta clean it up. And use some of the bleach that's under the counter in the shower and the toilet." Lara lectured.

"Can I use the bleach on the mirror to get your zit juice off of it, though?" I figured the best way to handle her demands was by passively aggressively grossing her out even more.

"Why is everything a joke to you?" She asked.

"Why don't you have a sense of humor?" I countered.

"Have it done before I get home from work tonight."

As if Lara didn't have enough going for her, she also worked at Baskin-Robbins scooping ice cream.

"For someone who's not my mother, you sure nag like you are."

"Consider me your fairy godmother then. You've got 'til midnight."

I taunted her to get a reaction, but instead of blowing up, she tried to use my sarcasm against me. That bitch! Who does she think she is trying to use reverse psychology on me? Sarcasm is one of my primary defense mechanisms and she doesn't get to take that away from me. And I wish I could say being sardonic didn't look good on her, but she wore it well, just like everything else it looked great on her.

I waited until she left the house in her forest green Honda Civic she'd bought with her own money she'd saved up from working before I did anything. I didn't want to give her the satisfaction that she'd won again. I wanted her to wonder the whole night if I'd done what she'd asked me to because what I really wanted was control. And if I couldn't have it, I'd settle for incendiary emotional damage. I picked up the half empty bottle of shampoo bottle and took off the top, taking a whiff to inhale it's strong artificial floral fragrance. Then I unscrewed the cap of the bleach before hastily pouring the last little bit that remained in the jug into the shampoo bottle with half of it splashing over into the basin of the shower. Exacting revenge isn't an exact science. I didn't know how much I'd need to achieve the desired result or even what the desired result was. Her hair falling out would have been the most disastrous one that came to mind, but I didn't really know what would happen. I didn't shampoo my hair for a week waiting to see the result of my impulsive bleach-shampoo retribution for her making me clean the bathroom. But, I never noticed anything different about her hair. It was as if it never happened at all. When things fall flat, there's a choice to be made: be relieved or take it up another notch. I, of course, opted for the latter.

While our days went on fairly routinely with my dad hibernating in the darkroom developing photos, Lara playing the role of my mom and me being the embodiment of the ultimate slacker-loser, I did some research. Adding bleach to shampoo only makes the person blonder, which as we know, only makes them more appealing. While pouring bleach in a gas tank completely immobilizes the car and thus, the person who drives it. First the car doesn't start, then it silently, but maliciously corrodes it from the inside. Before you know it, you've turned your sister into a freakish recluse without a social life, ruining her best years of high school. It was an easy way to bring her down to my level, ensuring I'd win. Although, there really was no prize for winning. I know that now, but in the moment winning something, anything meant everything. This time I was victorious; the engine in her car seized. But, the win was short term with long term consequences that completely backfired on me. She stopped nagging me. And she stopped trying to hold our defective little family together. Suddenly, I ceased to exist in her world.

It was the month after I'd sabotaged her car that she started dating Rick. He was tall and lean with dark eyes hiding under dark shaggy wavy hair. On the day he came to pick Lara up for their first date he was wearing jeans with a belt and a plain black T-shirt and Nike sneakers making him look cool, but also fairly clean-cut and respectable. The souped-up baby blue Camaro he picked her up in should've been the first clue that he was an insecure douchebag. It had two doors and technically seating for four, but the only thing anyone uses the backseat for in a car like that is having sex and even that seems impossible in such a confined space. In hindsight, I figured out Dickhead needed the extra two seats in the back to haul his inflated ego and his misogynistic tendencies. I blame myself for pushing her away from me and toward him. Maybe if I hadn't destroyed her car she wouldn't have gone out on a date with him that night and everything would've turned out different. Instead, she got an abusive relationship, cancer and died. And I felt responsible for all of it.

———————————

It was a Monday evening, my night off from work. I'd just put The Stooges to bed and was just about to pour myself a cocktail, as had become my custom, to celebrate the end of yet another excruciatingly, exhausting day with three demanding, ungrateful kids, when there was a knock at the back door. The streetlights illuminated an unfamiliar BMW parked at the end of the driveway, curiously closer to the street than the house. I hadn't seen him in years and he was the last person I wanted to see now. The last time I'd seen him was about five years ago after Max was born. His hair had thinned considerably since then. He was standing at the door of what used to be his house a deadbeat dad with a dad bod. Dickhead.

"I'd have let myself in, but the key isn't under the mat anymore", he said.

"You don't live here anymore, remember?"

"Lara and I own it." He said.

"Lara owned it. She was the responsible one with a good credit score, so the house was in her name, remember? You just occupied space here sometimes when it was convenient for you. You know, when you weren't at your side piece's house cheating on my sister."

"I forgot how funny you think you are Henny." He brushed his way past me and into the kitchen.

"Why are you here?" I asked. I wanted to ask him where he was when Lara died and why no one could find him. But, I decided I wanted him to stay lost more than I wanted to know the answer, so I didn't.

"Funny, I was going to ask you the same thing." He said while he walked slowly in a circle surveying the kitchen.

"I'm raising the orphans you created, Dickhead. I heard you love abandoning kids so much that you had another one with your hopelessly deluded girlfriend you left my sister for. Your commitment to overpopulating the world by only contributing your sperm doesn't make you more of a man. It makes you less of one."

For years, these words were pent up inside me waiting for the right moment to spew them into his face. Shouting at him released some of my rage, but I instantly regretted saying them. Not because Dickhead didn't deserve to hear them, because he did. I felt guilty calling The Stooges orphans because by doing that I was also saying Lara abandoned them, which makes it sound deliberate, but she didn't choose to die. Lara didn't intend for any of this, all she was guilty of was being naive, trusting and loving someone who wasn't capable of love. By the time the kids came along she felt trapped in her marriage and she didn't love herself anymore, but she loved them. And she deceived herself and them to think that was enough.

He threw his hands on top of my shoulders, threatening my throat with his thumbs. His eyes bulging with anger, but they were vacant at the same time.

"You'll regret those words." He said warning me.

He pushed me back, my body slamming into the edge of the counter top, my hand flinging back and smashing into a glass I'd just placed there before he came and invaded my home. I slunk down the cabinets until I was sitting in a heap on the floor surrounded by shards of the cocktail glass with my hand bleeding. I didn't see him leave, but I heard the back door slam and the screeching tires of his car as he pulled out of the driveway, so I knew he was gone. I hoped it was for good, but I knew I wouldn't be that lucky.

That's where Casey found me, on the kitchen floor sobbing, picking pieces of glass out of my wounded hand.

"What happened Henny?" She asked having just missed being an eyewitness to her dad physically assaulting me.

"Yeah..I tripped with a glass in my hand." I said, lying to protect her from the truth.

"It's ok. I have axe-idents too."

"We all do. I've got to try to be more careful from now on." I said, wiping the tears from my face trying to collect myself.

"When I have axe-idents, mama hugs me."

"You had a great mommy." I said wistfully.

"Mama's gone. I have Henna now."

Casey had cleverly combined Henny with mama and created a new moniker for me in the process. I hadn't known what The Stooges should call me. Aunt Hennessy was too much of a mouthful. Auntie was too formal and generic. And I'd always hated the nickname Henny. But, Henna was simple and perfect.

"I'm sorry." I was sorry for so many things.

"You needda bandaid?" She asked.

"I think I might." I smiled.

She hugged me, her arms stretching around my shoulders, her head nuzzling into my neck. I could feel her heartbeat and her deep, slow breathing. They calmed me. The loose waves of her hair tickled my neck. Casey looked so much like her mom. She had Lara's hair, full lips and small, perky nose. But, she had a feisty personality like me. I felt her body relax as she fell asleep holding me. I'd never wanted kids and now here I was responsible for 3.

I was never good to Lara. I never told her I loved her. I'd never said those words to anyone my whole life. I'd failed Lara. I didn't want to fail her kids too.

"I love you Casey." I whispered while twisting her curls around my finger.

CHAPTER 9

The stark reality of early mornings were the worst. Especially when I had a hangover from working at the club the night before. Drunk guys don't like to drink alone, so it was fairly common that customers bought me drinks making me their designated drinking buddy while they ogled the strippers. It was a buddy system for lonely guys and/or alcoholics and I wasn't one to pass up free booze. The first time a guy offered to buy me a drink at the club, I ordered Hennessy on the rocks as a joke since all the regulars at the club knew my name. After a while I started to develop a taste for cognac, but I only drank it at work because it was much too expensive for my meager crappy boxed wine budget. Alcohol seemed like a justified escape from the stresses of the day, until the alarm clock went off at 6am. Nothing's justified at that hour.

It was hard enough to get my own tired ass out of bed every morning, but to have to get up and take care of three cranky, ungrateful little humans is cruel, bordering on inhumane. If numerous attempts to wake them and threats that I wouldn't remind them again didn't work, I'd resort to pulling off their covers and tickling their exposed feet until they finally got their lazy asses out of bed. When they were finally vertical, that's when the fighting began. How could they even have the energy to fight about who gets to read the back of the cereal box during breakfast? Without coffee even? But yet, they did it every damn day.

"Did you finish your homework that's due today with Bethany last night?" I asked Max.

"No, she took us on a field trip," he said between loud slurps of his cereal.

Listening to kids eat is quite possibly the most disgusting sound on the planet.

"Oh? Where did she take you?" I asked.

"To her house." He said with his mouth full of a generous spoonful of Life cereal.

I had the sudden urge to throw up. Not sure if it was only from the disgust of seeing the soggy cereal in his mouth or if it was the cognac from the night before.

"Don't talk with your mouth full Max. I only say this every day."

I knew I was a hypocrite because I'm sure I had my own gross habits, but everyone knows someone else's gross habits are always more repulsive than your own.

"Mrs. Doom is going to keep me in for recess." Max said.

"No fair! You took all the powder and that's the best part!" Jack yelled while attempting to pour cereal from an empty box. Who got the prized powder of crushed cereal and granulated sugar at the bottom of the cereal box was the most common argument in the mornings.

"There's Cheerios in the back of the cupboard." I said, knowing it was their least favorite choice of cereal as evidenced by the fact that the same box had been in the cupboard for two months now.

"I FUCKNG HATE CHEERIOS!" Jack yelled.

"What did you just say?" I asked stunned he'd dropped the F-bomb.

"I SAID, I FUCKING HATE CHEERIOS!"

He obviously didn't understand angry sarcastic accusatory rhetorical questions, yet.

"Where did you hear that word?" Hoping to god the answer wasn't from me. Please don't be me. Please don't fucking be me!

"Last night at Bethany's." Jack replied.

"Fuck Cheer-os!" Casey chimed in.

"Let's start at why you went to Bethany's house last night." I asked.

"She said she had to do some stuff to do for work and we could help her." Max said.

"So what did you do there?" I asked.

"We put some weeds in bags." Jack said.

"Outside in the yard?" I asked.

"No, in her bedroom." Jack said.

"I wanted to weigh them, but she said only she could do that part." Max said.

"Max took the bags from me and wouldn't even let me help!" Jack argued.

"I gave bags to Beffany" Casey added.

My babysitter is a drug dealer. Unless she called herself a pot entrepreneur. Either way it's the same thing. Why didn't I think to ask her if she sold drugs? Come to think of it, I didn't actually ask her anything. Much less if she was a pedophile, serial killer, never mind drug dealer. It was just a natural assumption on my part that my babysitter wasn't a drug dealer and wouldn't use kids as free child slave labor to fill her dime bags. I was livid. At first it was at her for putting The Stooges in that situation. Before I realized I was even more guilty for putting them in that situation than she was.

I considered them a career investment, even though I didn't intend to make cocktail waitressing my career. But then again, Selena, a veteran stripper in her forties working at the Booby Trap never intended on making stripping her career either. One night after closing when we were changing out of our work clothes back into our sweatpants to head home after our shifts she told me that when she started she only planned to strip for a couple of years just to make some quick cash. But, there's never enough money and then you come to depend on the extra cash, choosing to live a more moderately comfortable lifestyle instead of saving it. She's been working as a stripper living paycheck to paycheck for over twenty years now. "I can quit any time, you think and then before long it's all you know how to do. And that's when you know you're hooked or trapped, depending on whether you're an optimist or a pessimist." Selena said. I wanted to be an optimist and think that I wouldn't be a cocktail waitress forever. But, the pessimist in me knew it was a real possibility. But, it was the realist in me that bought new black thigh high leather boots for work.

My transition from an exhausted, disheveled tomboy started after I left The Stooges with my dad, the only person I had to watch them since I'd fired Bethany and hadn't found a replacement yet, before heading off to work. I walked through the back door of the club in my old, comfortable engineer boots I'd worn since I was sixteen. But, before I started my shift, I sat in the backroom with the strippers and other waitresses putting on my make-up and getting dressed. I knew my tips were dependent on not only serving drinks without spilling them, but I was also required to put some effort into my appearance. I spackled on more make-up than a Sephora salesperson, being careful not to get any on my black Booby Trap T-shirt with two big white circles with a dot in center (which looked like tits and made mine look deceptively bigger than they were) when I pulled it over my head. It helped that I'd cut a generous hole out around the neckline so the shirt would fall over sexily my shoulder, exposing my bra strap. I found the black hot pants for my work uniform at the Salvation Army, hoping that the new dominatrix thigh high boots would help conceal my Pangea sized thighs. When I discovered they didn't, I wore black panty hose to help disguise the exposed cellulite and it make sliding off my boots at the end of the night easier. Or mid-shift if Devon was in the club, which he was religiously on Tuesday nights.

"They're exquisite!" He said. Extending his pointer finger at them longingly when I came for his drink order, even though I already knew his order was Amstel Light, we continued the ritual anyway.

I'd never felt sexy before I worked at a strip club and I admit, I kinda liked it. There was a component of power and control to it that I needed because my life felt so out of control. But, the price of feeling sexy was pain. The exquisite agony of constantly being on my feet for a 6 hour shift in 4 inch heels that needed to be broken in.

"Meet me," he said. Which I knew was short for "meet me by the men's room with your exquisite sexy boot so I can jerk off to it.

"I have other tables to take care of." I said and just like that I turned the tables on him and redistributed the balance of power by making him wait. Hoping my efforts would pay out with a bigger tip. I was on the cusp of giving him my boot's virginity after all. That's gotta be worth something.

I was making my way back to the bar with drink orders when he intercepted me.

"$250 in room #2," he said referring to the VIP rooms reserved for private lap dances.

He was a horny man, not a wordy one.

"I don't dance, remember." I teased him.

His piercing blue eye gave me a knowing glance before shifting his gaze down to my boots. He went in first and I followed a minute behind clutching my empty drink tray.

When I arrived he closed the door after me.

"Just to be clear, I don't give lap dances." I reiterated again. This time because I was a bit wary that he'd changed the venue of his tryst with my boot.

He guided me over to the couch intended for lap dance customers without saying a word. I sat down reluctantly and he got down on his knees in front of me. He placed his right hand on my knee while his left hand reached inside my left thigh to the top of the zipper. I couldn't help but notice that a bulge appeared in his jeans when he touched my boots. He unzipped my boot slowly, sliding it off over my panty hosed foot. Then he stood up, gingerly placing the boot on the cocktail table next to me like a trophy and proceeded to unzip his jeans, exposing his uncircumcised semi-hard penis. I couldn't stop staring at it. Not because I was turned on, because I wasn't. It was more of a clinical fascination because I'd never seen an uncircumcised man in that particular state of arousal before. He turned to face the object of his affection: my footwear, giving me a side view of him as he spat into his palm and started stroking himself. I turned my head away toward the back of the room, holding my drink tray up to my chest as a shield. In less than a minute he was done and began cleaning up with some baby wipes he removed from a ziploc sandwich bag he had stored in his jeans pocket. Which made me wonder if he had a baby and a wife waiting at home for him while he was here with me masturbating to my footwear.

"Great boots." He said handing me three crisp bills that felt like they'd just been printed at the mint.

"Oh you noticed?" He didn't laugh. He never laughed.

My boots had already paid for themselves.

———————

Max's bus was late. Usually, I was the one arriving late to pick Max up with the bus parked on the side of the road and the engine turned off because our stop was the last one on the bus route. When I approached the bus, I'd see the silhouette of Max standing next to the bus driver, Gary, asking rapid fire questions about the dials and pedals. His intense inquisitiveness was part of why I dreaded picking him up at the end of the day. Which might be part of the reason I seemed to lose track of time in the late afternoon. I knew that Max coming home from school meant that he and Jack would turn the afternoons and evenings into one long drawn out argument about everything. The boys were complete opposites, but also completely consumed with each other. Which left Casey to her own attention seeking destructive devices like cutting her hair into asymmetric shapes with the scissors from Lara's manicure kit. And the best game of all, flushing random objects down the toilet. The longer Max was out of the house and the boys were away from each other, the better.

We waited at the park next to the bus stop for Max's bus to arrive. Jack was riding the motorcycle on a spring rocking himself back and forth. The only time he seemed content was when he was moving. He even rocked back and forth when we were sitting down eating dinner together. Being in motion was a kind of comforting self soothing meditation for him somehow. I pushed Casey on the swing her legs stretching out in front of her, frustrated that she couldn't quite get the rhythm of pumping her legs to swing on her own yet. Even though she'd just grown out of the baby swings, she wanted to jump straight to complete swing autonomy. We were a disjointed family, all craving some independence when what we really were was interdependent.

Max came bounding off of a different bus than usual and just shy of an hour late, with a different driver.

"A car crashed into the back of the bus. The police and ambulance came with their lights and sirens on!"

"Cool!" Jack said with wide eyes.

"Are you ok?" I asked looking him over for signs of visible injuries.

"Yeah, everyone went to the back of the bus to see the car, but Gary made us sit down in our seats."

"All the kids on the bus were ok then?" I asked.

"Just the lady driving the car died."

"She died?" I asked stunned.

"Like mom?" Casey asked.

"People die sometimes." I said caught off guard. Realizing it was was the stupidest under exaggeration ever because people die all the time. No one knew that more intimately than The Three Stooges.

"Then the ambulance came. I overhead the police say she was texting and driving when they made us get off the bus and get on another one to take us home."

"Did you see the dead lady?" Jack asked.

"Everyone was looking out the windows trying to see. Then Gary made us sit on the floor in the middle of the bus so we couldn't see outside, but I think I saw her arm before that." Max said.

Max and Jack discussed the minutiae of the tragic accident on the walk back home.

"You want a piggyback ride?" I asked Casey, searching for some way to distract and comfort her.

"Carry me like a baby," she said.

"Like this?" I asked scooping her up, cradling her head with my elbow with her legs dangling over my arms.

She giggled, turning her head from side to side with delight making her curls spring.

When we got home I let her reach her hand inside the mailbox. Inside on top of the junk mail and bills was an unaddressed, unstamped envelope. I put Casey down, stood at the end of the driveway and opened it.

In The Circuit Court

For The Eighth Judicial Circuit of New York

Niagara County, Niagara Falls, New York

PETITION TO REVOKE GUARDIANSHIP OF A MINOR

Hennessy Greypath was appointed Guardian of

Maxwell Hack

Jackson Hack

Casey Hack

I, Richard Hack, ask that Letters of Guardianship be revoked because:

I am the biological father of said children.

Subscribed and Sworn to before me

Karen Green, Notary Public

CHAPTER 10

"This is totally worth starving myself for." Leslie said sipping her caramel Frappuccino, her full lips glossed in cotton candy pink puckering around the straw of her drink as she sucked it up slowly like it was a scene from a porn. We were sitting on the vinyl seats at the kids' play place in the middle of the mall while Jack and Casey played with the other germ infested kids whose parents couldn't afford to send their rug rats to preschool, so they too were looking for a free way to keep them busy for a while. You can always tell who the germaphobic parents are because they have a little container of hand sanitizer caribinered to their bag. And I'm sure there's Neosporin and antibacterial wipes inside the baby bag that they still carry with them even though their kid is five years old. I, on the other hand, was lucky if I remembered to bring my wallet and phone with me when I ventured out in public. I was an anti-germaphobe, assuming that exposing The Stooges to bacteria, viruses and even parasites would help boost their immune systems. That was my justification for my laziness anyway. That and the humiliation I'd cause The Stooges if I forced them into a lemon scented bird bath with an antibacterial wipe in the middle of the mall. The most neurotic parents weren't the germaphobes though. They were the parents of the ultra religious home schooled kids that met at the mall every Thursday morning at 10:00am. Their kids were so picked over and regimented it seemed like they weren't entitled to their own personality.

"It's Dickhead." Leslie said.

"How do you mean?" I asked taking a sip of my caramel Macchiato.

"He's bluffing. He forged the document to scare you and then he put it in your mailbox. That's why it doesn't have an address on the envelope and why it's not stamped. And there isn't a seal on it. The document is completely forged. Trust me, I've been with enough guys who are assholes and liars to know when things don't add up. Sometimes I've still stayed for the sex anyway though." She said.

"Well, it worked. I'm scared. The kids aren't safe with him."

"Why haven't you told me anything about the kids' dad until now?"

"I don't like to talk about him because I don't like to think about him. But, he's made that impossible since he resurrected himself from wherever the hell he's been. A couple weeks ago he came to the house, I'm not sure why. When I confronted him about what he'd done to my sister and the kids he threatened me, pushed me around and I cut my hand up pretty good."

"Why the hell didn't you tell me? Tell me you filed a police report at least!" "It was late at night and the kids were asleep. It just wasn't a good time. And then the next day I was busy with the kids. And then I felt responsible for allowing it to happen. I'm not even sure why I let him in the house in the first place." I confessed.

"Jesus girl!" Leslie said loudly. The group of homeschool parents in the corner turned to give us the evil eye. "You didn't allow this to happen...he physically assaulted you! And not filing a report with the police is what's fucking stupid. He's a despicable person and an abhorrent father. But, because he is their father, if this ever does actually go to court, they're going to favor the patriarchy, you know that. It's up to you to defend yourself and those kids by documenting everything he does or doesn't do." She advised.

"Lara's kids deserve better. Someone who knows what they're doing and is patient and stable. I'm not the best person to raise them, but Dickhead is definitely the worst option."

"If those are the stipulations for being a mother, most people wouldn't qualify. Especially me. Nobody's ever really ready to be a parent. Kids don't need perfect parents or every kid would be an orphan. They need just enough to get their needs met. So what you do is show up and try. That's it. So, stop making this about you and your failings, cause it doesn't matter. And no one cares."

"No one cares? What an unexpectedly, uninspiring pep talk." I said.

"I need to toughen you up and get you into fighting form. And honestly? With your pitiful victim attitude, we're starting with core. Sit-ups."

———————

I assumed she was joking about the sit-ups, but she wasn't. Except that sit-ups weren't her favorite way to exercise. That was sex and she talked about it all the time. How she lost her virginity, at age fourteen. With her older brother's friend who stopped over at the house when she was home alone. How many partners she'd had, which was a lot. And exactly what she liked sexually, which seemed like everything to me; a twenty-two year old woman with one horribly traumatizing sexual encounter and/or assault under my belt. How could a stripper that every man lusted over be so starved for sex? The answer eluded me. But, her recurrent conversations about her sexcapades made me excruciatingly intrigued. I was envious of her sexual confidence and freedom. Making me think it was no coincidence that her stage name at the club was Envy.

After sex, her next favorite way to workout was pole dancing. When she wasn't working the pole at the club, she practiced her tricks at home on the pole in her bedroom in front of a huge mirror she propped up in the corner. The room looked like a hotel room in it's starkness: a low platform queen size bed with nightstands on either side of it and one dresser. But it's the framed Manon Lescaut poster over the bed, with big red balloons, resembling women's breasts with knots for nipples on a pink torso with a small Eiffel Tower with the "Puccini Manon" printed in the bottom center that dominated the room. Her closet was brimming with pink and black, skimpy sexy dresses. She had as many stilettos as a shoe store lined up on shelves stacked floor to ceiling. And she insisted I pick out a pair I liked and put them on.

"Go ahead, play on it. Everyone wants to." She said.

"I must be the exception then. Because I don't see anything good coming from me spinning on a pole, especially in heels."

"You're right. I've noticed you walk like a trucker on speed at work. Like you're so focused on getting where you're going quickly, that you're unaware of the actual steps involved to do it. And that's when you start tripping over yourself and spilling drinks on customers."

"Balancing a tray full of drinks and maneuvering around all the tables and demanding customers is harder than you think. I'm just doing the best I can. We can't all be as graceful as you."

"Yes you can! I wasn't born knowing how to walk in heels or knowing how to dance. It's all practice. Lots of it. And you'd be better and more efficient at your job if you slowed down and walked like a stripper in your new boots. Plus, you'd get tipped more. It's all part of the show."

"No one cares how I walk when I serve them drinks. No one's looking at my frumpy ass. They come to the club to see you, not me." I said dismissively.

"See? Right there, that's your problem. Attitude. Everyone thinks it comes down to how they look. That you have to be a beautiful goddess or something. But, that's not it at all. The strippers and waitresses that make the biggest tips at end of the night aren't the prettiest girls. They're the ones who exude the most confidence. And you? You need to be empowered. Which is why I'm going to teach you how to walk with confidence in those pleasers you have on whether you like it or not. It's for your own good. "

"Is it too early for a drink? Or three?"

It was the Spicy Bloody Marys with extra horseradish she made that gave me the liquid encouragement I needed to give it a try.

———

It was that night, when I showed up at work with a buzz from the Bloody Marys, my feet already swollen from practicing my stripper walk. That's when my past and my future collided with my present. His walk when he entered the club had cocky asshole written all over it. He had shaggy, greasy hair with a ruddy complexion. The dress shoes he wore contradicted the casually thrown together baggy faded out jeans and untucked short sleeved button down shirt that hung over his belly. His scrawny companion had bulging eyes making him bare a striking resemblance to a chihuahua. It appeared that he hadn't finished dressing wearing only jeans with a white Fruit of the Loom crew neck T-shirt. They sat down at a table near the back of the club, usually frequented by businessmen trying to build camaraderie and/or close a deal with their clients at the table while pretending to be disinterested in the naked women on stage. Obviously, if they were really interested in building relationships or sealing a business deal they'd go somewhere less titillating to do it. But, what they were really doing was flaunting that they're big-time, successful businessmen for female attention. Or rather, flaunting the appearance that they were those things. Which is why we referred to this type of guy as a "peacock" spreading his tail feathers for all of us to see. The inside joke being that we all assumed their cocks were the size of a pea. Peacocks didn't waste singles on tipping strippers on stage, they blew their wad on lap dances in the private rooms. Dancers preferred working in private rooms where the tips were bigger and the effort involved was less than it was dancing on a pole. The only requirement to get a good tip lap dancing was acting interested in the guy you were giving it to.

Shaggy Hair, the spokesman for the table, motioned for me with two fingers outstretched like a flight attendant pointing out the emergency exits while he was talking to his buddy, Chihuahua Face and actively avoiding making eye contact with me. They were already patronizing, but even worse, they were going to be bad tippers. You could always tell.

"What can I get you?" I asked reluctantly.

I couldn't make out his drink order over the thumping music. He was watching the dancer on stage and couldn't be bothered to turn his head toward me so I could at least read his lips. Forcing me to bend down and ask him to repeat his order.

It was worse than I thought, he ordered a Cranberry and Vodka. A girly drink.

"We don't have cranberry juice. Vodka and soda work?"

"No cranberry? What kind of place is this?"

It's a titty bar where men can oogle women who wouldn't give them the time of day in broad daylight dumbass.

"Grey Goose or Absolut?" I asked knowing the answer before I even asked.

"Whatever's cheapest." He said on cue.

"And for you?" I nodded my chin towards his friend admiring the dancer's breasts.

"Budweiser for him." Shaggy Hair answered.

I knew I'd seen him somewhere before. The club had it's hard core frequent fliers and once or twice a year when their wives or girlfriends went out of town types too. He definitely wasn't former, but he didn't fit the latter either. I couldn't place him. I returned with their drinks making a wobbly stop in front of the table that I blame on the buzz from the Bloody Marys a couple of hours earlier. The tray of drinks tipped and landed in Shaggy Hair's lap. Shocked by the sudden cold spilled drink on his crotch, he made a face like he was having an orgasm. It was Tony Marino's O-face. I was face to face with the guy I had sex with in high school who might have raped me, but I wasn't sure what to call it. I was either a slut or a victim and I still wasn't sure which one. I didn't know what I'd say to him if I ever saw him again.

"I'm so sorry!" Of all the things I imagined saying to him, I'm sorry was never one of them.

He looked up at me for the first time, his eyes squinting. That's it, he recognizes me, I thought.

"Sweet. When you clean up the mess you made, don't forget this spot, it's really wet." He said with a smile pointing his finger to his crotch.

I'd had sex with this fucking vile misogynist and he didn't even know who I was.

"It's strictly self-service here. The bathroom's over there. There should be paper towels unless someone else has used them all up cleaning up after their masturbation session in there."

I expected him to make a scene, but he didn't. Tony went to the men's room and I picked up the empty glasses, putting them back on my tray and walking them back to the bar. Chihuahua Face was headed out the front door with a pack of cigarettes and lighter for a smoke when he stopped me.

"Hey, are you Hennessy Greywater?" He asked.

"Greypath." Why did I always feel compelled to answer a question, even when I knew I shouldn't?

"You hung out with Tonya Balinski back in high school?" Who is this guy?

I paused trying not to answer him.

"I used to party with her and remember seeing you with her sometimes. You worked at the T-shirt shop at the mall, right?"

A guy who had sex with me didn't recognize me, but this stranger knows where I worked and who my best friend from high school was. How fucked up is that?

He took my silence as confirmation.

"Whatever happened to Tonya?"

"She's in prison." I said and walked away.

It was true. She was arrested and thrown in prison for arson, but I didn't know if she was still there or not. We'd lost touch four years ago after we graduated from high school and I moved to Niagara Falls. I didn't think all that much of our growing distance at first. It seemed normal under the circumstances after we graduated and I moved away. But, a couple years later I heard a rumor there might be another more concerning reason I hadn't heard from her. She had schizophrenia. The structure that she set on fire was her childhood home and her dad and his dog were inside.

I'd always had a quietly complicated relationship with my dad. We avoided having any real meaningful conversations. Especially about my mom and Lara, the two people we loved and missed most. Both of us grieving on our own because we didn't know any other way. We were ignorant, stubborn loners and we liked it that way or so we told ourselves. Avoidance was our solace. And it was the one thing I was really good at. It was my protection, my thick layer of bubble wrap insulating me from the things I couldn't control. Which seemed like everything.

I'd left connecting with my father to Lara. She was a nurturing optimist like my mother, while I was a reclusive pessimist like my dad. She was the one who kept our family together. Calling my dad and me on the phone, coaxing us both to talk to her once a week, though I never reciprocated and called to check-in on her. Not until she got sick with cancer anyway. Gatherings for birthdays and holidays were always at her house. I just thought it was something she liked to do, I never thought about how much work it was until I inherited her life.

"It's Casey's birthday on Saturday. We're going to have something at the house at 2pm." I called my dad with a last minute party invite.

I usually took The Stooges over to his house. By usually I mean I did it a couple times before I stopped doing it because it was a huge pain in the ass. Not only was there nothing for them to do at my dad's house, they fought and whined even more than they did at our house out of sheer boredom.

"She'll be turning two?" He asked.

"She'll be three actually."

"Oh right.....time flies."

It had been three months months since Lara died, but neither one of us acknowledged that, even though we both knew that Lara's death was the benchmark for the passage of time now.

"Can you make it?" I asked.

"Of course."

His quick and easygoing acceptance of my invitation deceived his reclusive nature. I knew he didn't like going to anyone's house, not even mine. Especially for a party with people, kids jacked up on sugar, noise and small talk where he'd be trapped without a darkroom to escape to. My dad relished nothing more than peace and quiet. I know because I'm exactly the same way.

God knows I didn't want to throw a kid's birthday party at my house. There were three kids living there already and they were already more than I could handle. Plus, I didn't know who to invite. When I thought about it the only playdates Casey and Jack had been on were with the kids of the strippers and waitresses from the Booby Trap. Which meant that the party was going to consist of sex workers and their kids, adding a whole new element of stress and anxiety for my dad. And I didn't know what kind of party to throw for a three year old. Do I buy some cheap trinkety items from the dollar store and see which kid can flush them down the toilet the fastest without clogging it? It seemed like one of the more realistic options with Casey and her obsession with wearing big girl panties and her penchant for flushing random objects down the toilet. I desperately wanted potty training to be over. I tried to convince her to wear pull-ups. They offered all the big girl convenience of pulling them down like panties to use the toilet without any of the commitment in case she had an accident. Except Casey didn't buy it and was insistent on wearing real cotton panties, even though she constantly had accidents in them. It wasn't the pissing in her pants, so much as the shitting her pants in the most inconvenient public places, like the library and the grocery store, that was so frustrating. Not only that, she tried so hard not to poop that she had skid marks in her underwear, but she also suffered from chronic constipation. Requiring me to give her an enema once a week to clean her out. Which was a pretty distressing event for both of us.

"So you're coming then?" I asked.

"I told you I was, didn't I?" My dad asked defensively.

"Did you mean it?"

"Why would I say it if I didn't mean it?"

All of our conversations were a string of unanswered questions repeating on a loop. The truth is, neither one of us wanted the questions answered. Because the truth is brutal and harsh. And since we'd both had enough of that, avoiding disappointment was a priority in our relationship. If you could call what we had a relationship. We basically lived parallel lives in close-ish proximity to each other. We were a pathetic remnant of a family.

"Great! See you Saturday then. Oh, question, do you know anything about potty training?"

"Yeah, eventually kids use the toilet. Some earlier, some later."

"Casey has accidents all the time."

"Well, you're definitely related then. You pissed and crapped your pants all the time. Your mom and I thought about sending you to kindergarten in a diaper."

"Really? You're joking." I said even though my dad was never one to joke about anything.

"You don't remember? A while after you started school, you finally stopped. And then after your mom passed, you had accidents on and off for a couple more years."

That's when I remembered the sudden urgent need to poop and my inability to control it and then, when it was too late, being completely ashamed. Just thinking about it now, my face flushed with embarrassment.

"I took you to the pediatrician and he said it was stress from losing your mom. Maybe it's the same with Casey. She's only three, don't expect too much. She'll be alright."

But, would I be alright? I wasn't sure. But, I did know I was exhausted. When I wasn't taking care of The Stooges, I was working at the club. On my nights off after The Stooges went to bed I'd stay up late drinking cheap wine from a box, watching TV and scrolling Twitter (where I'd just opened an account) until I passed out. It was how I rewarded myself for having survived through another day.

CHAPTER 11

"I'd love to get out of my own head and into someone else's." After scrolling through Twitter and being a voyeur for months, I was finally brave enough to post my first tweet under the pseudonym Brandy@sullengirl. During my strutting 101 lesson with Leslie she started calling me Brandy, teasing me that the name Hennessy sounded too pretentious even for a fictitious stripper name. I combined Brandy with Sullen Girl, the title of my favorite Fiona Apple song to create my Twitter account. Leslie was the one who introduced me to social media. She'd used Twitter and Instagram for years, to market herself and entice new customers to come to the club to watch her dance. Unlike the other dancers at the Booby Trap, she wasn't an in-your-face booty shaking stripper, but more of a sensuous one, setting her apart from the other girls. Her pole tricks were slow, controlled, but also unbelievably athletic at the same time. On top of all that and being a classic beauty, she was also a brilliant businesswoman. Exposing just enough on-line to entice men to come into the club to watch her dance. Once they were there, she seduced customers with her refined allure. Ironically, it was the sense of mystery and restraint she had that men were drawn to and why she attracted so many repeat customers. She reminded me of Lara in that way. Only, Leslie was far more bold and confident than Lara.

Maybe that's why I used a picture of Lara as my Twitter avi, because I wanted to have that kind of mystique. And since I didn't have any in real life, at least I could pretend to have it on-line. She was about ninteen in the photo of her I posted to my timeline. Lara was wearing a white v-neck faintly see through T-shirt with a hint of her ballerina pink bra strap visible. The soft beach waves of her hair cascaded down past her shoulders, her face drenched in sunshine with her big blue eyes squinting slightly with a playful, genuine, shy smile. She looked sexy, but innocent at the same time. You could feel how happy she was in the photo. It was everything I wanted to be, but wasn't. Even if it was all a complete delusion, the way it was for my sister. I'm sure she was genuinely happy in that moment, right before her life changed forever. Because the photo was taken a few months before she married a narcissistic, loser, abusive dickhead.

"beautiful, gorgeous woman can't be sad" It was the first direct message I received on Twitter from Mr. Big Dick@ joeschmoo. Which was hilarious on so many levels. First, the lack of capitalization and punctuation. Then, grammatically. Either add an "A" to the beginning of the sentence or pluralize it to "women". And everyone knows that calling yourself Mr. Big Dick is just compensation for having a small dick, only proving that he's a really big dick with an inferiority complex. In addition, I think he meant Joe Schmo, as in just a regular guy, as opposed to Joe Schmoo, which rhymes with poo. But, what was even more glaringly obvious to me was his false belief that attractive people couldn't be depressed. The way Lara was shortly after her marriage to Dickhead. I was positive that the avi Joe Schmoo used of a large erect penis trapped in a g-string, was a stock photo. He could be anyone. Ranging from a horny fifteen year old boy to a grown ass, unemployed thirty-something living in his mom's basement. Hell, he could even be an elderly old man in a nursing home for all I knew. Whoever he was, I was positive I didn't want anything to do with him and decided the best course of action was not to respond at all, delete the message and block him.

But, there was always a new Mr. Tiny Dick; social media is full of them. The next guy who messaged me wrote: "I'm jerking so hard to you right now." Making me distrust him from the start. How could he type and masturbate at that level of intensity simultaneously? I highly doubt he could text with only his non-dominant hand. Something just didn't add up. And if you can't trust a complete stranger on the internet who can you trust anymore?

It's not that I was repulsed by male attention, because that wasn't it at all. It was that I was turned off by brash, iodiotic perverts. I was starved for male attention and sex; I needed to be wanted. I wanted guys to look at me the way they used to at Lara in high school and how men lusted after Leslie in the club. I wanted more than a man who paid me to jack himself off to my boot on Tuesday nights. Hell, my boot, an inanimate object, was getting more action than me. The only intimacy I was getting was from a silicone vibrator and it couldn't return my affection, clean up the wet spot or hold me when we were done. While, it still felt good, self love wasn't really doing it for me anymore. It had simply become part of my daily routine, like taking a shower. At the end of the day, it was another chore to tick off my list, although it was my favorite chore, it had become a kind of maintenance and mandatory stress release I needed to cope with life as an adult.

"Ms. Greypath, this is Beverly calling from Haven Hills Elementary. Mrs. Johnson has requested you come in for a meeting with her, Mrs. Doone and Ms. Funk at your earliest convenience." How could she even say Ms. Funk with a serious face?

The only thing worse than getting an e-mail from the school, which I got fairly regularly and ignored, was getting a phone call. I could delete an e-mail, but phone calls were more difficult to avoid because they meant that Max must've done something beyond getting his Good Neighbor card moved into the red zone. Since I had "disrespected" Mrs. Doom at our last meeting, now she refused to meet with me without the other two administrators and bonus, they could all team up against me. I'd never met Ms. Funk before, but I assumed she was screwed up the way a lot of counselors and therapists are. I'm convinced that people who go into counseling do it to solve other people's problems so they can make themselves feel more important with their condescending self righteousness.

"Today's not really convenient at all." I said.

"I'm sorry to hear that, but the panel is requesting to meet with you today. It's urgent."

Is panel just a nice word for war tribunal? Because whatever this was about, I was sure I was going to be convicted of being the world's worst stand-in-last-resort-parental-figure before I even set foot in the school.

"Today at 2:30, then?" She asked.

"Again, that's not really convenient." I responded.

"That would be the time that works best for the panel's scheduling." She said, countering her original statement that my convenience was a consideration in the matter.

It seemed I had no choice. Not that I had anything else going on besides breaking up fights between Jack and Casey, folding laundry while desperately searching for the mates of single socks and trying to figuring out what to make for dinner that The Stooges would eat without a huge bitchfest.

"Jack! Casey! Get in the car! We're going to the school."

Beverly was on the phone when Casey, Jack and I walked into the office of the school. Across from her desk sat a tiny, pale girl slumped in a chair looking like she might hurl at any moment.

"She's here in the office right now, if you could come pick her up at your earliest convenience. Okay. Ba-bye." Beverly said into the phone before hanging up.

Translation: Drop whatever you're doing and come pick up your kid immediately before she pukes. I think everyone throws up in elementary school at least once, it's almost as if it's a prerequisite for going to middle school. Long after kids forget how to do long division, they'll still have memories of being mortified when they threw up the school tacos in gym class in the 3rd grade.

"They can wait out here in the chairs for you." She said gesturing for Jack and Casey to sit down in the row of chairs next to the wall.

"All the way to the end." I instructed, motioning for them to take the seats at the opposite end furthest away from the sick girl. The last thing I needed was for one of them to contract a stomach virus on top of the usual chaos we had going on. I reached into my purse and handed them each a notepad and pens that had "Booby Trap" printed on them from the club to keep them occupied while I was gone.

"They're waiting for you inside." Beverly said urging me to go into the conference room.

When I opened the door I was greeted by a long fake wood-grained formica conference table where Mrs. Johnson, Ms. Funk and Mrs. Doone were already seated. But, down at the end of the table, there sat one more person. Dickhead.

He look directly at me with a little, douchey smirk on his face. My stomach dropped and I suddenly felt nauseous.

"Why is he here?" I asked pointing at him. Even though he was clearly the only "he" in the room.

I already knew why he came. Because to him it was psychological warfare. I just didn't know why the school had invited him when I was the legal guardian.

"Ms. Greypath, welcome. I trust you know everyone on the panel, including Mr. Hack. Please, have a seat." Mrs. Johnson said, motioning to an empty chair near her.

"Unfortunately I know Dick Hack." Over pronouncing 'dick' and speeding through 'hack' to make it sound as much like dickhead as possible.

"We contact all parents and/or guardians for matters regarding their children or the children legally in their care." Mrs. Johnson said sternly peering over her reading glasses to look at me.

"He abandoned his kids and doesn't have custody though...and I do. That's why the court gave me guardianship. I can show you the papers." I said pleading my case.

I'd learned early on after I became a guardian to keep the court papers in my purse to prove my legal status all over town for everything relating to The Stooges.

"That won't be necessary Ms. Greypath. That's a domestic squabble that you'll have to address elsewhere." Mrs. Johnson said.

And just like that domestic violence had been reduced to domestic squabbles.

Dickhead eased back into his seat smugly folding his arms over his chest. I wanted to tell them how he'd pushed me, but since I'd never reported it to the police I didn't have proof it even happened. Mentioning it would make me look like a hysterical and desperate woman without anything or anyone to back me up. I was alone and defenseless again.

Dickhead didn't say a word, waiting for me to lose my shit so he could appear like the stable one and win over the room by doing absolutely nothing, as per usual. My legs were shaking with rage, but I knew better than to give him the satisfaction of unraveling while he watched.

"Now, if you'll have a seat Ms. Greypath, let's get to the matter at hand...Max." Mrs. Johnson said through the worst fake smile I'd ever seen. She pointed at the chair next to her and I sat down.

"There was an incident involving Max earlier today that we'd like to share with you both." Mrs. Johnson said. "Ms. Doone can fill you in on the details."

"After lunch I opened my messages on the school website where I received an extremely vulgar message from an anonymous sender. I immediately contacted Ms. Lazarus, the technology teacher and shared the content of the threatening message with her to see if she could find out who had sent it. After some research, she determined it came from the school's computer lab and the message was sent during the time that my class had their multimedia special in there earlier in the morning. It was sent from the computer Maxwell had used." Mrs. Doone said.

"Ms. Lazarus would have joined us, but she has a class at the moment," Mrs. Johnson interjected. "Why don't you show her a printed copy of the message?" She said to Mrs. Doone.

The significance of Mrs. Doone handing the paper for Dickhead to see first didn't escape me. Further proving to me that he was winning and I was losing in the battle of public perception.

"He didn't use words like this when he lived with me." Dickhead said accusatorially.

You were never even home when he lived with you! I thought stifling a scream inside my head that could've caused an aneurism. He passed the paper on to Ms. Funk who sat between us who passed it on to me and I read it.

At the top was Mrs. Doone's e-mail address with the date and time of the message. Then the words:

I hate you fucking bitch!

"Max will be put on a two day out of school suspension starting tomorrow as a disciplinary measure." Mrs. Johnson said.

"Did you talk to Max about this? Why isn't he here to defend himself?" I asked.

"We thought this was the least disruptive way to handle the situation under the circumstances." Mrs. Johnson replied.

"So that's it? The concept of being innocent until proven guilty doesn't apply to kindergarten? I didn't realize Haven Hills was a dictatorship." I said.

So much for keeping my composure.

"The IP address and who was logged in to the computer when the message was sent is all the proof we need." Mrs. Johnson said.

"You don't want to know why he did it? Because I know why he did. Last week he came home from school and told me Mrs. Doone called him an idiot and a loser in front of the entire class. He was extremely humiliated and angry about it." I looked directly at Mrs. Doom when I said it.

"He's a liar! I most certainly did not!" Mrs. Doone said defensively.

"Now in addition to being an idiot and a loser, he's a liar too?" I asked.

"I only meant that he was confused." Mrs. Doone said trying to retract her original statement.

"Mrs. Doone has been teaching here for thirty years and she has an excellent reputation as an educator. Getting back to the matter at hand: Max's inappropriate e-mail to Mrs. Doone...in addition to being suspended, Max needs to apologize to Mrs. Doone." Said Mrs. Johnson.

"Wait a minute. So, Max is guilty because the IP address says he's guilty, but Mrs. Doom is innocent because she's an adult and she's worked here for a really long time? That's how this works? Why don't you ask Max or any of the other kids in his class?" I asked, purposely using her nickname because I was infuriated.

"How dare you come in here and imply that I said something demeaning to a student and that I deserved to get this message!" Mrs. Doone said enraged.

"I didn't imply anything, I said it. And you said demeaning things to a student. Plural." I said.

"We can't continue this discussion with you if you insist on being capricious and straying from it's intended purpose." Said Mrs. Johnson.

"I did recommend counseling at our last meeting." Mrs. Doone said for the benefit of Ms. Funk and Mrs. Johnson and to further deflect from the accusations made against her.

Reminding me that Ms. Funk, who looked to be only a couple years older than me hadn't said anything the whole meeting.

"What do you think Counselor Troy? You must have some therapeutic insight on this whole situation. Don't you think it's weird that no one talked to Max about any of this? And don't you think it makes sense that if a student felt like their teacher was bullying them, that they might then do something impulsive to get back at them? " I asked.

Ms. Funk looked terrified and sat speechless.

Mrs. Johnston interjected before she had a chance to answer.

"I'm going to have to ask you to leave the school premises now." Mrs. Johnson said.

"I'm going to have to ask you to get my kid out of class now." I said. It was the first time I thought of Max or any of The Stooges as being mine. Everyone being against us made me want to fight even harder to keep our little dysfunctional family together. I walked out of the meeting collected The Three Stooges and took them home.

CHAPTER 12

"What the hell were you thinking?" I said walking into his room in the ER. His imposing frame consumed every inch of the hospital bed and was covered by a thin cotton blanket.

"Henny! Where are the kids?" My dad asked.

"Whatever you were thinking, it was really stupid because there's no reason for you to be on a ladder." I lectured.

"I was on a ladder? What was I doing on a ladder?" He asked looking befuddled.

"That's the question of the day." I said surveying the damage. He had a deep bloody gash in his forehead above his left eyebrow, his left wrist was severely scraped and swollen up to almost double it's usual size.

"Where are the kids?" He asked.

"They're outside in the waiting room." I replied.

"What are they doing there?"

"They're waiting, Dad." I didn't want to tell him that I was previewing the extent of his injuries before I let The Stooges see him. Worried that they'd already been traumatized by visits to see their mother in the hospital when she had cancer.

I put my hand on top of his right hand and leaned into him to give him a kiss on the forehead. Not out of instinct, but because it seemed like something someone in this kind of situation would do if it were a Lifetime movie. And because I didn't know what else to do.

"You've been drinking." He said.

I flashed back to an olfactory memory of the musty gin smell emanating from my dad's skin in the mornings when I was getting ready for school when I was a teenager.

I stood up, slowly removing my hand from his and sliding it back into my pea coat that I'd hastily thrown over my sweatpants on the way out the door.

"Yeah, well...I didn't exactly expect to get a call from Mrs. Everet saying you took a stage dive off the roof. Then have to pack up the kids and get them into the car to drive to the hospital. This wasn't exactly how I planned to spend my night. And I hadn't talked to Mrs. Everet since you kissed her in the kitchen after mom died." I said deliberately dredging up the past to distract him and make him feel guilty. I wanted him to hurt, which seemed especially cruel under the circumstances. How dare he question me having a glass of wine...or three...while I helped Max with his homework?

All those years he was physically present, but emotionally absent from my childhood were punctuated by his drinking. Who the fuck was he to judge me? I'm just doing my best.

"Drinking won't erase your mom dying or me kissing Mrs. Everet. Trust me, I know because I tried." His voice took on a hushed ruminating tone I'd never heard before. Probably because we'd never talked about how he coped with my mom dying, even though we both knew the answer was gin.

Cue the lecture about drinking from an alcoholic. As if there's anything I didn't already know from growing up with one.

Then, a blank look took over his face.

"Henny! Where are the kids?" He asked.

"I already told you, they're in the waiting room", I said.

"Why are they there?" He asked.

Why was he asking me this again?

"Because they're waiting, Dad." I said, annoyed.

"How's our patient doing?" A tall, thin man with short cropped red hair and blue eyes checked his medical chart. I wasn't sure if he was addressing me or my dad.

"Question for you doctor: Why doesn't he remember the accident? Or that we were in the middle of a conversation?" I asked taking a small step away from my dad.

"I'm not a doctor, I'm his nurse. And it's very common after severe head injuries." He said peering up from the chart to look at me. That's when I noticed he had a cleft chin covered in a day's worth of ginger scruff that accentuated his perfect lips. Not too full, but not too thin either.

"Oh I'm sorry. Not that you're a nurse, but because I assumed..." My sentence trailed off and I felt both embarrassed and sexist.

"No worries, it happens all the time. My name is Chance." He said extending his hand.

"I'm his daughter." I said shaking his hand, glancing at his fair, but lush and masculine eyebrows.

"You must be Lara. He was talking about you when they brought him in." He said with a sincere smile that made his eyes squint a little.

"No. I'm his other daughter, Hennessy." I said.

Even dead Lara lived more in my dad's memories than I did.

"Is his memory loss temporary?" I asked.

"It's too soon to know. He's being moved up to the ICU for observation over night, which is standard protocol for a head injury like this. The neurologist will know more after he examines him again in the morning."

"Ms. Greypath?" A rail-thin middle aged nurse with a mousey brown wavy bob wearing pink scrubs poked her head into the exam room.

"That's me." I said quizzically.

"Your daughter's had a bit of an accident in the waiting room."

"Of course. I'll be right out." I said. Hoping that Casey had peed her pants and not pooped them this time. The day had already been shitty enough.

"I guess that's my cue for an ungraceful exit. So, I'll check in with you in the morning then?" I asked, hopefully. Looking him directly in the eyes in what was my pitiful attempt at flirting with him.

"No, you should go to the ICU upstairs, that's where he'll be."

"Right, of course." Dammit. I'd never been attracted to a pale redheaded guy before. But, there was something intriguing about him. And I wanted to see him again. Was that too much to ask?

"But, you can come down here and say 'hi' if you want." Chance said.

Oh my god, he's flirting back!

"I'm working the morning shift tomorrow and I'd love to hear how your dad's doing. Working in the ER, I don't always get to follow up on patients once they move up onto the floor."

Right, my dad. He's concerned about my dad, not interested in me. Of course, how stupid of me.

Devon's visits to the club had become erratic. The fluctuation of his schedule was irritating me. I'd come to depend on the predictability of his Tuesday night romps with my boot and the supplemental income I earned from it to relieve some of the stress caused by my overburdened finances. I didn't make near the tips the dancers did. None of the waitresses did, that was the price of keeping your clothes on in a strip club. I knew I should be horrified at what I was doing and feel used that I was trading sexual favors for money. That, technically, I was a foot fetish prostitute, but, I had enough cognitive dissonance to rationalize it. After all, I wasn't taking my clothes off or touching him in anyway, much less having sex. So, I wasn't doing anything wrong. He was the pervert, I was just the conduit. Actually, technically, the shoe was. I was just an innocent bystander who owned and wore the shoes. And if I didn't provide the service, he would've found another provider in one of my competitors; either a waitress or a dancer. Any of us could be fired for engaging in a sexual act with a customer. Which just added an element of danger to my otherwise mundane life. Did I mention I really needed the money for things like paying the rent? That was my justifiable excuse.

Maybe if I was in a relationship I would've felt guilty about what I was doing with Devon. Sadly, my secret rendezvous watching Devon masturbate at the club was as close as I'd gotten to having sex with a man since high school. My sex life was so pathetic there wasn't even any sex in it, unless my vibrator counted. Which I named Bob, to make it sound like I had a lover (if only to myself), so I'd feel like less of a loser.

The weirdest part was that I started missing Devon in his long absences from the club. The way his fingers would gently graze my leg before he brushed the top of my foot with them when he anxiously shimmied my boot off before placing it on the table to start the ritual. With my permission he'd added caressing my foot into his routine. No one had ever rubbed my foot before. And now I was getting paid for the privilege of getting a free foot massage. If there was a jackpot for a tired, lonely, broke cocktail waitress with sore feet, this was it.

But, winning the lottery comes with the lottery curse. That everything you've won could all be gone in an instant. Soon, Devon stopped coming in altogether. At first I thought maybe he was out of town on business, although I didn't even know what he did for work, never mind whether it required him to travel. I wondered how he developed a foot fetish in the first place. Was it something that happened in his childhood? Which led me to wondering other things about him. I'd noticed he didn't wear a wedding ring. Maybe he was too busy at work to date. Or maybe he had a girlfriend or wife who was repulsed by his attraction to women's feet forcing him to find an outlet for his fetish. To put my mind at ease I'd created a fictitious narrative about Devon's life. He was the chief financial officer for a large corporation and flew out to London to work out a merger. His frequent travel made it hard for him to keep a relationship alive, so he resigned himself to cat ownership, buying a BMW and searching for companionship at strip clubs. I didn't even address the fetish in my fantasy, because that's what fantasies are for; erasing the unwanted details.

Didn't I mean anything to him? I know what we had was fucked up. That it wasn't a real relationship, but more of a silent, shady, under the table business deal kind of thing. But, now that it was over and I didn't know why, I was left to wonder. Did he move to London permanently? Get a girlfriend? Find a new club to go to and negotiate a new contract with another cocktail waitress? Was she prettier than me? Skinnier? Or were her boots more upscale, with a higher heel and less of a malodorous stench? Why did it even matter to me? It was just a business transaction.

Lying awake in bed at 3:00am it was all clear to me. I knew the next logical step was to ask him to move in with me. That if we wanted to take our relationship to that next level that we needed to share space and time together. To allow ourselves to be vulnerable with each other. And I knew I had to be the one to make the first move because he was too obstinate and proud. Morning came at 5:30am when Casey woke me by gently poking at my closed eyelids and whisper-shouting, "I'm hungry, Henna". With my face still imprinted with creases from my pillow, I promised myself I'd make the commitment and do the right thing this time. Even though I could barely take care of myself and three kids, I had to take care of my ailing father during his recovery from his accident.

With Leslie watching Jack and Casey, I checked in with the receptionist at the desk of the ICU. She escorted me back to my father's room with methodically reverent footsteps usually reserved for church. Though hospitals had a similar somber feel, but with more latex.

When I rounded the corner and saw my dad laying in the hospital bed hooked up to wires and tubes. I felt even more guilty for the things I'd said to him the night before, hoping he wouldn't remember any of it.

"Hey Dad. How was your night?" I said rubbing his uninjured arm lightly.

"I've had better." He said fidgeting with the hospital blanket.

"You know, if you wanted more excitement in your life you could've just taken a trip to Vegas or something. I'm sure it would've been more fun and a lot cheaper too."

"Vegas is overrated." He forced a smile that came off as more of a grimace.

"So's getting on a ladder to clean out your gutters dad." I replied.

"I don't remember getting on a ladder."

"Do you remember me coming to see you in the ER yesterday?"

"I don't remember much about yesterday. I'm sorry about all of this. You came to the hospital? How'd you know I was here?" He asked.

Thank god, he'd completely forgotten about our conversation yesterday. And that I'd been drinking prior to driving to the hospital with The Stooges in the car. It was a stupid thing to do. I could've taken a taxi or an uber instead of driving. Clearly, I wasn't thinking clearly. I was reacting instead of doing the responsible thing, again. At least the incident was expunged from my dad's memory. If only I could delete it and the guilt that came with it from mine. If I got a DUI I'm sure they'd take The Stooges away from me and put them in foster care or worse, give them back to their father now that he'd resurfaced.

"I'm Dr. Sengupta," said a short Indian man with wire-rimmed glasses that accentuated his big brown droopy eyes. A badge confirming he was a neurologist at the Lostport Hospital dangled from the pocket of his pressed light blue shirt.

He had a warm smile, but avoided pleasantries, diving straight into the extent of my dad's injuries.

"The radiographs of the left arm show a comminuted, displaced, and angulated fracture of the distal left radius. The right knee has a supra-patellar contusion and soft tissue edema. The CT scan indicated three skull fractures, fluid and debris in the sphenoid sinuses and a tear within the cavernous sinus, which is the large venous structure running between the two cerebral hemispheres."

It sounded like my dad was on the brink of death.

"What does that mean exactly?" I asked.

"That he's extremely lucky. The testing this morning indicates he won't suffer any long term neurologic damage. We're going to start discharging him now, but, you'll need to contact an orthopedic surgeon within 48 hours in regards to having surgery to correct his shattered wrist. His orbital and skull fractures should heal up on their own. And his knee will need a brace and to be immobilized. I'd suggest a cane for more stability until it's completely healed and absolutely no stairs."

That's how my dad came to live with me and The Three Stooges.

CHAPTER 13

Max was begging to go on the tilt-a-whirl while Jack and Casey formed an alliance making their case for the spinning swings.

"The swings win by majority vote!" I announced.

"What's jority boat?" Casey asked.

"Who cares, we're going on the swings!" Jack said leaning down into her face to explain their win.

"That's not fair! The swings are boring!" Max said in protest.

"Look dude, life isn't fair, even at the fair. And boring? Both rides are pretty much guaranteed to make you puke. And if you do barf, then with the corn dog you just ate out of the way, you might just have room for some cotton candy." I rationalized.

I'd been at this substitute mom thing for several months now. Long enough to know that logic doesn't work on kids. Hell, logic is lost on most adults. But seriously? I have to bribe a kid to make him stop fighting and go have fun at a spring fair by forcing him to go on a ride? Life doesn't get better than this kid. I know the parenting commandments say "thou shalt not bribe", but I don't care. Sometimes giving rewards works and I'd get a minute or two of peace, making it all worth it. When you think about it, the real world runs on incentives too, I'm just mirroring real life for them. Besides, no matter what I do, I'm pretty much guaranteed to screw The Stooges up somehow anyway.

"How about a fried Twinkie?" Max countered.

"I don't bargain with Twinkie terrorists. Cotton candy was what I offered. Look, you don't have to go on any rides. You can sit here with me and grandpa and take bets on who's going to puke first on the swings Jack, Casey or some other random person we don't even know. But, if you don't go on the ride everyone will think you were just scared that you'd be the first puker. The choice is yours."

I'd learned from my on the job training that parenting often requires not only bargaining, but also that multiple layers of manipulation be applied liberally and reapplied frequently, like sunscreen.

Kids learn how to be parents from their own parents. Maybe even more important, kids learn how not to parent from watching their parents. Not that my dad didn't do his best to check the boxes of being a father. He gave up lucrative photography jobs to be at home for me and Lara and we always had everything we needed. It's just that I wanted more of him, but he wanted to be alone in his darkroom surrounded by the toxic fumes of the chemicals developing his photos. I knew the process well. The developer converts silver halides exposed to light into silver metal revealing an image. The stop bath halts the development and the fixer transforms the image making it permanent. A water bath eliminates the residue from the photo and prevents discoloration. Then, the photos are hung to dry, bathed in an eerie red light. Senior pictures, weddings and babies; pictures of life juxtaposed with the faded photos of my mom he kept in the corner of the darkroom as a kind of a photographic shrine to her. It seemed like I lost both my parents the day my mom died. I didn't have much of my dad's attention growing up, but I wanted more for The Stooges. The day my dad moved in with us, I felt like The Stooges gained a grandpa.

"Hurry up Grandpa! I think you're using that cane as a crutch." I said teasing him.

"Go on ahead, don't wait up for me." He said, slowing down looking for a place to sit.

"Can't we revisit getting you a wheelchair?" I asked.

"Once you get in a wheelchair at my age, you don't get back out."

"Don't be a stubborn old man and suffer through it." Even though I knew that's exactly what he was doing because it was what he had always done.

"Have you thought about the havoc having a wheelchair in the house with the kids would create?" He asked.

"Good point." I said motioning to a bench near the tilt-a-whirl with a good view of the swings. "Here's a spot for you to sit down."

"If it stops you from bringing up this wheelchair nonsense I will." He said slowly lowering himself onto the wooden bench.

"I'll be right back. I'm gonna go take some pictures of the kids while they're riding the swings.

My eyes scanned the ropes of the queue line of the swings, looking for The Stooges. I was getting alarmed that I couldn't find them and started to panic thinking that someone might have kidnapped them. I don't know what kind of sicko would want the responsibility of three little kids so desperately that they would steal them from someone else, but it seemed to happen all the time on the news.

"No running! Walk!" I heard a wiry, old carny with unruly eyebrows peering out from under a dirty, frayed trucker hat yell.

It was his firm tone and loud, raspy smoker's voice that honed my gaze in his direction and then on the kids rushing in to choose their swings. What a relief to find The Stooges safe and sound under the watchful supervision of a complete stranger who could be a sexual predator for all I knew. The Stooges transitioned from a run into a Joan Benoit worthy race walk while maintaining the same speed as they circled around the swings until they found a row with three open seats next to each other and sat down to claim them. It was amazing to me that The Stooges could be such masters of semantics at such a young age. Determining what an adult wants of them, like slowing down, and then cheating the system by changing just enough of their behavior to make it seem like they complied, when they really hadn't.

After all the riders were seated and the curmudgeonly carny checked that all the kids had their safety bars pulled down, the ride started slowly. When the swings floated out, Casey squealed with delight. I watched her spin around until she was hidden behind the center post of the ride. That's when I caught sight of a familiar face on the far side of the swings. He was holding hands with a young blonde woman wearing a henley shirt half unbuttoned to display her large breasts that were heaved up to what seemed like her neck. The only thing I noticed about her face from a distance was her exaggerated, over arched, drawn on cartoon eyebrows. She looked like a she could've been a dancer from the club, but no stripper I knew looked like a stripper when they weren't going on stage because it was simply too much effort when they weren't getting paid for it. Which meant the guy I recognized wasn't the boyfriend of someone from work that I'd met in passing at the Booby Trap. I knew him.

The man bent down over the little boy that stood between them. The blonde said something and the man stood up, grabbing the toddler firmly by the hand, pulling him in the opposite direction towards the men's room. When he starting walking, I knew who he was immediately. I'd recognize his douchebag saunter and bad attitude anywhere. How didn't I recognize it was him right away? I knew the answer was that he was out of his usual context. Because he had a kid and a woman with him. It was Dickhead.

I found it ironic that I was taking care of his kids while he was taking care of someone else's. What the hell? Not that I wanted him to take care of his kids, because I didn't. I just wanted him to disappear, the way he did from The Stooges lives years ago. But, I wanted him to be gone for good so I'd never have that sinking feeling in my stomach again, wondering if we'd run into him. And what he'd do if we did. As fucked up as I was, The Stooges needed me. I was all they had.

It was odd timing for the motherly instincts I didn't even know I had to kick in. I had to go talk to her, even though it was the last thing I wanted to do. Even though I didn't know what I was going to say. Not for her benefit, but for her kid's. I felt like I didn't have a choice.

I looked over at the swings, still spinning with The Stooges lost in the thrill of the moment, then I made a bee line straight for her. I knew I didn't have much time before The Stooges were finished on the swings or Dickhead returned from the bathroom. I didn't have time to find the right words, any words would do.

"Hey." I said standing in front of her trying to get her attention. But, her head was buried in her phone and with the whir of the rides, she didn't hear me.

"Hey!" I said again gently tapping her shoulder with my finger. Startling her into nearly dropping her phone.

"Sorry, I didn't mean to scare you." I said with a nervous laugh while she stood staring at me. "Look I don't mean to be creepy or whatever, but I saw you with that guy and a kid that I'm guessing is yours." I continued.

"What the fuck? Are you stalking me bitch?" She asked with eyes that could kill me.

"Just listen, Rick, the guy you're with is a deadbeat dad and physically abusive." I said.

"Oh? I get it, I stole your man and now you're gonna talk shit so you can get him back." She said stepping forward, throwing her hands back, almost dropping her phone again and posturing like she was in a rap video.

"God no! Not me, he was with a friend of mine." I said concealing that the friend was actually my sister for anonymity's sake.

"Right, a friend," she said using air quotes with her finger around the word friend. "Cause no one's heard that bullshit before. And I suppose you're being my 'friend' right now telling me this." She could've clawed my eyes out with her perfectly manicured sparkly pink nails.

"I just wanted to warn you to protect your kid." I said.

"Well, aren't you Mother-Fucking-Theresa? You know what you and your little 'Save the Children campaign' can do? FUCK RIGHT OFF CUNT!" She shouted. The talons of her right hand came dangerously close to grazing my face while she clutched her phone in her left hand.

While I'm not normally one to take advice, especially from a potentially homicidal stranger, this time was the exception. I fucked right off. Before the situation escalated even more. Or Dickhead returned. Or The Stooges saw Dickhead. It was a stupid idea from the beginning. Why did I go talk to her? What did I think was going to happen? That I was going to help change something for someone and make a difference? I couldn't even do that for myself.

I'd gotten Max off to school and dropped Jack and Casey off at Leslie's house so I could take my dad to his outpatient surgery to put a plate in his shattered wrist. I don't know who was more uncomfortable since his accident, him or me. It seemed I'd just settled into the routine with The Three Stooges when my dad came to live with us. Which disrupted everything. I gave up the last sliver of privacy I had in my own house semi-willingly when I surrendered my bedroom for my dad to sleep in, while I slept on the couch in the living room. There wasn't any other choice really. My dad was too tall to fit on the couch. I knew because I was four inches shorter than him and I didn't fit. There were two other good reasons he was entitled to my bed: he's old and disabled and I usually passed out on the couch every night anyway. It didn't much matter where I slept because I didn't sleep well anywhere. My dad has three distinct snores: a subtle almost cute dog snore, a loud freight train snore and the one where he puffs air out of his mouth in what sounds like a duck call. Add into the mix Jack's screaming night terrors, Max rolling off the top bunk with a thud onto the floor and Casey waking me to tell me she wet the bed again. And once I was awake in the middle of the night, I couldn't fall back asleep. Leaving me to lay in the dark for hours on end ruminating, alphabetizing my mistakes, worrying about The Stooges, my dad, my finances and wondering how I was going to fix everything. But, answers never come in the dark of night. And in the mornings I was too exhausted and depleted to bother searching for answers to the big questions because I was too busy attending to all the little things that everyone else needed every day. I was the caretaker of the family, but there was no one to take care of me.

"We're leaving in about half an hour, that should get us to the doctor's in plenty of time." I said while putting the milk away that I'd reminded Jack to put back in the fridge several times, but he conveniently forgot.

"I'm going to drive home and check my mail then," my dad said.

I knew he wasn't going to his house to check the mail. He needed his own space for a while to get a break from me and the ritualistic morning chaos of the kids. I felt the same way, but there was nothing I could do to get a break.

"You're not supposed to be driving Dad!" I said, knowing he was too stubborn to listen to my advice.

"It's one mile away, Henny, I'll be fine." He said pouring the last dregs from the coffee pot into his cup.

"Promise me you won't use the stairs then. All we need on the day they fix your arm is for you to screw up your knee worse than it already is."

"I'm not even going in the house, Henny."

We both knew that was a lie.

"Alright, I'm going to jump in the shower real quick while you're gone." I said.

Taking a hot shower in my outdated, mildew infested bathroom with a tub full of kid's bath toys and soap scum was one of the few pleasures left in my life. Especially if I pleasured myself while I was in there. Which was just what

I needed to take the edge off. I took the hand held shower head off of it's base, aiming it at my nipples until they were hard before spreading my legs letting the water flow between my thighs. With the shower head in my right hand, I stroked myself with my left, imagining it was the strong, capable hand of a handsome, selfless stranger who wanted nothing more from me than to orgasm for him. His finger easing its way inside me, gently and slowly at first. Then gradually getting faster and inserting another finger. That's when I adjusted the shower head into a concentrated, pulsing flow until my heart beat so fast and waves of pleasure radiated from my vagina, spreading out to the rest of my body. Giving me the temporary release I so desperately needed.

It was only when I turned off the water that I remembered I'd forgotten to wash myself while I was in there. Then I heard the long low creak of the bedroom door. Dammit, I always forget to grease that door. Mental note: add WD-40 to the grocery list and then grease the damn door. Shit. I must've lost track of time. I grabbed the crumpled up towel that hung over the top of the shower door that was saturated in a musty stench to dry myself off with. Mental note #2: Remember to separate the towels and wash them all in hot water and add some baking soda to the load.

"I'll be right out, Dad!" I shouted while scurrying to get dressed into my usual, everyday slacker special of loungewear. After a bit of a struggle with my body still damp, I managed to put a sports bra on, followed by a sweatshirt I picked up from the floor that I'd worn the day before. When I realized

I didn't bring panties into the bathroom with me, I threw the bathroom door open bare bottomed to run and grab a pair from my dresser.

"Well...you're as fat as ever." Said Dickhead.

He was reclined on my bed wearing his work boots caked in dirt that left a dusty residue on my comforter. He stared at my bush before quickly panning his eyes down to my sizable thighs. I reached down to the floor to find something to cover myself with. Grabbing Max's underwear he'd thrown next to the hamper and held it over my crotch like a loin cloth.

"So tell me...do fat bottomed girls get any action like in that Queen song?" He asked with a chuckle.

"How'd you get in?" I asked trying to pull my sweatshirt down for more coverage with one hand while clutching my loin cloth in the other.

"Does it matter?" Not only was he right, it was also probably the most profound thing he'd ever said.

"You know what the fattest part of you is Henny? Your big fat mouth. Didn't anybody tell you not to talk to strangers?" He paused trying to coax a response. "Well?"

"There's no one stranger than you." I rebutted.

He got up off the bed slowly and deliberately. His eyes fixed on mine as he walked toward me until he stood in front of me a couple of inches away from my face. We were about the same height, but it was clear he had the upper hand in the situation.

"See what I mean about your mouth?" He whispered into my lips with the stench of cigarettes on his breath. His eyes seared through me and the veins in his forehead throbbed forming a "v".

He reached down and ripped Max's boxer shorts out of my hand, reaching his other hand around my shoulder and pushing me back onto the bed. Pinning me down with the weight of his body on top of mine, he wadded the underwear into the ball with one hand and then forced it into my mouth. His hand pushing harder and harder forcing my head to sink deeper into the mattress.

This must be how I die.

Then suddenly his hands loosened over my mouth, his head jolting into mine, his body jerked and then went limp before landing in a heap on the bed next to me like a spent lover. I looked in the doorway to see my father standing holding the weapon he'd used against Dickhead still in his hand: his cane.

CHAPTER 14

"Wait, slow down and start from the beginning again." I said, gently stroking Leslie's hand my fingers running over the bandage on the top of it. More than her boobs, long legs or any other body part, her strong capable, calloused hands she used to grip and spin around a stripper pole were her livelihood.

"He was standing at the bar for probably a couple of hours. I wouldn't have noticed him except that he had his back turned toward me and he was wearing a Ryan Fitzpatrick Buffalo Bills jersey. Like who wears those anymore? Then American Woman started playing and you know that's my song. Have you ever heard the original by Guess Who? It's weird. The Lenny Kravitz version I dance to is so much much better. Anyhow, I KILL that song! All four long, damn minutes of it. You've seen me. And you know that part where I lick the pole. That's why I get my best tips dancing to that song. So, he's standing there milking his drink and he didn't turn around once while I danced. Not once. Fuckin' pissed me off! What kind of misogynist goes to a strip club and doesn't watch the strippers dance? I was the last dancer of the night before we closed for the night."

"Had you seen him at the club before?" I asked.

"I don't think so." She said squinting her eyes a little trying to remember.

"And then what happened?" I asked.

"It was just a regular night closing up. Jimmy was the bouncer last night and he walked me to my car, like always, and then I headed home. But, I had to stop at the gas station for some milk for the boys in the morning and I picked up my Tuesday night cheat snack, a Snickers bar and a bag of Doritios. After that I drove straight home."

"King size? Or regular size? And who has their cheat night on a Tuesday?" I said, attempting to use humor as an antiseptic again.

"Tuesday is amorphous and the tips always suck, which is exactly what makes it the perfect cheat day. I can't believe I need to explain that to you, it's so obvious. And what kind of a rookie do you think I am? King size...duh!"

"What time was it?" I don't know why I asked as if what time of night it was mattered.

"Um... I probably got home about 2:45 in the morning. Somewhere around there anyway."

"Ok, so now you've arrived home..." Prodding her for the rest of the story.

"Right...so I pull up in front of my house and park on the street cause my fucking garage door clicker needs new batteries or something and I can't get it to work. I get out of the car to grab the groceries, my dance bag and purse from the backseat. Shut the door, walk around to the front of my car, lock it, and then drop my fucking keys. I'm about to bend down to look for them when I see something moving on my front lawn next to the magnolia tree. Then the motion light clicks on and I see a shadow moving toward me and as it gets closer, I see it's wearing a Buffalo Bills jersey." Her hand started trembling when she was talking.

"It's the guy from the club?" I asked.

She nodded.

"How'd he know where you live?" I asked.

"Hell if I know. Then I said 'Hello? Can I help you?' like I'm some horror movie cliche. It's a lot harder to come up with a really good salutation for a stalker on the spot like that than you think, especially when you didn't even know you had one. Now, all I'm thinking about is hitting the panic button on my keys that are somewhere on the road near my feet in the pitch dark. But, bending down to blindly grope for them when I had no idea where they were didn't seem like a good idea." She explained.

"You are anything but a cliche..." I chimed in.

"I just want to talk to you', he said. He was a big, bulky guy like he was a football player himself back in the day or something, but his voice was soft and effeminate. Kind of like that singer guy. You know the one with the big mole on his face."

"Ahhhh...Enrique Iglesias?" I asked.

"Are you kidding me? Does he look like a linebacker? No...an old guy that sings that horrid 80s song......Don't know much, but I know I love you..."

"Ohhhhhh....Aaron Neville!"

I said feeling like I'd won Jeopardy.

"Yaaaaaaassssss, that's him. Except a white version of him with blonde hair. So, I say to him, 'Now's not a really good time. Why don't you come by the club tomorrow?' Then he said there were too many people there, that he was shy and needed to talk to me alone." Leslie said.

"So, he needs to come stalk you at your house because he's socially awkward?" I asked cringing.

"And I'm thinking of Luca, Enzo and my mom inside the house sleeping. Are they going to wake up and find me face down dead in a pool of my own blood on the road in front of our house? God, that would fuck the boys up forever. Then I thought what if he did something to them already and they're all dead in the house with blood everywhere like in an episode of Snapped? I started walking to the front door, trying to pretend I wasn't freaking the fuck out. My heart was beating so fast, the adrenaline was making me shake and my knees almost buckled underneath me. Then, when I was about to walk past him, he grabbed my shoulder and pulled me into his chest. I screamed and he covered my mouth with his hand. So, I start nailing him in the back with the milk jug, which isn't a great weapon FYI, because it kinda absorbs the blow. If only I could get to my purse which was wedged between me and him, I've got some heavy shit in that purse and I could've done some damage. I dropped the milk and just starting nailing his body with my fist. I might have gotten his head a couple times, I don't know. I just kept swinging. I don't know how long it was. It was like it happened in slow motion or something. And, then I don't know what happened, he just let go and I face planted on the sidewalk."

Even with abrasions on her forehead and a broken nose covered in medical tape, she looked stunning. It was her deep, soulful sultry dark brown eyes. They made her look mysterious and sexy.

"So what? He just took off on foot and left?" I asked.

"Yeah, I guess. I was kinda preoccupied face down in a pool of my own blood wondering if I was still alive or not. Turns out I only cracked a tooth and broke my nose. And my knees are all torn up. Basically, I look like a crack whore right now." She said.

"But, like a really gorgeous, upscale crack whore. Guys would still do you." I assured her.

"Guys'll have sex with anything. Not only do I have a broken nose, now I have to take time off work and lose money while I heal. That's my punishment for getting stalked." She said.

"You gonna be ok?" I asked.

"Dancing's always the thing that made me believe everything was going to be okay. I make enough money to support me and the boys and I have lots of time to spend being a mom to them which is great, but also drives me completely insane at the same time. I feel young and sexy when I dance. Desirable. When the DJ says "Next to the stage, Envy!", I become her for the night. No kids. No cares. No bills. It's complete freedom. I know it sounds weird, but I love what I do. It's empowering. But, what if being a stripper is a threat to my family?" She asked.

"Lez, a psycho stalked and assaulted you. This could've happened if you were a receptionist too. It's not your fault. You didn't do anything wrong!" I said knowing everything I said was true, in her case anyway. In saying the words out loud I was trying to reassure myself that they applied to me too and that I wasn't to blame for Dickhead assaulting me.

"Yeah, well, I bet this kinda stuff happens less often to receptionists wearing turtlenecks and sensible shoes than it does to sex workers."

"I don't see you trading in your pleasers for penny loafers anytime soon." I replied.

"All I know for sure right now is that since I need to get my nose fixed anyway, I'm gonna trade in this oppressive Italian nose for a sleeker, straighter model. Because why not?"

"You're not going to go with that pert upturned nose that's gonna make you look like a soccer mom like Jennifer Grey did are you?"

"Oh god no! Too obvious and snobby. I'm going for a more sumptuous Sophia Loren kinda vibe, just a little subtle sculpting of what I already have. I figure I'll turn this tragedy into a happertunity."

"Happertunity?"

"When happenstance meets opportunity."

"You're on pain meds aren't you?"

"Oooohhh...I'm not feeling any pain! But, I'd like to be feeling my doctor up right about now. Have you seen him?

He's older than I normally go for, probably about fifty with sympathetic blue eyes and a strong jaw line."

———————————

All I had for protection was a couple of pieces of paper with some words written on them and they didn't make me feel safe at all. Not the court document appointing me legal guardian of The Three Stooges and certainly not the new restraining order I had out on Dickhead. There's nothing more fragile than words written on paper because both the words and the paper are extremely incendiary. But, it's the unspoken words swirling in the dark crevices of your own mind that are the most damaging. Words that wake you up in the middle of the night terrified. Fear that everything that you never even wanted but was thrust upon you, could be taken away from you in an instant.

To the police I was the same old story. To the school I was hostile. To the strip club I was easily replaceable. To my dad I was a ghost of my mom and my sister. But, to The Stooges, I was everything. Even though I wasn't good at anything. They accepted my inadequacies. They didn't care that I didn't know how to cook and they seemed content to live off of charred grilled cheese sandwiches, cereal and granola bars. Housekeeping wasn't a skill of mine either. I found cleaning and tidying up to be utterly pointless. Putting things away only made it more fun for The Stooges to dump out their toys and make a mess again. While I was logging on the computer to check to see how the check for my mortgage bounced, I caught a headline that confirmed that natural consequences are what's best for disciplining kids. While I didn't bother to read the article, I still used it for justification of my slacker approach to parenting and living in filth. If The Stooges stepped on enough legos with their bare feet maybe sooner or later they'd pick them up. I used to call it karma, but "natural consequences" sounded more intellectual and less accusatory. The unnatural part of natural consequences is that they negatively impacted me. Because I was the one coming home from work in the middle of the night, tiptoeing barefoot across the living room in the dark only to step on a lego landmine. My only retribution at that late hour was whisper-shouting "mother fucker" under my breath so as not to wake anyone. And apparently, the natural consequences of not having enough money in your bank account to cover your mortgage payment is bouncing a check.

They say, the best things in life are free. But, the only free things in my life seemed to be polluted air and Twitter. They both had a cost, the way all free things do. Lara's dilapidated piece of shit house was built in the 1970s or the asbestos era as I prefer to call it. I didn't know if the house had asbestos or not and I didn't want to find out. I couldn't even pay the mortgage, let alone have anything extra left over for asbestos removal. All I knew was I had an incessant cough. Maybe it was dust embedded in the shag carpeting or mold behind the loose tiles in the bathroom. I consulted WebMD and it confirmed it could've been either of those things and/or asthma or cancer. That's when I decided it didn't really matter anyway. I wasn't going to do anything about it because it was far cheaper and easier for me to die from whatever it was than to go to the doctor. Ironically, I considered it a fundamental delusion necessary for my survival as a woman living on the poverty line.

Twitter was my escape where I entertained my delusions of grandeur. I was growing a following on Twitter by being Lara. I tried to portray her as accurately as possible. Cheerful, encouraging, confident and level headed. All the things I used to see in her before I was bequeathed her life and learned nothing was what it appeared from the outside. I thought that everything came easy to her. She drew people in with her beauty and charisma. Who wouldn't want that kind of adoration? I'd never considered that being admired could also have a downside until I acquired Lara's life and her problems. But, now I could see that Lara's compassion compelled her to want to make other people happy because it was easier than trying to gather the courage to make herself happy.

"Hi Brandy :)" A message appeared in my inbox from BenThere@traveling.

I'd forgotten I used Brandy as my alias on Twitter to protect my anonymity.

"I just wanted to tell you that I really like your tweets. They're insightful and witty at the same time. It's a combination that's really rare on here." He wrote.

Just when I assumed it was a dick pic from one of my horny followers, which seemed to be all of them, I got a missive typed in proper English with capitals, punctuation and a genuine compliment even. Usually, I only got compliments about my photo, which of course wasn't even me. But, this wasn't about the way I looked. It was about my words. And those were all mine.

"Thanks! You probably tell that to all the girls." I replied and hit send.

"Nope. I'm actually quite selective about who I message on here."

I studied his photo. He looked to be in his mid-thirties with dark hair and light eyes framed with classic Ray Ban eye glasses, an easy-going smile and straight teeth. Whatever he did for a living, he must have a decent vision plan and dental insurance. The white button down shirt he was wearing wasn't wrinkled, but wasn't meticulously pressed either. He was sitting at a bistro table in what looked to be a coffee shop. The casual setting made me imagine he brought his laptop with him. Maybe he worked from home, but preferred the background noise that the din of a small coffee shop provided and where he knew the barista by name. He looked like the guy next door, except the guy next door is never actually handsome.

"Well, it's nice to meet you, Ben." I typed.

"Wait...is your name really Ben?" I asked.

"Yes. Is your name really Brandy?"

"No, it's Lara." I panicked. Then somehow felt I owed a complete stranger an explanation for this initial act of deceit. "It keeps my coworkers from finding me on here."

"What do you do?" Ben asked.

"I'm an oncology nurse." Please god, don't let him know anything about anything in the medical field, because I don't.

"Oh, you're a nurturer then?" He asked.

Um....not really. But, I couldn't say that. I paused waiting for my brain to come up with a good reply when I received a second message from him.

"Just my type ;)" He wrote.

Technically, I didn't lie. He filled in the blank, I just didn't correct him.

"So what do you do Ben?"

"I'm a structural engineer."

"I thought maybe you were a sherpa or something." I said trying to be witty.

"There's not much need for sherpas in California. And why would you think that?" He asked.

"Your Twitter address is @traveling." I responded.

"Oh, right. I was in the Peace Corps when I started this account."

"Well, well, well...who's the do-gooder now?"

"Touche. Look, I gotta run right now because I'm finishing up some plans that are due tomorrow."

Dammit, I wanted to keep chatting with him.

"It's 2am, you better get cracking!" I typed.

"If I were on the east coast. But, it's only 11pm here in California. Buying me a bit more time ;)"

"I hear even time is virtually unaffordable in California." I was determined to prove to him that I was more than a pretty face.

"Drop me a message next time you're on here, I'd love to chat with you again Laura."

"It's Lara." I said correcting him on my fictitious name.

CHAPTER 15

I woke up late with a wicked hangover from imbibing my insecurities the night before. Wine took the edge off being an incompetent guardian, living with my dad and the financial quicksand that was slowly and steadily sucking me under. My dad's huge hand was on my shoulder gently rocking me back and forth on the couch to rouse me. The motion made my stomach upset and my head pound.

"You look like shit," he said.

"I feel like shit." I said in a hoarse, sluggish morning voice.

"You're not the only one, Max came into my room last night looking for you while you were at work complaining he had a stomach ache. Maybe you've both got the same bug."

My dad went from being an alcoholic who drank gin to teetotaler who drank beer. But yet, he was blind to my burgeoning dependence on alcohol while he was still battling his own addiction. I thought him coming to live with me would bring us closer, but we were as emotionally distant as ever. With The Stooges he was more attentive, patient and a bit softer around the edges. Maybe emotional intimacy skips a generation. From what I could see, the legacy of parenting seemed to be passing down stress, anguish and uncertainty to your kids. I didn't want to do that to The Stooges, but I didn't know how to stop the cycle either.

"He doesn't have a bug, he just doesn't want to go to school. He probably didn't finish his homework or something." I said bitterly remembering all the other times that he'd done the same thing.

"He looked pretty bad, Henny," my dad said.

"He's a really good liar Dad. Remember his vague stomach ache a couple of days ago when I asked him to take the garbage can out to the curb? He's fine, really."

"Ok, you're the mom." He said backing down, but obviously disapproving of my decision while overstating my relationship as The Stooge's mother. Even though I sometimes felt like their mom, I always felt undeserving of the title. Henna, The Stooge's term of endearment for me, was the most befitting title for me, especially since I was sure I'd leave a permanent stain on them.

I looked at my phone: 7:57 am. The bus would've already left the bus stop two minutes earlier. Max had tried to convince me for months that his refusing to wear pajamas and choosing to sleep in his clothes instead saved him time in the morning. This was the first morning I saw the genius of his choice. Not only was it more efficient, especially this morning when we were short on time, but it was also really economical because I saved money by not buying him pajamas. And since I was always short on cash, that was a double bonus. I'd have to remember to concede that he was right at another time when I wasn't so rushed or hungover. I grabbed a black banana from the fruit bowl for him to eat for breakfast on the drive to school and handed him two tattered dollars from last night's disappointing tips from work to cover school lunch. Hopefully that would be enough. In my current state I couldn't remember how much a school lunch costs. Over Max's protest, I forced his listless body into the backseat of the car, one hand on his arm, the other one protecting his head from inadvertently hitting the roof of the car on his way into the station wagon the way a police officer would escort a criminal to jail.

I hated going to Max's school for any reason, but especially since the last conference where I got "confrontational", in the school's words, and it ended in Max getting suspended. After which I considered switching Max to another school. But, it seemed too daunting to shop for another one, only to drive him across town to go to it and then after all that work and inconvenience, he'd have to make new friends which seemed especially difficult mid-year for a kid who didn't make friends easily. When I told Leslie about the incident at the school, she suggested I e-mail the other parents in Max's class to see if their kids had ever mentioned anything to them about Mrs. Doom insulting other students at the school. I didn't think it would help anything, but I was wrong. My one little measly e-mail to the parents of the twenty-three kids in her class opened the floodgates for parents from the entire school to rally together against Mrs. Doom. Apparently, no one liked her or the way she treated their kids and all they needed was someone to bring them together to share their mutual hatred of her. One of the parents started a Facebook group to document the collective misdeeds of Mrs. Doom at Haven Hills and discus what could be done about it. Then the parents organized a letter writing campaign to complain to the superintendent of the school district. Within three weeks Mrs. Doom had a new attitude and soon after her early retirement at the end of the school year was announced by Haven Hills Elementary. While I wasn't making any friends with the administration, the results were well worth the fake cordiality that masked the animosity they had towards me.

I pulled into the school parking lot only to be blocked by the school librarian who stood in front of my car holding her hand up to stop me, motioning wildly in the other direction with her other hand. She was giving me the death glare from underneath her overgrown gray bangs that were perched high on top of her wire rimmed glasses. She shouted something I couldn't make out while I watched her arm flail, the motion made my head pound even harder and my stomach churn. I rolled the car window down to hear what she was saying, hoping the cool air on my face would revive me and somehow make me feel better.

"Wrong way! This is the exit!" Now she was using both arms to gesture causing her entire body to sway aggressively, which must've been the most exercise she had in quite some time because she was out of breath.

I turned my head to look back at the long line of cars in the left turn lane blocking the road into what must have been the entrance for dropping off students. Then I looked back at the librarian.

"No way dumbass." I said indignant.

She stopped gesturing and approached my car. Exiting traffic had slowed to a stand still to watch the elementary school morning student drop-off drama unfold. With the drop off lane clogged, drivers started honking their horns. Whatever was about to happen was sure to be on the agenda as the topic of discussion at the next PTA meeting.

"Henna, everyone's looking at us." Max said from the backseat.

Shit. In the commotion, I'd forgotten Max was in the car.

"Did you say something?" The librarian asked accusatorially, cocking her head.

"Almost outta gas." I lied. Even though it turned out my lie was true and the needle was on empty.

I couldn't stifle it any longer. I stuck my head out the window and puked on her brown Dansko clogs.

"Oh god!" She shrieked in horror jumping back, losing her balance and narrowly rescuing herself from falling backwards on to the blacktop.

"I'm so sorry, I have the flu." I lied, wiping my mouth with my hand before putting the car in reverse and backing out of the exit nearly hitting an oncoming car. I dropped Max off at the curb a block away from the school. Mortified, he got out of the car as I watched him walk slowly the rest of the way to the front entrance of Haven Hills.

I'd just gotten home and laid back down on the couch when I heard Casey and Jack loudly slurping their cereal while my dad sipped his coffee and watched CNN with the volume blaring. I pulled the blanket over my head and then my cell phone rang. I checked to see who it was before I answered. Haven Hills Elementary. Fuck. I let the call go to voicemail. I couldn't deal with being ridiculed about vomiting in the student drop off line at the moment and closed my eyes hoping I'd doze off.

"Why are you sleeping?" Casey's thumb was resting on the bags under my left eye while planting her forefinger under the top of my orbital socket using it for leverage to pry my eye open.

I swatted her sticky hand away. She was probably playing with the honey in the cupboard again. Her favorite toy wasn't even a toy at all, it was pretending the bear shaped honey container was Winnie the Pooh. She'd rearrange the food in the pantry to make it into a tree house. She always laid a box of mac and cheese on it's side for his bed. This was usually the time that Jack decided to clear the Hundred Acre Wood and took the old Tonka truck I got him at a garage sale to level all the trees (which are usually represented by ramen packets) because, from my observation, that's what boys do best; obliterate things.

"Because I'm tired." I muttered.

"I'm not tired. I'm awake, Henna." She climbed on top of me, a spiral of her curls grazing my cheek as she bent down to kiss me, but blew a long, wet raspberry on my face leaving a puddle of drool behind instead. Then she pulled away with a jubilant belly laugh.

It was a moment I wanted to get lost in forever. That one perfect one that makes the billion other shitty ones all worth it.

"Henny, the school just called me to say they couldn't reach you. Max threw up and needs to be picked up." My dad said.

And just like that, the perfect moment was ruined.

"Uhhhhhhhhhhhhhh you've got to be kidding me of course he does!" I smacked my palm on my forehead.

Jack came running in from the kitchen, his bare feet crunching the Cheerios that were spilled on the floor.

"I wanna see Max's puke!" Jack shouted.

"Me too!" Casey said.

"You don't even know what puke is!" Max said.

At least I had something that would entertain the remaining two Stooges for twenty minutes at minimum.

"If you clean up the kitchen and brush your teeth, you can come to the school with me. But, you've gotta be quick, I'm leaving in ten minutes."

I'd brilliantly exploited the unfortunate circumstance of one kid to bribe the other two to do something they needed to do anyway. I'd also secured myself some human shields to protect me, or at least act as a diversion, from the glares I was sure to get now that the gossip from the morning's drop off debacle had sufficient time to spread throughout the school. This must be what winning feels like.

When we arrived at the school, Beverly, the school secretary, had the phone sandwiched between her ear and shoulder, the same position I saw her in when I came for the emergency conference last month. I wondered if she saw a chiropractor for her neck, which must be constantly crooked. We made eye contact and she held up her arm raising her index finger to indicate she'd be with me in a minute. Her day must be one long continuous interruption in the form of demands from annoying parents, kids and teachers.

"Can I help you?" She asked after she hung up the phone in a tone more suited to the phrase, *can you go to hell?*

"I'm here to pick up Max." I said.

"Are you his mother?" She looked at Jack and Casey suspiciously.

"His legal guardian. Do you need to see my I.D.?"

"That won't be necessary. I remember you now." She said.

Being remembered is never a good thing. Everyone knows that a bad reputation is what makes people memorable.

"Follow me," she said. Escorting me to a small room adjacent to the office filled with boxes of candy bars with white labels and red lettering for the upcoming school fundraiser. In the center was an exam table with Max laying on top curled up in the fetal position. He looked how I felt.

"Hey bud. How ya feeling?" I asked.

Max opened his eyes, groaned and promptly closed them again.

Jack carefully surveyed the room. "I don't see any puke!"

"Where is it?" Casey chimed in.

"It's gotta be here somewhere." Jack said searching the room trying unsuccessfully to push the heavy boxes of chocolate out of the way.

"Can I talk to the school nurse?" I asked.

"You're talking to her. I'm also the security guard and the peanut allergy patrol." She said.

"There's no nurse at this school?" I asked surprised.

"There's no nurse at any schools in the district anymore. Hasn't been for years with the budget cuts because of the declining property tax revenue after the plant closed and all the jobs got shipped overseas. My husband hasn't worked in over eight years. That's why I'm still working at my age. There's a district nurse at the administration building shuffling immunization paperwork if you want to call her I can give you her number. But, I'm the one who doles out the Epi pens and Zyrtec here on the front lines day to day."

Her acerbic demeanor made complete sense now.

"That won't be necessary. I'll just take him home then." I acquiesced.

"I wouldn't do that," she said.

"You wouldn't? What would you do?" I asked, putting emphasis on the word would. "While I'm not a nurse, I'm a mom and a grandma who's worked at an elementary school for almost thirty years. So, I know when a kid needs to go to the emergency room. You just get a sense about these things."

Mother's intuition must come gratis with a vaginal delivery. Which must explain why I didn't seem to have any. Oddly, not being the biological mother of The Stooges didn't make me immune to mom guilt though, because apparently it doesn't discriminate the way intuition does. Why did I send him to school in the first place? I knew the answer. And I also knew it made me a horrible person. Because I was hungover and sending him to school gave me one less kid to deal with because I'm stupid and self absorbed. Which is normal for the average twenty something year old. But, I wasn't the average twenty-two year old, I had inherited three kids and all the responsibility that came with being their guardian.

CHAPTER 16

I don't think there's anything less ergonomical than a hospital vomit pan. Whoever designed it was seriously deluded about how the physics of spewing the contents of your stomach works. It is virtually impossible to throw up into a shallow pan curved in the shape of a macaroni noodle. I'd run out of wine the night before and scoured the house until I found a bottle of tequila that Lara had hidden back in the pantry behind an old barely used bread maker. I hadn't had tequila since the night I got trashed at that party in high school, passed out and either had sex with or got raped by Tony Marino. It was six years after the fact and I still wasn't sure what to call my first sexual experience besides horrifying. And now here I was stealing a puke pan from Max who was admitted to the hospital. He was really sick with an acute case of appendicitis, while I just had an acute case of too much tequila and needed to wretch. I was consumed with guilt, not only because I deserved to feel the way I did, but because I missed all the signs that Max was seriously ill. If Beverly, the secretary at the school, hadn't urged me to take him to the ER, he could've died. Not only did I screw things up again, but underneath it all I was distressed that Max pushed me past my limits daily and I didn't know what to do about it.

Max exasperated me. He was fidgety, bossy and argumentative. Constantly challenging my authority choosing to do things his own way instead of how I had asked him to do them and then acting entitled and righteous while he did it. In addition to that, he had an annoying habit of taking household items apart in an attempt to figure out how they work and then not putting them back together. When I saw the lamp in his bedroom in pieces, I was pissed. I was so incensed, it took me about three days to realize that he could've electrocuted himself and that I should probably be thankful he didn't. My thankfulness didn't last long though because his compulsion to break things down into it's parts only grew into a full on obsession. When my alarm clock went MIA, it was because Max had transformed it into a robot. But, what made me even more irate is when he took the front panels off the washer and dryer to try to dismantle them. I was so annoyed I wasn't concerned with his safety any longer. Maybe a little gentle jolt of electricity was just what he needed to stop destroying our home because nothing I did seemed to help. Ultimately, I felt guilty that I found Max far more likable when he was immobilized laying on a hospital bed in pain. Because this way, I could actually feel empathy for him, rather than just feeling sympathy for myself because I didn't know what to do with him.

"We need to take him down to pre-op now." A thin nurse with a short boyish haircut and glasses with purple frames appeared in scrubs from thin air.

I looked over at Max who suddenly looked so small and fragile.

"Am I gonna die?" He asked.

"Oh, you're definitely going to die. Everyone dies. Just not today." I said with a smile.

"How do you know?"

"Because your job is to torture me until I die, remember?"

"You look like you're gonna die right now. Maybe you have appendicitis too."

"No, I don't. But, I feel like I could die, but I'm not going to today either. Not yet. Because I'm going to nag you for years and years to come. The only thing that won't live to see another day is that stupid, useless bully of an appendix of yours. It's time is up." I made a line slicing my throat with my finger for comic effect not sure if I'd taken it too far until he cracked a shy smile.

"Love you Henna." He said.

"Love you too, Max." I said, my eyes pooling with tears.

With Max headed to surgery, the other two kids at home with grandpa, and me with a throbbing uncaffeinated head, a queasy empty stomach and a couple of hours to myself, I headed down to the hospital cafeteria. I wound my way through the white hallways with florescent lights assaulting my eyes and my mind heavy with worry about Max. Even though I tried my best to calm his fears, the truth was I was scared too. Not only about him having surgery, but also how much an appendectomy was going to cost and how I was going to pay for it when the bills came.

I ordered a black coffee and a plain toasted bagel with butter to try to settle my stomach and found a table in the corner with a USA Today newspaper and some empty

Splenda packets on top that I pushed out of the way with a napkin. I sat down and pulled out my phone.

When I opened Twitter I hoped to see a message from Ben who I'd been chatting with for a couple weeks now. While there was a message in my inbox, it wasn't from him. "Night."

Sent from AverageGuy@anonymous at 2:30am. I didn't remember messaging with anyone the night before and scrolled up to the beginning of the conversation while I picked at my bagel and sipped coffee.

Average Guy: That's a very pretty and sexy profile pic.
Brandy: You don't look so bad yourself. Bold choice to go with a shirtless pic.
Average Guy: Not as bold as if you had a shirtless profile pic. Ha ha
Brandy: I don't like to show off my assets publicly.
Average Guy: How about privately? I bet you've got a smokin' hot body!
Brandy: Maybe I do.
Average Guy: Let me be the judge of that.
Brandy: You mean like send you a nude pic of me?
Average Guy: Uh-huh.
Brandy: Of what exactly?
Average Guy: Of what's underneath that sexy pink bra peeking out of your shirt in your avi.

When I scrolled down I saw a hideous photo of my small, pathetic, asymmetrical boobs with the backdrop of my unmistakeable dirty bathroom with mauve tiles and the plastic Solo cups the kids played with in the bath lining the tub, staring back at me. The line where my bra had been was still imprinted on my skin. What the fuck was I thinking? Why did I take a picture of my boobs and send them to a stranger? And if I was bound and determined to send this guy nudes why didn't I think to google and screenshot a photo of a porn star's boobs to send to him?

Average Guy: You're so beautiful! I need to see the rest of you.
    Take your panties off and take a picture.
Brandy: I can't.
Average Guy: Of course you can. Unless you've got something
    to hide...

Then there was a picture of what would've been my panties, if I was wearing any. But, to my horror I wasn't. I was face to face with a close up photo of my own crotch. I don't imagine anyone's crotch is particularly photogenic, but mine was nothing short of revolting. Razor burn isn't sexy. Also, while I'm sure that there are some angles that could look make a vagina look artistic as opposed to pornographic, this definitely wasn't one of them. And sending it to a complete stranger I had absolutely no interest in made me feel like I did after I had sex with Tony Marino in high school: empty and ashamed.

Suddenly, my arm went limp and I spilled my coffee in my lap burning myself. I let out a high pitched yelp that sounded like a chihuahua bark in the crowded cafeteria, jumping out of my chair to tent my pants out away from my skin with my fingers. The whole room got quiet and all the eyes in it were firmly affixed on me.

Before I knew what was happening someone was dabbing my crotch with a handful of napkins.

"Oh you poor thing!" She must've been in her seventies.

"It's ok." I said trying to gently brush her hands away and sit down to divert the attention of the cafeteria patrons away from me.

"Don't sit, there's a pool of hot coffee there, sweety." I normally despised strangers calling me by generic terms of endearment, but in this case she sounded sincere instead of condescending the way most other people did, plus she was old.

"I'm fine, really." I said. She pulled on my arm to try to prevent me from sitting down.

"You could have a third degree burn. Come with me." She insisted grabbing my hand.

I only complied, because I didn't want to make any more of a scene than I already had and there was nothing I wanted to do more in that moment than get out of the cafeteria.

"Women always say they're fine when they're not. It's what we do. You must be a mom, aren't you?" She asked.

"Aaaaaaaahhhhh..." I said not knowing how to respond.

"I knew it, you're the worst of the lot. Never taking care of yourself." She said making conversation as she guided me into the hallway.

"Excuse me, young man." She said to a passerby wearing scrubs. "I wouldn't normally impose on you, but my granddaughter here burned herself with hot coffee and I think it should be looked at. But, I was just summoned that my husband is ready to be discharged from the hospital. Could you take her to the ER for me?"

"Of course, that's just where I was headed." He said.

"Thanks, dear." She said with a quick wink at me before she headed off in the other direction.

"I can relieve you of your contractual obligation now." I said looking up into the face of the nurse from the ER the day my dad fell off the ladder. Of course I'd run into a handsome man in what was my most embarrassing moment to date when I have a hangover and look like shit.

"What are you talking about?" He asked.

"She's not my grandmother and I don't need to go to the ER. She's very sweet, but I'm ok." I said turning my face away from him a little to try to conceal my coffee breath.

"Did you or did you not burn yourself with hot coffee? Or was that a lie too?" He asked with a knowing smile.

"Unfortunately, that part is true." I confessed.

"Wait. I've seen you somewhere before." He said.

"That is also true, unfortunately. I came to see my dad in the ER after he fell off the roof a month or so ago."

"Right, that's it. Tragedy follows you everywhere, huh?" He joked.

"That about sums up my life." I replied.

"How's your dad doing?"

"I'd say he's doing well, but he's moved in with me and three kids temporarily. So, clearly he's suffering from some kind of a brain trauma."

"Are you here for a follow up appointment for him then?"

"No, I have a kid with acute appendicitis. He's in surgery right now. See...you were right about the whole tragedy following me thing."

"Oh, I'm sorry to hear that." He said stopping in front of the doors to the ER.

"I've got to get back to work. I could have a look at that burn while you're here?"

"No!" I said emphatically. "That's not necessary, I'm fine. Really."

The last thing I wanted was for anyone else to see my crotch today, especially a nurse who also happened to be an extremely attractive man.

"At least let me get you something to put on it. I'll be right back."

He returned two minutes later and handed me a cold can of Dr. Pepper.

"We're all out of ice in the break room and I'm not a doctor so I can't prescribe you anything, so this was the best I could do." He said sweetly.

"Just what the nurse ordered!" I said trying to be witty. "Perfect, because I need the caffeine more than ice right now. Thanks."

"What's your name again?" He asked.

"Hennessy."

"And here Hennessy, if you need anything." He handed me a napkin with Chance scrawled above his phone number.

"Thanks for the medicine Chance." I said giving him a mock toast with the can of soda he'd given me. I walked away mortified by the whole incident and that I'd acted like a complete idiot in front of a hot guy.

I needed more hours at work to pay my bills. But, there weren't enough hours to go around as it was. Barbara, the owner of the Booby Trap, was a stripper herself over thirty years ago. It was hard to imagine her as a dancer. She was short and portly with a penchant for wearing yoga pants with T-shirts that were two sizes too small, which only brought more attention to her physical flaws. Even though her looks weren't what they used to be when she was young, she still had the confidence and business savvy of a stripper, except now she owned the place and called the shots. She'd been a Mary Kay consultant for over a decade before she got breast cancer and a double mastectomy a couple of years ago. Oddly, it was losing her breasts that prompted her to buy a strip club and rename it the Booby Trap. Cancer took her boobs, but not her courage. You could always tell when she was in the club because her pink cadillac was parked out front.

"Business hasn't been great since the goddamn church protesters showed up a couple of weeks ago. Did you know that they've started taking pictures of our customer's license plates and posting them on-line? And don't get me started on the hateful abusive things they say to all of you when you're headed in to work. They're not Christians, they're hypocrites, is what they are. Thank god for Jimmy pulling double duty as bouncer inside the club and crowd control outside of it. Speaking of which, I heard you encountered some of the riffraff on the way in today." She said.

"Yeah...they surrounded my car when I pulled into the parking lot. And when I got out they formed a circle around me and started praying that I'd start respecting myself and stop taking my clothes off and find Jesus. I didn't know if they were going to grab me or what, so I just kept pulling my arms in tighter clutching my purse to my chest trying to make my way through them. Jimmy must've heard them and came out to escort me in. Then some woman in the back of the group said 'Who'd want to see that fat, ugly slut take her clothes off?' When I looked to see who'd said it it was a fat, ugly middle aged woman. Can you believe that?"

"Please tell me you said something witty back to that bitch."

"I turned back, looked her in the eyes and said, 'Your husband.' "

She laughed loud and long with a throaty chortle. "Perfect! You're nominated to be the official spokesman of the Booby Trap for the battle of Heaven vs. Heathens. " She joked.

"Seriously, I don't know what I'm going to do to pay the bills."

Which I completely understood because I was in the same predicament. But, instead of employees and protesters. I had kids and bill collectors.

———

Lostport wasn't the safe, idyllic place that I'd grown up in anymore. Though my childhood was turbulent, my hometown gave me a sense of place and made me feel grounded. Ever since the Ford factory that employed most of the adult population living in Lostport closed just shy of a decade ago, things in the city went downhill rapidly. Most notably, property values on the old historic homes built at the turn of the century declined. Many of them going into disrepair, while others were sectioned off and converted into low income apartments and others were foreclosed altogether. That's when the evangelical churches moved in to capitalize on the low cost of housing. Before they arrived, the city was mostly comprised of quiet Protestants and Catholics who pretty much kept to themselves. But, with the more outspoken fundamentalists in the mix, combined with an influx of people moving from Buffalo to the suburbs of Lostport to cash in and be house rich, it created tension. Not only for business owners like Barbara, but for people like me who worked for people like Barbara. Who had to walk through a crowd of people chastising them to get to work. Regular, everyday people who were just trying to survive by providing a service where there's a demand. I don't know why anyone would waste their time trying to save my soul from the evils of working in a strip club when there were people living on the street without enough food to eat or kids selling drugs. While I knew I didn't have my priorities straight, it seemed to me that the priorities of the protesters were even more screwed up than mine.

CHAPTER 17

I thought about calling Chance. But, what would I say? And he couldn't possibly have actually been flirting with me anyway. He was too handsome, personable and put together to be interested in me. I rationalized that he just gave me his number to be nice, like some kind of Nurses for Train Wrecks outreach charity campaign. It's in their job description to be empathetic and altruistic, they can't help themselves. It was a meaningless reflex on his part and it didn't mean anything.

I'd been avoiding Twitter for a week after I deleted the thread with the nudes I'd sent to Average Guy and blocked him from my account. Now I could pretend that it never happened.

"Where've you been stranger?" Ben asked.

It was ironic that he choose the word 'stranger' as a term of endearment when he was actually talking to a stranger pretending to be her dead sister.

"My son had appendicitis." I typed as if I were Lara.

"You have kids?" He asked.

Dammit. I couldn't keep track of my own fictional narrative straight.

"Didn't I mention that last time we talked?" I typed.

"Nope. I would've remembered, trust me."

"Well, I have 3." I typed hoping that this wasn't a deal breaker and that he wouldn't stop talking to me.

"And their dad?"

"We're divorced."

"What about you?"

"Never married. No kids."

"Ah, the simple life."

"I don't know about that. But, less complex than yours, I'm sure."

"That's not saying much."

"Was it a rough divorce?"

"Rough isn't a rough enough of a word for what it was. Followed by breast cancer and now raising these 3 kids on my own."

"Are you ok now? Damn, you have had it tough!"

"It's in remission now. The bills aren't though."

"So, you treated patients with cancer while you were fighting cancer?"

Oh shit, I forgot I was an oncology nurse. Now I've gone and layered the martyr on too thick.

"You're an amazing woman Lara." He said.

Phew. I'd have to make a Venn diagram of my lies so I could reference them in the future or something.

It was the sympathy I wanted most. Even if I was getting the hand me downs from my sister, just like I always had with her clothes. Even if the sympathy wasn't warranted because I wasn't divorced and didn't have cancer. And I wasn't a nurse or a mom. I just wanted someone to acknowledge how hard my life was. Even if I had to change all the facts of my truth to get it. I only did it because I know being a cocktail waitress at a strip club didn't make me seem like a very sympathetic character to most people. It made me look like a miscreant to the average person, when all I was trying to do is make a living and pay my bills. Social media was the most cost effective and efficient delivery system to get what I needed to fill the void. It was the next, new opiate of the masses after religion. And everyone else seemed to be doing it, why not take a hit? Good thing, I was going for quantity of sympathy over quality. This way, it didn't matter who was doling it out, it was pity just the same. And I was not above being pitied or lying to get my emotional needs met. Obviously.

"Jack, I saw you wrote your name there." I said peering over his shoulder while he was sitting at the kitchen table.

"No." He said sitting with his back hunched looking down at the floor.

"I can see it Jack!" I said raising my voice.

"It wasn't me!"

"Well how is your name written here in your own handwriting then?" I asked.

"I didn't write it!" He said stubbornly.

"Why would you lie about this when your name is written in your handwriting on the kitchen table in Sharpie pen?"

"It was Max!" Jack said.

"Max is at school and this wasn't here at breakfast before he left."

"Must've been Casey then." He said.

"Casey just turned three and she scribbles. These aren't scribbles. So, tell me the truth."

"It wasn't me!" Pleading his innocence while waving his hands wildly and avoiding eye contact.

"You know... saying it doesn't make it true. And lying, well...lying eats you alive."

I was shocked by what I'd just said to a child. Even though I knew it was true and that I was a huge hypocrite with all the lies I told. It's just so much easier to preach the truth than it is to live it.

"It does?" He sat quiet, staring at his right hand for a minute. "Like on the show Monster Inside Me?"

"Yup. Pretty much." I said, laying it on thick.

"I did it," he whispered.

I was envious of the courage it took him to confess and come clean.

"Nice handwriting. Your 'a' looks a lot better. I'll bring you some toothpaste and you're going rub it into the table until your name comes off."

"It comes off? I thought it was permanent and it'd be there forever."

"Nothing's permanent." I said, even though I was convinced it was a lie. It was a white lie.

I wanted him to believe the fairy tale that anything is possible and that mistakes are easily cleaned up. It was my attempt to preserve his innocence and protect him from the harsh, complicated realities of adulthood. I wanted to give him hope in what, he was sure to come to realize once he got to be my age, was a hopeless world.

I went to get the toothpaste for Jack from the bathroom, but the door was locked, as it often was with five people sharing one bathroom.

I knocked furiously, "Casey, I told you not to lock the door!"

"It's not Casey," my dad answered.

"Oh, sorry."

"Just a minute." He said, unlocking the door.

"Just need to grab the toothpaste," I said, squeezing my way in through the doorway while my dad dried his wet hands off on the bath towel. I'd dispensed with the formality of putting hand towels next to the sink months ago.

"Where the hell is it? It's normally sitting out without the cap on oozing onto the counter." I said opening the drawers and cabinets of the bathroom vanity to search for it.

"You really need a new job." My dad was standing over my boots and hot pants I'd left sprawled on the bathroom floor from the night before.

"I know, I'm just not getting enough hours because of all the damn protestors. I haven't gotten the bill from Max's procedure yet and I have to make some cash until things work themselves out at the club." I explained.

"No, you need a real job, Hen. Something respectable where there aren't any men leering at you or any protesters threatening you." He said concerned.

"Respectable? I don't take my clothes off, so no one's leering at me Dad. I'm a waitress and that is a respectable job. "

"It doesn't matter what you're doing in a strip club. The fact is, the men that go there have one thing on their mind. And some will take things too far."

I purposely hadn't told my dad about Leslie being attacked outside her house. And god knows, I hadn't mentioned that I earned extra cash on the side with Devon. They were lies of omission to protect him from worrying about me.

"Don't worry, I'm safe Dad."

"It's not up to you. You don't have control over what other people do."

Little did he know that I'd learned that lesson years ago when I was drunk at a party in high school.

"Not even in my own house." Bringing up what neither of us had spoken about since the day Dickhead showed up and assaulted me in my bedroom.

"Which makes it even more important that you have a job that's safe and stable."

"It's not like there are lots of options for someone like me out there with kids and without a college degree Dad."

"Make some." He said looking me straight in the eyes like it was a threat when he said it.

"Yeah, with all the extra time I have between taking care of the kids and work."

"You need to stop making excuses for yourself and make it a priority."

"I've made feeding the kids and taking care of you my priority! I can't catch a break."

"Things would be even worse if you get a DUI. I got up to use the bathroom last night and saw you stumbling in through the door from work drunk Henny."

"I had a couple drinks, I wasn't drunk. And let's talk about all the beer cans that are in my recycling bin every week since you moved in. They aren't mine. Maybe drinking is the great Greypath tradition." I wanted my words to sting, the way his judgement had stung me.

"I just don't think what you're doing is good for you or the kids."

"Maybe you living here with us isn't good for me or the kids."

CHAPTER 18

I learned how to do the sign of the cross at St. Christopher's where I was forced to go to Sunday school at 9am every week before going to mass at 10:30. It was a lot like elementary school, sitting at desks and reading aloud in front of the class, except the only subject we studied was Jesus. I'd count the number of kids and then the paragraphs to figure out which passage I'd be forced to read for the class and practice it. Going through several possible pronunciations of Pontius Pilate until I finally decided to go with Pontiac Pilot. The class erupted in laughter, except for Sister Helen. My attempt at humor made her even more dour and irritated than she already was. The only things I learned in Catholic Sunday school was that my one skill was doing the sign of the cross faster than anyone else in class and that I was definitely going to hell.

After my mom's funeral, I never went to church again. Until now. Although technically, I was't going inside the church. I was sitting on a lawn chair on the sidewalk on a Sunday morning in front of New Day Church holding a "Jesus Loves Boobs" sign in my work uniform: black booty shorts, black transparent compression hosiery to suck in my gut and disguise my cellulite, paired with a Booby Trap T-shirt and my sexy, bordering on whoreish thigh high boots. Leslie wore a tiny Mediterranean blue string bikini making her perfect set of 34 C's look even bigger in comparison to the teeny triangles that comprised the top. She stood near the No Parking sign next to the street holding a sign that read "Free the boobs at the Booby Trap". Most of the other strippers and cocktail waitresses who came to protest at the church of the people who'd protested the Booby Trap, wore more or less what they did to the club. Making sure to keep their nipples covered, leaving just enough to the imagination so that no one could be charged with public indecency. Even the bouncers came out to show their support, not to mention their feminist sides. Though Barbara stressed that this was a peaceful protest, she wanted them, not just for unity, but also for protection just in case things got out of hand.

Barbara had decided to fight fire with fire. It was a faction of the congregation from New Day that was protesting relentlessly in front of her business for weeks. Harassing the customers and staff and chasing business away. Given the situation, she did the only thing she could think of in an effort to get them to stop; hosting a demonstration in front of their church on a Sunday morning when most of the congregation would be going to church to see it. She insisted on taking the high road to make her point. We weren't going to resort to the tactics that they'd used against us; verbal harassment and taking pictures of their license plates to post on line. Barbara didn't want to match their sleaziness. After the club closed on Saturday night she went over the rules of engagement at New Day, where we'd assemble the following morning.

"You're going to see protestors who were total assholes to you outside the club. It's going to be emotional, but you've gotta reign it in and stay in control, just like you do with difficult, grabby customers at the club. Reacting is the worst thing you can do. We're not here to make trouble. We're here to make a statement and stop them from driving our business away. We're fighting to keep our jobs here. Keep that in mind." It was oddly befitting that she adjourned our meeting with a bible verse from the Book of Matthew: "Love your enemies and pray for those who persecute you."

Her kill-them-with-kindness approach made sense; it was smart. But, it still pissed me off because it seemed so submissive compared to the slut shaming smear campaign they'd waged against us. We all knew what society thought of us. We also knew that while people talk shit about strippers, they fill a need in society. If the Booby Trap wasn't filling the demand, some other entrepreneur would.

Barbara stood closest to the sidewalk leading up to the front entrance of the church, the first in a receiving line of about twenty scantily clad women and two bouncers. As our matriarch, she wanted her face to be the first one churchgoers saw when they rounded the corner from the side parking lot. She was wearing her usual stretchy pants paired with a tight petal pink T-shirt that had a pink ribbon with the words Breast Cancer Survivor printed on the front.

"Good morning!" She greeted the first wave of churchgoers with a big smile, sticking out her hand to offer them a handshake the way a pastor does when they welcome their flock.

The congregates looked bewildered, reluctantly shaking hands with her, not knowing what else to do. The rest of us stood or sat on lawn chairs behind her like we were her backup singers, waving and welcoming them with "Good morning", "Hi there!", "How are you?" with the occasional "Pretty Blouse!" or other such compliment thrown in to mix things up. The church crowd began to fan out away from the side walk, quickening their stride and cutting across the grass to avoid us before seeking asylum inside the church. A woman in her thirties tripped and fell on the grass when the heel of her pumps got stuck in the lawn.

"Here let me help you!" Leslie said jogging over to the woman. All eyes were on Leslie's boobs bouncing seductively in her bikini top. I'm sure some of the men watching her were praying her top would fall off, but by some miracle it stayed on. She bent over offering her hand to help the woman while the lady's husband who was walking behind her ogled Leslie's ass in her cheeky bikini bottoms.

"I don't need help from.......you!" She said, editing herself while she scrambled to pick herself up off the ground. She turned around to whisper into her husband's ear, but it was clearly audible to everyone. "The audacity for them to show up here like this!"

As if they didn't have the audacity to show up at the club and slut shame us for weeks on end. They were the ones who'd forced us to do something to stand up for ourselves and protect our jobs. I was trying to hide how outraged I was behind a ridiculous fake smile I had plastered on my face. It was only ten minutes until the church service started, I could hold it together for that long and then go pick up The Stooges at Leslie's moms house and go home to resume the regularly scheduled chaos that waited for me there. That's what I was thinking about when I saw him. Devon. He was wearing the same white button down shirt he always wore to the club, but instead of jeans he wore khaki pants with a preppy striped tie which made him look like he had just stepped out of a J. Crew catalog. His wife was a petite Asian woman who was holding her two young daughters close to her body with her hands covering their eyes.

"Mom! What are you doing?" One of the girls giggled while the other one tried pulling her mom's hand away.

"We're playing a game." She said sternly.

"What game?" The giggly one asked.

"How many steps does it take to get to church with your eyes covered." She said.

"ONE, TWO, THREE...." The girls counted as she rushed them past us.

I got out of my lawn chair and stood up, shifting my weight onto my left leg jutting out my right hip to make sure Devon saw me and the boots he paid me to have sex with. He pretended not to see me, walking behind his wife with a sheepish look on his face. *You had sex with my boot remember? I fucking exist you fucking bastard! Acknowledge me!* I had to do something. That's when I walked up to him and grabbed him by the tie. His wife looked back and saw me fact to face with her him and let out a squeal.

"Get your hands off my husband!" She demanded.

"SIX, SEVEN..." Her daughter's continued counting and walking.

"I'm just straightening his tie." I said with my back to her looking him straight in the eyes, tightening his tie around his neck like a noose. "Don't want you to look unseemly or indecent in front of the whole church now do you? Now... there that's better." I said fixing his collar after I'd adjusted his tie. "You appear dignified now." I said putting the emphasis on the word 'now' as a threat. He knew I knew where to find him now and that I could expose him if I wanted to. It was the only time in my life I felt like I had all the power. And I didn't have anything to lose. But, he did.

———————

It was 8:00pm on a Monday night when there was a loud knock on the door. I don't know why I opened it, but I imagine it was because I thought that whatever was waiting for me outside the door of my house couldn't be worse than what was happening on the inside where I trying to get The Three Stooges ready for bed. Max had just remembered he had math homework due the next day and if he didn't finish it he'd lose his recess time. Jack insisted on making every excuse he could think of to avoid taking a bath. And Casey wanted me to read her the book <u>Love You Forever</u> for the third time that night. She was fascinated by the story and the fantasy that her mom lived to get old and that she'd be able to take care of her, the way her mom had done for her before she died. But, once again, I was wrong. What was waiting outside the door was far worse.

A middle aged balding man with a polo shirt, jeans and sneakers wielding a large black tactical flashlight stood at my stoop.

"You Hennessy Greypath?" He asked. It seemed like a trick question. So I didn't answer, I just stood there with a blank look on my face.

"I said, are you Hennessy Greypath?" He asked again louder.

"We call her Henna." Casey's voice said from behind me.

"Who are you?" I asked.

"You've been served. There's a court date on the bottom of the document." Then turned around and left.

Richard Hack________________________ Name

82 Walnut Street Apt. 2____________ Address

Lostport, NY 14090________________ City, State, Zip Code

716 842-6619_____________________ Telephone number

IN PROPER PERSON

DISTRICT COURT NIAGARA COUNTY, NEW YORK

In the Matter of the Guardianship of:)

) Case No. _D 857246_____

Maxwell Hack

Jackson Hack

Casey Hack,

PETITION TO TERMINATE GUARDIANSHIP

TEMPORARY GUARDIANSHIP   ❑ Person

❑Estate
❑Person and Estate

SPECIAL GUARDIANSHIP   ❑Person

❑Estate ❑Summary Admin.   ❑Person and Estate

GENERAL GUARDIANSHIP   ❑Person

❑Estate ❑Summary Admin.   ☒Person and Estate

❑NOTICES / SAFEGUARDS   ❑Blocked Account

❑Bond Posted

Petitioner(s), *(first Petitioner's name)* ___Richard Hack
_________ and *(second Petitioner's name or "n/a" if only
one Petitioner)* ___Darcy Camp_________________,
in accordance with Chapter 159 of the New York Revised
Statutes, respectfully represent the following to this Honorable
Court:1. An Order appointing *(guardian's name)* ___Hennessy
Greypath_________________ and

28

1. Relationship to Ward. Petitioner(s) are the (***check one***) ☐ guardian(s) / x parent(s) ☐ other (*state your relationship to the ward*) _________________________ of the Ward.

2. Guardian(s). The names and addresses of the Guardians are: Guardian's Name: ______Hennessey Greypath __________

3. Address: __232 Maple Street __________

Lostport, NY 14090__________________________________

Co-Address: ________________________________

____

____

4. Reason for Termination. The guardianship is no longer needed because: (***check all that apply***)

1   ☐ **Death**. The ward has died.

2   ☐ **Age of majority**. The minor ward is now 18.

3   ☒ **Parents request termination**. The parents have corrected the reasons that the guardianship was granted because (*explain what has changed since the guardianship was granted and how you will provide the child with food, clothing, shelter, medical needs, and educational needs*):

4   ☐ **Moved out of New York**. The court granted permission to move the ward to the State of _______________________. Guardianship and/or conservatorship has been obtained in that state (*attach proof of the other state's case*).

5   ☐ **Competency**. The adult ward has been deemed competent by at least two physicians (*attach documentation from each physician*).

6   ☐ **Other**. (*explain the reasons the guardianship is no longer needed*)

CHAPTER 19

This time it was for real and I had exactly one month until the court hearing that could change everything. I had exactly zero ideas on how to prepare for it. Did I need a lawyer? Not that I knew how to get one and god knows I couldn't afford one. All I knew was I couldn't lose custody of The Stooges. The kids that I'd never wanted were now all I wanted. And I was fucking it all up, just like I'd always done. But, I couldn't afford to do that this time. Because this time it was about them and what they needed, not about me and my needs and failings. They couldn't go back to an abusive excuse for a man who'd already given them up twice before. Abandoning them the first time when he left them and Lara for another woman and then another time when he disappeared into thin air when she died and I got guardianship. I knew I wasn't the best caretaker for them and that The Stooges deserved better than me. But, I also knew for sure that Dickhead was an abhorrent father and that they'd be better off with me. How would a judge see it though? I remember the lady at the counter at Child and Family Services telling me that the state places kids with their parents first. That's exactly how the court's going to see it. That he's more worthy of custody because he's their biological sperm donor and I'm just their immature, inadequate, insolvent aunt who works in the sex industry.

I frantically searched the house. Starting with the pile of bills in the dining room, before moving to the mass of memorabilia that was The Stooges' artwork in my bedroom that I had reclaimed when I made my dad move out. With a box cutter I slashed open moving boxes in the garage to find the remnants of my old life wrapped up in old newspapers and sealed with packaging tape. Charcoal colored twin sheets from the bed in my old apartment where I wasted years pining over a gay man who I was destined never be anything more than a roommate to. A Niagara Falls ashtray I'd bought for my dad when I was little that my best friend Tonya stole from my house. The night after high school graduation when I was at her house for a party, I stole it back and that was the last time I saw her. A T-shirt from The Sweatshop in the mall with the words "Made in China" written across the front that Amitty had given me. It was at the bottom of that box that I found my sketch pads filled with doodles of my mundane everyday adolescent life. Drawings of my dad's photo lab in the basement, the phone booth that was out of order at the mall, my mom's overcrowded shelves of books and near the end of the last book, sketches of Lara's face. Hers was the only face I'd ever drawn. And while I drew her smiling, there was something that was unconvincing about it. Something was missing from her eyes. Maybe I just wasn't good at drawing facial features. Or maybe something was always missing from her eyes, an emptiness that I was just too self absorbed to see until now.

I sat with my legs crossed on the cold garage floor sandwiched between Lara's car and the stairs to her house twisting a metal pencil sharpener over the dull tip of a charcoal pencil letting the shavings fall in my lap. I flipped the sketch pad to one of the few remaining blank pages and started to draw her face from memory. Her covetable cheekbones, noble forehead, bantam, almost child-like nose and pillowy lips. Shivering, I started to sketch her eyes in soft layered strokes, but I drew them with the same void I did when I drew them years earlier. Annoyed, I erased her eyes that I'd redrawn and started over. But, when I drew them over again, they were still indistinguishable from the original sketch.

"Henna!" Jack shouted from inside the house, his voice buffered by the door to the garage that was closed.

"In here!" I shouted back.

"Where?" He inquired. His voice muffled from shouting inside behind the closed door that separated the house from the garage.

"Here in the garage!" I yelled.

The door to the garage flew open.

"You're not here!" He shouted in frustration. I'd noticed that Jack wanted to be next to me constantly and he got anxious when he couldn't see where I was. And when he got anxious, he got angry and took it out on Max, Casey and me.

I looked up from my sketch pad at him and waved my hands over my head like a game show contestant.

"I'm right here, buddy!" My voice an octave higher and trembling from the cold.

He came up beside me and put his hand on my shoulder like he was trying to balance himself, only he was firmly planted on both feet while he studied my sketch of his mother.

"Mom used to get cold like you are before she died." He said. His hand sensing I was shivering.

"I'm not sick like your mom was. I should've come in the house out of the cold garage, But, I got distracted." I explained.

I don't remember if he was an anxious kid before his mom died. I barely knew him back then. Or maybe he got anxiety after she died worried that he'd be abandoned again. He would be a different kid if she hadn't died. We all would, but now we're all changed.

I handed him the drawing of his mom and the pencil I'd drawn it with.

"Take this inside for me, while I grab this box ok?"

His eyes widened studying the portrait and then retracted into a squint before burying his face in it and inhaling.

"It looks like her. But, mom always smelled like rain."

For months I'd taken refuge in Twitter: a dumping ground for anyone with an internet connection and some time to waste with an opinion on politics, a porn addiction, something to sell, a statement or joke to attempt to validate their intellect, wit or stupidity. I steered away from writing inspirational tweets and gravitated more toward confessionals. It had become a public diary where I'd post the thoughts I couldn't say in front of The Stooges or my dad. Not that I'd spoken to my dad since I kicked him out of my house over a month ago. Not that it mattered because our conversations were always forced and cursory anyway.

It was the daily direct messages with Ben that I looked forward to most. I'd never been good at talking to people. But, it's surprisingly easy to type the things you don't feel like you can say, especially when the person reading it is a non-judgmental stranger who thinks you're incredibly smart and sexy because you're impersonating someone else. At first I felt guilty about my deception; using a photo of my sister and backing it up with lies about being a devoted nurse instead of a lowly cocktail waitress. It's just that the deeper I got in conversation with him, the easier the deceit got, until it started to seem less like fiction and more like a fantasy I was entitled to. Before I knew it there were feelings involved. I wouldn't call it love so much as an excessively intense lustful like.

My thoughts were filled with ridiculous romantic comedy plots on how we'd meet accidentally when he flew into Lostport for work to design a new bridge to replace it's old claim to fame, the widest bridge in America that was crumbling downtown. He'd be on the bridge inspecting it wearing a hardhat, unpretentious khakis with sensible, yet timelessly classic shoes and that white button down shirt from his avi. I'd be walking hand in hand with Casey down the street wearing a sundress. I'd be twenty pounds lighter with a smaller, sculpted nose, long wavy blonde hair and cellulite free legs shaved smooth. Suddenly, Casey lets go of my hand and wanders into the street when she sees a stray dog in traffic. That's when Ben, who's watching us because he was checking me out, darts into the street and rescues Casey and the dog. Then we'd realize we knew each other, that he was the Ben I was talking to on Twitter and I was that completely amazing Lara-Brandy-Hennessey (my exact name didn't matter anymore because it was the real me he'd come to know and love) woman he'd been talking to on-line. Where he told me I'm everything he's always wanted in a woman. Wait...why didn't he tell me he was coming to town? Oh right, because he wanted to surprise me with some grand gesture. The rest of the delusion is filled with charming mishaps the way romantic comedies are and it would have the same kind of happy-sappy ending too. I'd move out to California with The Three Stooges and we'd be a family. The stray dog was even part of the subplot. We'd adopt him and name him Snickers and he'd never do gross things like pee in the house or eat other dog's poop when we took him on a walk. And we'd all live happily ever after.

I knew the whole thing was ridiculous fantasy from beginning to end. That it was offensively over simplistic, gender stereotypical and completely, ridiculously stupid. But, that's the addictive thing about fantasies; they are absolutely devoid of any and all reality. That's why we have them in the first place. I just didn't know the reality of the situation could be quite so terribly erroneous.

"Good morning my beautiful Lara! *wakes you with a kiss" Ben wrote.

"Hold on, let me brush my teeth first! *brushes teeth, gargles mouthwash straight from the bottle, returns to bed with you & kisses you back" I replied.

"While that's thoughtful, it's not necessary. I'm sure I'd even find your morning breath adorable!" He typed.

"Not after that fettuccini alfredo and garlic bread I made for dinner last night." Which I didn't actually make, so much as I took it out of my freezer and heated it up in the microwave, but I left that part out.

"Even that couldn't dissuade me from kissing you. I'd start at your lips and inch my way down your body."

A tingle ran through my body reading his words. It was far from the most sexually explicit our conversations had gotten, but the mere suggestion of intimacy between us was a turn on because of the emotional connection between us.

"How selfish of me, I forgot it's Wednesday and you have to work! Can I make you breakfast before you're off to the hospital to rid the world of cancer?"

Dammit, I forgot I'd told him about my fictitious work schedule yesterday.

"I wish! I have a 12 hour shift today and I'm already running late. Gotta get Max to school and then run Jack and Casey over to Euphegenia's house."

Euphegenia was my fictitious babysitter, I stole the name from Mrs. Doubtfire. I'd watched the movie with The Stooges a couple months ago. The reality was...Leslie's mom, Manuela, had been watching them at her house since my dad moved out. She was doing me a huge favor by babysitting them for free when I had work. After my shift at the Booby Trap, I'd stop at Manuela's house to pick up The Stooges who would be sound asleep on the floor in her living room. Waking them up to get them into my car and home in their beds, only to wake them up a few hours later to get Max up and ready for the school. It wasn't an ideal arrangement, but she was willing to watch them and wouldn't accept any money for doing it, which was good because I didn't have any to pay her with. Even though the protests at the Booby Trap stopped after our visit to New Day Church, where it turns out Devon was an elder with considerable clout, customers were still reluctant to come back. The hospital bill for Max's appendectomy had finally arrived in the mail and totaled a whopping $22,352.18. I spent countless hours on the phone with the Lostport Hospital crying to the billing department before the manager of the department took pity on me and reduced the charges down to $15, 672.99, which was negligibly less daunting. After several more phone calls and sobbing on the phone with every employee who worked in the billing department, they finally offered to put me on a payment plan, that I'll probably be making payments on for the rest of my life.

"Well, you go save the world, while I see about demolishing this old condemned building downtown." Ben typed with a heart and a kiss emoji.

Why did I say I had a twelve hour shift? Truth was, I had hours to kill until my shift at work started at 6pm. And now, I'd have to maintain complete Twitter silence until tomorrow to keep up appearances that I was at work when all I wanted to do was text him. Leaving me alone to attend to Jack and Casey while Max was at school without any shiny, sexy distractions to get me through the day.

That's when the phone rang and my day got even worse.

"Are you home?" It was Leslie's voice.

"Yup, livin' the dream." I said sardonically.

"My ma's car broke down and she's stuck in Rochester 'til it gets fixed. And I have a class in twenty minutes." She said.

"What kind of class? Are you going back to school?" I asked wondering why she'd never mentioned anything about taking a class before.

"I don't have time to explain right now. Luca and Enzo are home from school today and she was supposed to watch them. I'll drop the boys off at your house in about ten minutes. Thanks." She said before hanging up.

Jack and Casey were a handful, but Luca and Enzo were a full on terrorist organization. Now I remembered why her kids weren't at school, Leslie had mentioned the boys got caught throwing a rock through the window of the science room at school shattering it. Luckily, the room happened to be empty at the time, so no one got hurt. The boys were taken to the principal's office, but neither one admitted to throwing the rock. The school secretary couldn't reach Leslie, who'd picked up an afternoon shift and worked a double until late into the evening, so the boys sat in the school office for the rest of the school day. When she listened to the message from the school on her voicemail the following morning she'd already sent the twins to school on the morning bus. That's when she called the school back to find out the boys were sent home with a Behavior Reprimand form the previous day that she was supposed to sign and the boys were supposed to return to the school the following day. Only the boys never mentioned the incident or the reprimand form which is how they got suspended and why they are home from school. I had nothing but sympathy for Leslie because I understood exactly how difficult raising hellions is, because I was doing the same thing. And now that I'd become their unwitting babysitter for the day, I only had sympathy for me. I owed Leslie so many paybacks for all the things she'd done for me: getting me a job, loaning me her boots so I could earn a supplemental income at work and offering up her mom to babysit my kids at no charge. Not to mention her friendship and support, which I had a very short supply of these days. Babysitting her boys was the least I could do for her. But, I knew if we were all to survive the day unscathed I needed a plan.

I fetched the box of art supplies I'd brought in from the garage the night before from my bedroom. It consisted mostly of Lyra Rembrandt pencils covering the spectrum of subtle, dreary shades of graphite, two beige Sanford Artgum erasers and a few remaining blank sheets of Strathmore drawing paper. All of which were gifts that my dad had given me on my sixteenth birthday. He saw my need for an artistic outlet long before I did. Unfortunately, nothing contained in the box was going to work to keep four rambunctious kids occupied all day. But, the box did stir up my emotions, suddenly making me sentimental about my dad and the overwhelming guilt I had for insisting he move out after the argument we had. How could I turn my back on my dad when he needed me the most? And for saying something I needed to hear, but I was too stubborn and defensive to listen.

When Luca and Enzo arrived, I was as prepared as well as I could've been on such short notice. I'd gathered an empty bucket from the garage and some food coloring from the kitchen I'd used to color the frosting for Casey's mermaid cake I'd made for her birthday months ago that looked more like a manatee by the time I was done with it. I sent the kids outside into the backyard on what was a dreary, but unseasonably warm spring day out to Lara's garden, which was barren except for the chives that I somehow hadn't managed to kill, with a bucket. And a little prayer: God, I hope this works.

CHAPTER 20

After my obligatory twelve hour hiatus from Twitter to keep up appearances that I was in fact who I was pretending to be and working a long, completely selfless shift at the hospital as an oncology nurse, the thread of messages from Ben was gone. It must be a glitch I thought, searching his handle to find his timeline. 'Sorry that page doesn't exist!' The exclamation point seemed especially definitive and mocking. I typed it again slowly to make sure I didn't mistype BenThere@traveling. 'Sorry that page doesn't exist!' And then I tried it seven more times until I was absolutely certain that it wasn't a glitch or a typo and that he was gone. Why would he delete his Twitter? We'd been talking for months. In my on-line persona, I'd fixed all the things that were wrong with me. Allowing me to give him the flawless, perfect version of me. So much so, that I was actually someone else altogether. How could he not want me? That's when the answer appeared in my inbox.

The avi was a photo of a woman wearing a pair of wonder woman underwear with the handle The_Panty_Christ@ Alicianator. At first glance I thought it was a spambot filling my inbox with advertising for a lingerie company or something like that. I tried to avoid following people on Twitter who only wanted to sell me something, but sometimes it's hard to distinguish who just wants your business from who just wants to know your business. While you can escape reality on social media, you can't escape junk mail. That shit follows you everywhere. I clicked the message anyway though.

"Lara- I'm Alicia. You don't know me, but I hate you. While you were sexting with Ben you were systematically destroying my relationship. You probably do it all the time. 'Innocently' reeling in unsuspecting victims so you can ruin them. Using your pouty lips and your sweet and witty words to seduce them. I stayed up all night reading through your messages with Ben. God...it was like a dagger in my gut at first and I could barely breathe. But, I couldn't stop reading, even with my stomach churning with disgust. While you two were sharing your secrets and desires with each other, I was looking after the family Ben and I have together. How could you be so selfish and break up my family? Our sweet little adopted girls, Gertrude and Alice. They were the smallest dogs at the pound and not just because they're chihuahuas. They were starving for love, just like I was before I met Ben. That's when everything changed. Or so I thought anyway, not realizing what was going on behind my back. I wasn't getting the adoration that was supposed to be mine, because it all went to you. Some chick on the internet. This was the love that I thought was finally going to last. That we were going to be together forever. Until you fucked it all up! This morning at 4:30am when I finished reading the whole thread of messages between you and Ben, I wanted to set both of you on fire. But, then when Gertrude and Alice woke up and I saw their little faces, I knew I needed to find a way to make it work. Not only for me, but for them. Somehow I found the courage inside me to forgive the person I trusted most in the world. Only to be rejected by the person I loved most in the world for you, the cyber girlfriend. I was devastated! That's why I deleted Ben's Twitter account, so you can't talk to each other anymore. Just so you know, Ben was my girlfriend of two years and her name is actually Jessica. I know. I was as shocked as you. I had no idea she had created a bogus account (as a guy even...wtf) and catfished you until I was going through her phone when she ran out to the store to buy tampons and accidentally left it at home. I wasn't going through her phone looking for evidence of her cheating, if that's what you're thinking. I'm actually a very trusting person, it's important to me that you know that. It's just that when I got into her phone, it was open to the last message that you sent her. I assure you, it wasn't a discovery I wanted to make. I'm not writing to you because I want you to feel sorry for me, but so that you know you were talking to a lesbian in a committed relationship. She deceived both of us. The real reason I'm writing you is because when I read your words, even though I hated you, I also kinda fell in love with you a little bit. I know this is unconventional and maybe you're not into girls, I don't know. But, maybe all this happened to bring you and me together. Please say you'll give us a chance. ~Alicia"

While a neurotic, Chihuahua loving lesbian was falling in love with the fake me on the internet, the real me was falling in love with art again. I rediscovered my passion for it by accident the day that Enzo and Luca were left in my care.

I don't know where I got the idea of making paint out of mud and food coloring, but it was probably on Pinterest. I'd opened an account there before I realized that pinning crafts I was never going to make because I wasn't actually the crafty type was a complete waste of time. And that Twitter was a more fun, entertaining and efficient way to waste my time.

The kids reveled in scooping up the mud and squishing it in their hands, letting it ooze between their fingers. That alone kept them occupied for almost half and hour. I didn't know it was possible for something without a screen that didn't get plugged into an outlet to capture their attention for that long. After they thoroughly fondled the mud, they separated it into small piles on the driveway. This is when I got nervous that my idea wouldn't work at all and that it would become utter anarchy. Because anytime something (it could be anything really) is broken down into smaller subsets, there's always risk involved. Someone always wants to be in charge and inevitably that someone becomes a tyrannical autocrat. Who could blame a kid for power tripping when there's a mound of dirt and fun to be had? Being the curator of mud and it's equitable dispersion was bound to go to someone's head. But, that's not what happened.

Enzo and Luca suggested they move the mud to designated locations on the driveway, marked clearly by

Casey's sidewalk chalk instructional diagram. Jack was in charge of quality assurance and making sure the mud was evenly distributed so everyone could color two piles. It was like a hippie art commune, but without the pot and patchouli smell. I was finally doing something right, I just didn't know exactly what it was. But I think there was something therapeutic about how tactile it was. They were talking to each other and playing together, but while they were doing that they were also learning how to work together to organize and plan. It probably helped that Max, my resident control freak, wasn't home because he was in school. Even so, I still got four kids age five and younger to cooperate and play together. And it felt like a major victory. Why don't kids play in the mud anymore? Why didn't I let them play in the mud before now?

Then, I encouraged them to use the mud as face paint, which turned into body paint, which would've been fine if they were wearing swimsuits instead of clothes. The grand finale was when they got to spray each other off with the frigid water from the garden hose after hours of playing in the mud. They looked like the cast of Lord of the Flies and their clothes were stained when Leslie came to pick her boys up. I tried to explain how much fun they had and that their clothes were actually tie-dyed. The truth was, I think I enjoyed the day more than they did. I wasn't continually breaking up fights like I normally did and I wasn't constantly checking my phone for notifications (and validation) from Twitter either. I was in the moment and so were the kids; sharing it together and it felt really good. The bonus was that there was no carnage or destruction of personal property, depending on your take on tie-dye of course.

Art had always been an outlet for me. I just forgot about it for a while, distracting myself with other things I thought were either more fun or more important. But, actually most of the things I was doing were self destructive. I thought that feeding my passion for drawing was a frivolous waste of time. But maybe that's because I didn't see it's full potential, the way I didn't see my own potential. I'd never been playful or had fun with with art before. Not realizing that doing something I loved could help fortify me and make me a stronger person.

There was always a moody urgency and intensity to my drawing. It was a solitary and solemn event I pursued as a selfish endeavor. I never shared my sketches with anyone. Instead I archived them, stashing them away in cardboard boxes, compartmentalizing the emotions I'd associated with them. Much the same as my father had done with the photos he'd taken of my mother, squirreling them away in the darkroom where he could brood over them in seclusion. Thinking he was sparing Lara and me of his muted agony of having lost her. But, instead, we lost him to his grieving. I knew, if I didn't change something, I'd lose myself to my own grief the way he had. And I'd pass the grief on to The Stooges, one day like an unrelenting inheritance. I needed to break the cycle. And I knew that art had to play a role somehow. I just didn't know what it would be or how to make it happen.

CHAPTER 21

It was two weeks until the court hearing and I didn't have a lawyer or any idea how to prepare for it or what to expect. It'd also been two weeks since I had a drink. I could say it was because I was too busy, but no budding alcoholic is ever too busy for a drink. It was more than that. Being on the brink of losing your kids is a sobering experience. And yes, I admit it... I'd begun to think of The Three Stooges as my kids. How couldn't I? I was doing everything a mother does, but without any of the acknowledgment for doing any of it. Which is precisely what qualified me to be their mother. Because mother's never get the recognition they deserve.

Now that I was free-to-be-alcohol-free, I declined free drinks men bought for me during my shifts at work. Politely refusing Sex on the Beach, or whatever other girly cocktail with a sexual innuendo for a name that they offered me, while I fantasized about throwing their complimentary drinks in their patronizing faces. Baptizing them in rejection. I didn't want their drinks, stares or compliments anymore. In the beginning, the attention from men was kinda nice. Even though the attention was superficial, based on how slutty I dressed, how dark the club was or how drunk the guy was, I soon grew dependent on it to validate me. But it never did. I still went home feeling empty even when I had a pocketful of cash at the end of the night. Without booze and with my newfound clarity, I was the one in control now, not the other way around. I could see how some strippers got addicted to the power they had at the club. It's a potent drug I found myself wanting more of, but just not at a strip club, I wanted power and control over my life.

It was one of the reasons why I closed my Twitter account. I opened it as an escape, but it quickly became a delusion I grew to rely on to try to replace the negative feelings with positive ones. Except, it didn't work anymore and when I think about it it never actually did even at the beginning. Even before I found out that Ben was fictitious. Ben who I still missed horribly even after I found out the truth of the situation and we stopped talking. I ached for him, even though he never even existed, I mourned the loss of the idea of him and how he made me feel. Now, I just felt so alone. As for Alicia, I never replied to her. What would I say? That I thought she was crazy. Even crazier than I was. I didn't think that confessing I was guilty of catfishing her girlfriend would do anything help the situation. And I knew from experience that no matter what I did, she'd hurt just the same. Corresponding with her would just prolong her hurt and mine, so I decided blocking her was the best way to go. Even, without her or Ben on Twitter, I noticed I was getting more anxious about it. When I wasn't on-line, I was worried I was missing out on something, when in actuality I was missing out on real life by being on social media. I'd become more wary about posting tweets and retweeting other people's tweets wondering why it didn't fill me up like it used to. I found myself needing more and more validation just to maintain my high the way drug addicts do. And even that didn't work anymore because I constantly felt depressed. The way I did when I was seventeen and attempted (and then aborted) suicide. Now that I had The Stooges who loved and depended on me, that wasn't an option for me anymore. Not like it was ever a good solution for my problems. Instead this time, I tried a healthier option to try to find some contentment. I deleted Twitter from my phone and my life.

I never imagined I'd like the way restraint felt. But, I did. I liked everything more without Twitter and booze: The Stooges, the old dilapidated house I lived in with them and even the constant distress that it could all be gone two weeks from now. Without the diversions, I was feeling things I hadn't allowed my self to feel before; both good and bad. Something I should have done years ago in an effort to get my shit together. I'd even stopped obsessing about my body issues and my weight, although with all the stress and the absence of alcohol, I'd probably lost a pound or two. In the big picture, it didn't seem as important as it once had. Fear has a way of providing a deafening clarity. Injecting me with an impassioned live-like-you're-dying approach. Instead of using social media, I got on-line to look up activities for The Stooges to do and healthy recipes to cook for them. I'd become Mrs. Cleaver overnight. Except that she probably wouldn't have a house full of smoke from burning dinner that would've set off the fire alarm if she hadn't taken the batteries out of it months ago to use in her vibrator. Which is why I also promptly bought new batteries to put in the fire alarm.

But for all my changes, I still needed to make things right with my dad. We hadn't spoken to each other for a couple of months. I just didn't know how to do it. Just like I didn't know how I was going to win custody of The Three Stooges, only that I had to do it.

The thing I hated most about shopping at Walmart was that I didn't have much of a choice about it because that's where the working poor shop. On the plus side, I had to admit that they usually had relatively clean bathrooms. With the dust settling after the fall out of the protests at the Booby Trap a couple of months ago, I still wasn't getting enough work hours at the club and desperately needed a steady income. Also, I wanted to have a job that I didn't feel compelled to lie about. It seemed everywhere I went we'd run into one of Max's classmates with their mom requiring me to make obligatory, awkward small talk chit-chat. As if that weren't uncomfortable enough, sooner or later in the conversation the mom would ask me where I worked. Then I'd pause much longer than is socially appropriate to consider my options. Do I take the easy way out and say I sell Tupperware? Which is a great conversation ender because no one wants to get asked to host a party. Or do I tell the truth and over explain my situation? It was enough to make me consider picking up a job application to work at Walmart. If the working poor shopped here, they probably worked here too. But, then I'd be right back in the same predicament as I am now. I still couldn't afford to pay someone for childcare while I worked.

I lifted Casey hoisting her up from under her arms in front of the faucet so she could wash her hands. She swiped her hands over the soap sensor several times, collecting the soft oozy fluff in the palm of her hand as she giggled. She hadn't had an accident in her panties in a week, which was cause for celebration. In fact, she'd taken on a new disturbing trend of wanting to visit every public restroom everywhere we went. She was fascinated that each women's room was different. And she noticed everything. From the toilet seat liners to the sanitary pad dispensers. Because she was inquisitive, she always asked the purpose of things she was unfamiliar with. "Those are to put on the toilet seat, like the crunchy paper they put on top of the exam table at the doctor's office. And that box is for big, used band-aids." Unfortunately, that last explanation only made her more curious. Enough to open the lid of the sanitary napkin trash next to the toilet to gaze in wonderment at how big some adults boo boos must be.

Casey was well on her way to knowing who she was at only three years old. She didn't like the soap dispensers you had to push to make soap come out because they were hard for her to manage and usually took several attempts at pumping before anything squirted out. She wasn't a fan of stiff, scratchy brown paper towels to dry your hands with. But, she liked those better than the loud air dryers that she flat out refused to use. Which is why she resorted to drying her hands on a pair of her brother's hand me down track pants she was wearing. Ultimately, she wanted independence. I couldn't blame her, I wanted it too. I think most women do.

"High five! Well...when your hands are all dry, no hurry." This was one of the first times I'd said 'no hurry' and meant it. It was all part of my new plan to be-in-the-moment instead of dwelling on the past, worrying about the future or distracting myself with delusions. I found it relaxed me and that when I was more calm The Stooges seemed to be too.

We walked out of the bathroom and headed back to the electronics department where I'd left Max and Jack to wait for us.

Jack was sitting crosslegged in front of the row of TVs mesmerized watching Dr. Phil, his head swerving from screen to screen. Max was standing in front of the cell phone cases trying to pick the lock off the end of the rod they're all hung from with a paperclip he'd stretched out straight.

"Max, what are you doing? Stop before you break the lock!" I said.

The lady at the counter turned her attention away from the customer she was ringing up to look us over suspiciously.

"I just wanted to know how to get it open, like MacGyver." Max said innocently.

"And I'm sure you were really close, MaxGyver. But you can't do that in the store, ok?"

"This girl likes to potty!" Casey shouted. I'd forgotten to reward her for using the toilet with my usual silly potty cheer of "Who likes to potty?" after she flushes the toilet. I high fived her with the eyes of everyone in the electronics department on us.

I turned to the clerk, "I assure you he wasn't trying to steal a phone case. He doesn't even have a phone." I said, trying to smooth things over. "But, if you haven't heard we're potty animals over here!" My attempt at humor had no effect on her, but The Stooges giggled. The clerk rolled her eyes before turning back around to finish up with her customer.

I was headed to the check-out in the front of the store with The Stooges following behind me pushing the cart when he approached me.

"I thought it was you!" A male voice said.

"Look, I promise you he wasn't trying to steal anything..." I said trailing off and stopping mid-stride for emphasis.

"I know, I saw the whole thing." He said.

The Stooges crashed the shopping cart into the back of my heels.

"Cheezus Crackers!" I exclaimed using the kid friendly almost swear word I spontaneously invented in the moment.

"It was Max!" Jackson and Casey announced.

Then I looked up and saw his blue eyes and ginger hair.

"Ouch! I can imagine that happens a lot by the looks of your brood." He said with an empathetic smile. "Chance, we met at the hospital some months ago."

"I remember." I said nodding.

"I remember I gave you my number and you never called." He said.

He was flirting with me after all. I could feel my face blushing and my heart beat faster.

"As you can see, my life has some complications. I figured I'd spare you from them. It was an act of kindness really." I said.

"I'd say that the first thing that struck me about you was your kind eyes, but I think it was your wit. Or maybe I was intrigued because you didn't seem interested in me." He said.

Me...not interested in him? He's joking right? Quick, think of something flirty to say. Or witty. Anything. But, nothing came to mind.

"This is the third time we've run into each other. We probably owe it to superstition or cliches to at least get together for coffee. I think it might be the only way to break this pattern of seeing each other under strange and unusual circumstances. Then we could finally find out if the third time's the charm or if bad things really do come in threes." He said. It was a super corny thing to say and I loved it.

"You do make a very valid point there. I guess we don't really have a choice when you think about it." I said.

"Do you know Perkatory, the coffee shop on Transit Road?"

"Yeah, Perkatory, I feel like I live there sometimes." I said looking at The Stooges.

"How about we meet there Saturday at 2:00?"

"It's better than meeting in hell, I suppose." God, why do I always say the stupidest things when I'm nervous? "I think I can do that." For the first time I was willing to risk rejection as the real me because I didn't have anything else to lose.

What the fuck was I thinking? This couldn't be happening at a worse time. I was supposed to be getting my shit together and focusing on how to keep custody of The Stooges. Not going out on date with a hot guy who's just going to realize he made a huge mistake and wasted his time and effort to go out to get coffee with me.

CHAPTER 22

It was the second time Leslie convinced me to get on a stripper pole. Except last time the pole didn't move, but this time she pulled out a pin at the base, allowing the pole to spin. I grabbed it with both hands pulling up with my arms and grasping the pole between my knees like a fireman the way she'd taught me. Between the sensation of my body spinning and the colored lights swirling around the dimly lit room, I'd started to feel nauseous. It reminded me of the time my mom took me and Lara to the amusement park and we rode the Scrambler around in circles. The three of us packed tight into the bench seat with the safety bar laying across our laps, tilting and jutting us out before reeling us back in. Laughing as our bodies were compressed together by the force before changing direction and throwing us in the opposite direction. When the ride was over I was so disoriented and dizzy I could barely walk to the exit. On the way to get back in line to ride it again, I stopped next to a tree, knelt down and threw up. My mom tried to convince me to go on the carousel instead, to spare me from getting sick again. But, even at seven years old I was stubborn and attracted to things that weren't good for me. I could not be reasoned with. There wasn't much I could do about being obstinate. But, what I needed to do was channel it to propel me forward instead of allowing it to hold me back like I'd always done before. No one could save me from myself except me.

"That's it Lez, I'm done being your guinea pig!" I put my bare foot down dragging it on the floor to stop myself from spinning and stubbed my toe in the process. "Goddam it! I blame you for all of this!" I said sitting down on the wood laminate floor to cradle my foot. Pointing to my foot and then around the room at the six stripper poles in her new spacious pole dance studio.

"Don't be like that!" She said, playfully swatting my hand with hers.

"Man, I can't believe this used to be a book store. You sure do know how to put the strip into a strip mall though." I said. The fact that she named her pole dance studio Stripped and it was located in a suburban strip mall made it all the more perfect.

"Why thank you! The Stripped sign goes up out in front next week. Then, I should be open for business if everything goes according to schedule. I'm really proud of this, you know?" She said.

"I know you are, as you should be! I know you worked your ass off for this. Literally. How'd you do it though?" I asked.

"You know I had anxiety about dancing at the club ever since that psycho stalker followed me to my house and attacked me. So, I starting thinking about quitting dancing altogether, even though I really didn't want to. Then when the protests started, I wasn't making the money I used to so

I knew I really needed to find something else. But, I love dancing and I'm really good at it so I didn't want to give it up. Then I saw this video of a pole dance class on Instagram. I figured if I opened my own pole dance studio, not only would I be able to dance on my own terms, but how fun would it be to teach other women to dance on a pole like a stripper? And who knows, maybe they'd feel empowered and sexy dancing the way that I do. I was never ashamed of stripping. And at thirty years old and after popping twins out of my vagina with the stretch marks to prove it, I look pretty damn amazing naked! Anyhow, I'd squirreled away some money from trips out to Vegas where I'd strip for a week here and there. That helped with the start up costs. And I got my mom to invest too. Can you believe that, my traditional Italian mom is part owner of a pole dance studio? And she loves that she's a business woman now. I'd never thought of starting my own business before. But, once I had the idea, it just seemed so perfectly obvious I wondered why I hadn't thought of it before. And somewhere in between all the other stuff going on in my life, I started taking classes in Buffalo to get my certification to be a pole dance instructor."

"So...those were the classes you were taking! Why didn't you tell me? Way to abandon me at the club!" I sulked.

"It's not like I was keeping it a secret or anything. I was just busy driving back and forth for classes, then I was looking at properties, trying to figure out how I was going to come up with the money for all the overheads, that's when I recruited my mom to be my business partner. Then there's the boys...and basically, I was just trying to keep them alive. Which is a huge feat because they're so fucking determined to kill each other. Come on, you know how it is Hennessy. Forgive me!" She begged.

"I'm happy for you. I really am! But I'm also really jealous that you have everything already figured out before the club closes at the end of the month. Things are working out for you and I'm completely envious. Because from the looks of things, I'm going to be unemployed, homeless and have the kids taken from me all at the same time."

"Yeah, I know I've been wrapped up in my own shit storm of a life lately, but I'm here for you, you know that! You're going to find a job, keep the house and the kids. I know because you're the most tenacious, level-headed, big hearted person I know. And you're a hell of a lot smarter than you give yourself credit for. You'll figure it out. Those kids need you and you're a much better mom to those kids than I am to mine. I know that's not saying much, but I mean it as a compliment. The judge would be an idiot to give custody back to their father." She said.

"While we're on the topic of idiots...on a scale of 1 to 10, how stupid is it to go on a date when you're on the precipice of losing everything that matters in your life?"

"That's not stupid at all, that's exactly what you need, some Vitamin D to lift your spirits and distract you!" She said excited for me.

"Vitamin D? Really? You're such a pervert. I can always count on you to turn things slutty. It's not like that, it's not about sex. I mean, he's really good looking and all that don't get me wrong, but it's more than that, there's something about him that's intriguing."

"I'm intrigued by your choice of the word intriguing.... who is this guy?"

"The nurse who took care of my dad after he fell off the roof."

"A nurse and an afternoon date? Then there is cause for concern. Either he wants a quick escape in case you're schizoid or he wants to take things slow because he sees some potential."

"Which is worse?"

"Depends on him really. And you."

"So, can I drop the kids off with you tomorrow afternoon so I can go brutally disappoint this guy?"

"First of all you're not going to disappoint him! I mean sure, you're a bit of train wreck right now, but you're a snarky, good-natured train wreck with the very best intentions. But, you're going to kill me...because tomorrow I have the final exam for my certification to teach pole. And I'd offer up my mom, but she's out of town for a funeral of a distant relative that I don't even know in New Jersey. So, I had to my farm my boys out to this mom I barely know from their class at school. Honestly, I was shocked she agreed to take them with the reputations they have at Haven Hills Elementary. But, if I'm bragging, I am extremely persuasive when I beg."

My life had become a constant search for childcare, which is precisely the reason I went to City Hall. Leslie's new business venture had given me an idea. If I had a hard time finding someone to watch The Stooges, there must be parents who were in the same predicament that I was. I couldn't be the only one. There was zoning to check, on-line classes to register for and an exam to schedule. But, ironically, the first thing I'd have to do to make any of this happen was find someone to watch The Stooges while I did. And there was only one person I had left to do that; my dad. Further complicated by the fact that we weren't on speaking terms since I'd gone and fucked things up when I savagely threw my ailing dad out of my house.

I stood on his porch, the memories flooding my brain. Thinking about all the times I'd walked through that doorway. It was the devastation the day I came home to find out that my mom died twelve years ago that overshadowed all the others though. I still dreamt about it. How I left that day headed out into the frigid winter weather on my bike, not telling anyone where I was going. Coming home with my fingers and toes numb seeking the warmth and shelter of home. How I left my winter coat, hat and gloves carelessly in a damp heap on the floor of the entry way. The look on Lara's face when she told me mom died. How everything moved in slow motion. How I'd been stuck, stranded in that moment for twelve years. How I'd never moved on. Just like my dad hadn't. And I was the only one who could do anything about it. I'd taken in Lara's kids when they needed me. But, now I needed to rescue me.

The doorbell was broken so, Casey knocked on the old warped wooden screen on the front door.

"You have to knock a little harder or grandpa or won't be able to hear you." I said.

Jack and Max took this as their cue to pound the door rapidly with both of their firsts making it sound like machine gun fire.

"Ok guys, we're here to visit with grandpa, not scare the bejesus out of him. Remember he's a bit fragile so don't attack him. Also, we don't want to break his stuff, so no one goes in the darkroom in the basement to scare each other like you did last time. All of his expensive cameras and chemicals to develop photos are down there."

I said nervously not knowing what I was going to say to my dad.

"You mean when I grabbed Max's shirt pretending to be a zombie chasing him and I scared a fart out of him?" Jack laughed with delight.

"I wasn't scared, I knew it was you! I saved up that fart for you, fart face." Max insisted.

"Remember the special camera lens you guys broke knocking it off the shelf when you did that? That's what I'm talking about." I warned.

"That was Max's fault. It was his arm that hit it." Jack said.

"It's your fault! I wouldn't have hit it if you hadn't snuck up behind me." Max countered.

"You were both at fault because you weren't supposed to be down there in the first place. Remember?" I said, firmly assigning blame with both of them. The same way my dad and I shared blame for the distance between us.

How was I going to fix something as daunting as the rift with my dad if I couldn't break up a little spat between The Stooges?

I saw the silhouette of my dad's tall frame lumbering slowly to the door. His face lit up with a huge smile when he peered out the window and saw The Stooges. When he opened the door the rusty hinges let out a prolonged squeak. Since I'd seen him last, his face had grown more drawn and his steps more shuffled. He seemed to have aged a couple of years in two months.

The Stooges hugged his stomach gently.

"I'd stoop down to hug you, but I don't think I'd be able to get back up again if I did." He snickered, cradling their heads in his massive hands. The same way he'd done with me the day my mom died. I remember the comforting tingle it sent down my spine and the smell of Lava soap he always used to wash the chemical residue off his hands after he developed photos. Contrary to the rest of his weary appearance, his hands looked just as strong and capable now as they did back then.

"Now, go head out in the back yard and take turns on the tire swing." I'd spent countless hours of my childhood swinging there myself. Studying the sturdy trunk of the the chestnut tree it was hung from. Collecting chestnuts when they fell to the ground for no reason in particular, other than it made me feel safe to know I had an arsenal of them to throw for protection should I ever need it.

"This was unexpected." He offered cautiously.

"You don't use a cane anymore?" I asked while walking into the entryway.

"Nah. I figured if I kept depending on it, I'd never stop using it. So I started going to the mall to walk in the mornings with all the other old people to build up strength in my leg so it'd heal faster."

It was just like my dad to snub the advice of the doctors and create his own medical treatment plan instead.

"Sounds like you, thinking you know better than the doctor. You'd rather go without a cane and risk falling and hurting yourself even worse next time?"

It occurred to me I'd been doing the same thing in my life. Choosing to assume risk over being cautious and calculating at every turn.

"We Greypath's are stubborn, as you know. And I'd rather go without a cane if I'm capable and independent enough to stand on my own two feet like I am. No one wants to rely on anything outside themselves." He paused. "Did you come here just to scold me?"

"I came to apologize. Because if there's anyone you should be able to rely on it's me. And I abandoned you when you needed me most. Everything you said to me that day was true. I was acting recklessly and risking losing everything in the process. But, I'm gonna make everything right now. I'm sorry for making you move out and the things I said to you." I said with tears welling in my eyes.

"Everything you said was true too Hennessy. I was never there for you. You were just a kid the day we lost your mother. I was never much of a father, Essie was the one who always took care of you girls. Then, when your mom was gone, Lara stepped up to take care of you and I stepped back and let her. I thought that because she'd always taken after your mother that she'd do a better job at parenting you than me. I probably couldn't have stopped her if I tried, but, my biggest regret is that I never even tried to. In the end, I failed both of you. It's me who's sorry. For not being there for you or Lara."

He rounded the corner into the adjacent living room and slunk into his favorite armchair, his hands covering his face sobbing.

I sat down perching myself on the arm of his chair, leaning into him, nestling my head on top of his.

"We can't go back now and change anything either of us did or didn't do. But, it's not the end. Mom and Lara are gone, but, we still have each other and Lara's kids. It's not too late for us to fix things."

"I wouldn't know where to start." He admitted.

"I do. And I need your help. You could help me figure out how to keep custody of the kids. Rick is petitioning to end my guardianship and the court date is in two weeks. We have to fight to keep our family together. And as you know, the Greypath's are stubborn." I said using his words to rally him before I caught him up on the events of the last two months including the closing of the Booby trap and my plans to open my own daycare. "Oh, if you could babysit your grandkids tomorrow afternoon, I have a date. And Dad? I love you." It was the first time I'd ever told my dad I loved him, it was one of the many unspoken things between us. I was always scared that he wouldn't be able to say those words back to me. But, then he did.

"I love you too Hennessy."

CHAPTER 23

At over 90 degrees, it was the hottest day in May on record and I was standing in an open field being brutalized by the sun surrounded by excited elementary school kids. My punishment for signing up to volunteer at field day was getting assigned to be in charge of the three-legged race without a sliver of shade. I figured it was Mrs. Doom's final act of retribution against me after I'd reluctantly started an e-mail campaign against her that accidentally turned into a coup that ousted her from the school and ended her teaching career. With the school year nearly over I was looking forward to opening my daycare and having The Stooges at home with me for summer vacation. Unless they wouldn't be with me because the court had different plans for them. I tried not to think about that though, but it was constantly on my mind.

"Hi, I'm Jennifer Wilkerson, President of the PTO." If she was thinking I'd be impressed that she had the title of president, she was talking to the wrong person. "I don't think we've met before and I know everybody." She said placing the emphasis on everybody while assaulting me with her coffee breath. The blonde highlights she used to disguise the grays in her mousy brown hair made me think she was in her late forties. She extended her perfectly manicured hand with a big condescending smile.

"I'm Hennessy Greypath." I said returning her handshake.

"Greypath? I'm usually pretty good with matching people with their kids, but I don't recall a student with that last name." She said, giving me the indication she was the nosy type.

"Max Hack is mine, he's in kindergarten." I said hesitantly hoping she hadn't heard about his reputation as a troublemaker. Or worse yet, mine.

"Oh, I'm so sorry, you must be divorced. That was so insensitive of me!" She said with a flimsy, unconvincing apology.

"Actually I'm his aunt. And also his legal guardian. When my sister died of cancer she left me her kids."

Her prying for information was pissing me off, so I went straight for sympathy in the hopes she'd stop with the small talk and cut straight to the point already.

"When I put my foot in my mouth, I just jump in with both feet, don't I?" She quipped with a giggle. "Well, we're glad you're here to help today!" She flippantly changed the subject while pulling out her clipboard, careful not to spill her venti sized Starbucks cup with a ring of pink lipstick surrounding the hole in the lid. Then she proceeded to give me overly detailed instructions on how to set up the three-legged race, including an entire segment on how to tie the bandanas around the kids legs. "Below the knee, but above the ankle, because anything above the knee well it's basically the same as molesting their privates. And not too tight, so it won't cut off their circulation or leave a mark." I waited for her to acknowledge the awkwardness of having just treated me like a sexual offender. Maybe a sympathetic head tilt or a disclaimer that she tells this to all the parents or something like that, but she didn't. Thankfully, her monologue ended abruptly when she got a call on her walkie-talkie that the juice boxes at the water station weren't organic and she made a quick bee-line back to the other side of the field.

"Sounds like you got the Haven Elementary initiation," a voice from behind me said.

"Is she always that um.....intense?" I asked, glad that someone else had witnessed the absurdity of her commander-in-chief of field day power trip.

"You have to be pretty Type A to run for PTO president. It's a pretty thankless volunteer job. All stress and no fun. Hi, I'm Angela." Said a skinny brunette in an expensive looking athletic spandex sundress; the kind with the built in bra.

"Hennessy."

"Now that's a unique name." I knew, because I only heard how unique it was from everyone I met.

"Not completely, I actually share it with the cognac. My middle name isn't XO though, it's Victoria. Apparently my parents thought I was going to conquer something."

"My name just means I'm a 'messenger from god' just like the millions of other Angelas on the planet. Hey...you look really familiar. I'm horrible with names, but I'm really good at remembering faces." She said studying me.

"Huh. I haven't been around the school much, you're probably confusing me with someone else." I seemed to have one of those faces that people always told me I looked like their distant relative who lived in Albuquerque.

"Oh, you must be a working mom then. What do you do?" Angela asked.

It was the inevitable question of status and worth in society, as if people are defined by their job. I had to make a conscious effort not to roll my eyes at her. I could've told her I was a waitress, but now that I was in a career transition, I decided to use it as an opportunity to market myself.

"I have two younger kids at home and I'm starting a day care in my house, if you know anyone who needs child care." The best marketing is word of mouth they say.

"Oh so you are a stay-at-home mom too. It's really the best thing for kids to have a mom who's home. Just like breastfeeding is; it's so natural and simple. I mean what kind of mother gives their kid formula or drops her kids off at daycare to let someone else raise them? Oh...no offense." The no offense comment was out of respect for my impending daycare, not for her being myopic misogynist.

I was about to go into a tyrannical feminist rant. About how there's all kinds of mothers and women in all kinds of situations. Some of whom don't even consciously choose to be mothers. That working and dropping a kid off at daycare doesn't make anyone less of a mother any more than being a stay-at-home mom makes someone a good mom. But, that's when the first class of kids paraded over for their turn at the three-legged race. The teacher was following behind her class with a stern look on her face while giving the wiry boy with a brush cut in front of her the stink eye.

"Sorry, I've got to run him to the office real quick. Field Day can bring out the worst in some students. I'll be back before they rotate to the next game." She told me walking off with the boy hesitantly trailing behind her.

I went down the line while they counted by twos, separating them into two teams just like Jennifer had instructed, then urged them to partner up with someone on their team so I could carefully and gently tie bandanas to hold the two kids' legs together. But, not too high or low or tight as to alert CPS. Just as I was about to explain the rules of the game, I felt a tap on my forearm.

"My shoulders are burning. If I come home with a sunburn my mom is going to kill me." A tiny, pale blonde wearing a tank top and athletic shorts with big blue pools for eyes looked up at me.

"Do you have any sunscreen on?" I asked.

"No. My mom told me to put some on this morning, but I forgot." She said.

"You're going to be fried being in the sun all day. No worries, I've got some in my bag." I pulled a tube of Coppertone out of my purse. For the sake of efficiency and even coverage, I rubbed some between my hands before slathering it on her forehead, cheeks, nose and then shoulders and arms. I knew better than to touch her legs. "There...good to go!" I pronounced.

With the class standing at the starting line cinched just above their ankles, they looked like a chain gang picking up trash from the grass along the highway. "On your marks, get set...," I blew the whistle to start the race. A couple of overzealous boys bound together went down straight away and lay sprawled out on the grass. It was mid-race when the shrieks started. Emanating from a girl covered with the vomit of her partner, a small freckled face boy named Garret. I knew his name was Garret because the rest of the class, already at the finish line was shouting... "Ewwww.... it was Garret." And "Gross Garret!" Which sounds like one of those monikers that can really stay with a kid his whole lifetime. Angela, the messenger from god, appeared out of nowhere from the sidelines and crouched over him. Since he was being taken care of, I grabbed wet wipes from my purse to help clean the puke off his horrified classmate. Their teacher had just returned from the office and was now headed back to the office with Garret and the unfortunate girl he threw up on.

"I know where I know you from now!" Angela said. "You're the one who threw up in the drop off line at school a couple of months ago. I told you I'm good with faces." Her moment of pride was recollecting my disgrace. Never mind what I'd done to bring the parents of Haven Hills together to rid the school of a verbally abusive teacher, I'd always be known as the woman who puked in the morning drop off line. It's hard to escape the worst of yourself when it's the most memorable thing about you.

Jennifer was doing a slow Baywatch style slow motion jog through the field towards me holding her clipboard under one arm and her walkie-talkie in her other hand. She must have finished her coffee, because there was no Starbucks cup in sight. Also, she was probably picked last in PE class because she had a gawky, uncoordinated stride. She seemed more the secretary of her class type anyway. She stood in front of me out of breath and panting.

"I was told you applied sunscreen to one of the students," she said.

"I'm glad I had some in my bag, she was already a bit pink." I said, proud that I'd come prepared the way mothers always seemed to be.

"We don't do that here. Not without written permission from a parent." She scolded.

"You're joking right?"

"We don't joke about sunscreen here at Haven Hills." She said with a straight face.

"You'd probably need written permission from a parent to joke about it."

"I'm going to have to ask you for your whistle. You've been stripped you of your duties as head of the three-legged race. We won't be needing you anymore, I'll take over from here." She said haughtily.

"But, I didn't even apply sunscreen to her legs, which honestly, I thought was kind of negligent on my part if you asked me."

"No one asked you anything. We have rules here."

While I didn't like her and I thought it was utterly ridiculous that I was convicted of the crime of applying sunscreen to a minor, I knew on some level she was right. If I was going to run a daycare working with other people's kids, I needed to reign myself in. I needed to think like a businesswoman. I had to start thinking before I said and did things. I needed to establish rules and boundaries. Because there's nothing more important or potentially contentious than taking care of other people's kids. Basically, I needed to cover my ass.

Being chronically late to everything had become the new normal since I'd moved in with the Three Stooges eight months ago. Sometimes it was because Casey had disappeared without a trace again; a cruel one-sided game of hide and go seek she liked to inflict on me when we were in a rush. But, usually it was because the kids couldn't find their shoes. Requiring a ten minute search at minimum and a rescue mission to find something to put on their feet. And hopefully what they found was a matching set of shoes, not that it really mattered. I was more concerned that the boys refused to untie their shoes and merely slid their feet in and out of them, ruining the structural integrity of their sneakers. Which was one reason they destroyed them so fast. I nagged them about it constantly. But, by the time we were finally leaving the house I was so frustrated and rushed, I didn't care if the kids were walking outside barefoot in the middle of winter through six inches of snow. If my tardiness wasn't explained by one of those reasons, then it was probably because I lost track of time yelling at The Stooges to stop them from yelling at each other. Or that in all the chaos of trying to get out the door, I lost the car keys again. The reason didn't matter. The fact that I had a built in excuse (or three) for any and every occasion did.

I pulled into Perkatory thirty minutes late. I fully expected that Chance would've already given up on me and left. It was a thought that dissolved my pre-date nerves and allowed me to relax and think about consoling myself alone with a cup of coffee for an hour without any nagging kids or pressure to try and act normal on a date, which I didn't know how to do. That's when I saw him sitting at a round cafe table for two by himself reading the newspaper. Who reads the the newspaper anymore? Why wasn't he scrolling through his phone like a normal person? Why did he wait for me? And why the hell did he ask me out in the first place? My stomach started churning and I prayed I wouldn't have to make an emergency run to the women's room for the nervous shits that were one of the usual embarrassing results of my anxiety.

His ginger hair peeked out from over the day's edition of the Lostport News that his head was buried in. I could turn around and walk out and he'd never even know I'd been there. That's when he looked up and smiled at me with a big toothy grin. He'd gotten a hair cut since I'd seen him last and sat wearing a grey t-shirt, making his slightly small, sympathetic blue eyes stand out even more. With a day or two of stubble on his chin, he was perfection right down to his jeans and Adidas sneakers.

"There's no excuse for me being this late, but I'm going to give you one anyway. My boys made mac and cheese in the coffee pot. Now, they've made ramen soup with the coffee pot before which I thought was kinda clever. But, there's no cheese involved in that. There was cheese everywhere and I mean everywhere. Then they fought about who was going to clean up the mess. I was tempted to just do it myself, but then I'd violate the rules of every parenting book and then the good parenting brigade would show up and impound my station wagon or something like that. I probably just should've lied and told you I had car trouble. But, I feel like you should be forewarned that these are the realities of my life with three kids. In fact, I should probably just go and let you get back to reading and enjoying a quiet afternoon without me complicating it." I said after rambling on clumsily the way I do when I'm nervous.

"Kids cooking food in a coffee pot is easily the most inspiring thing I've heard all day. You can't suck me in with an intriguing story like that and then walk out, leaving me here with today's depressing news and a cold cup of coffee. Look, I know you're a busy mom and that you have your hands full with your kids. But at least, sit down and let me get you some coffee. From the sounds of things you might not be able to make any at home for a while in that pot of yours."

I studied his handsome, sincere face for a socially inappropriate amount of time.

"The first thing you should know about me is that I'm not a mom." I pulled out the chair with a loud screech and sat down. "The second is that I really want a black coffee with some apple pie and whipped cream if they have it."

Something about him made me comfortable immediately. Comfortable enough to tell him the truth. About being reluctant to take care of my niece and nephews after my sister died, working at a strip club, drinking too much, kicking my dad out of the house, using my sister's persona on-line (although I left off the on-line relationship with a lesbian which I thought was more embarrassing than significant in the big picture), losing my job, giving up drinking and being on the verge of losing custody of the kids. Once I started telling him about my life since The Stooges came along, I couldn't stop. The narrative came flooding out of me with surprisingly little emotion in my delivery, as if I were telling someone else's story. But, it was mine and the first step to owning it was to say it out loud. I figured why not just pull the existential bandaid off and push him away quickly rather than go through the agonizing process of it happening slowly over an indeterminate amount of time. Provided that I actually told him my saga later on if we had a relationship. When I finished talking he was still sitting across from me, his body leaned in toward mine with his forearms propped up on the table top, his eyes focused on my face and his eyes filled with compassion.

The date didn't end there. He told me about his parents divorce when he was nine and how his mother forced him to see a psychologist for years afterward, because she worried he'd become a screwed-up drug addict as a result and it would all be her fault. So, while all the other boys were playing baseball and soccer after school, he was seeing Dr. Beal and learning how to cope and talk about his feelings. And he had a lot of feelings not only about the divorce, but about growing up as a red-headed boy. It wasn't easy on him being teased and called devil boy by his classmates. On top of all that, he wasn't into sports and felt like an outsider with boys his own age. Being that he was unusually emotionally mature for his age from years of therapy, he found he got along better with the girls at school and hung out with them. Instead of being on the football team, he was in the school musical. That's when some kids at his school started bullying him for being gay. Except, he wasn't gay. But, the rumor followed him all through high school anyway. Even when he'd dated Bethany in his junior year, the gossip didn't stop. It was just a cover, they said. But, it got worse the last half of his senior year when he and Bethany broke up and word spread that he'd gotten a scholarship to go to college to study nursing. Through all of it, he'd never challenged the rumors. First of all, he thought it didn't matter if he was gay. That and he didn't want to offend his gay friends by denying he was, like it was saying there was something wrong with it. Then, he figured they weren't going to stop even if he did confront them and it was probably only going to fuel the fire and make the situation worse.

I'd never met anyone like him before and when I left Perkatory, I knew I was screwed.

CHAPTER 24

I t was the last day the Booby Trap was open and I fully expected the place to be dead. For it to slowly fade out into oblivion. After all, the club had been on life support for months. But, instead, it was the busiest night I'd ever worked. Turns out, while I was busy taking CPR classes and maxing out my credit card to buy shelves and stock them with art supplies in preparation for my daycare opening, Barbara had been busy advertising the closing of the club all over town and had even enticed new customers to come out to the club by hosting an amateur night for dancers. While she was closing the Booby Trap, she was opening a new upscale strip club called Jezebel in Buffalo. She figured relocating to a bigger city and buying property downtown would entice businessmen in to unwind and spend their money. Plus, it would provide a much bigger radius of potential customers, especially with the Peace Bridge making it a short commute over the border from Canada where the clubs closed earlier.

We were all starting new adventures, even if we were all generally doing the same things. Leslie was still dancing, except she was dancing for women instead of dancing for men. Barbara was still a club owner, except she moved to the Queen City (the second biggest city in New York state) without the small town mentality. And I was still raising kids, they just weren't mine. Not that they ever were. But, over the last few months I'd come to feel that they were. It was Casey who came up with the name for my new business. Henna's Hands Daycare. It was surprising how relatively small the financial investment to becoming a child care provider was. Thank god, because I was already in serious debt. I was surprised I hadn't thought of it before, but who am I kidding? Before I got served with court papers with the possibility of losing The Stooges looming over me, I was doing the bare minimum just trying to survive. Now that I was investing time and energy into organizing art projects to do with kids, somehow it seemed like less work instead of more because the more they did, the less they fought. The creative outlet helped focus Max's excess energy away from systematically destroying the house and everything in it. Jack was less anxious and learning to be more independent and entertain himself. And I discovered that Casey had a natural talent for art, especially painting. Because The Stooges were happier, I was too. Instead of wasting time, I was spending it with the people I loved doing something I'd always loved: art. I even planned on recruiting my dad to help out when we did some photography projects.

I assumed brutal honesty would doom any possibility of a relationship with Chance. But, just like I'd been with so many other things up until this point, I was wrong about that too. It seems sarcastic women with rambunctious kids, thick thighs and low self-esteem who make poor life choices then attempt to redeem themselves at the last minute before it's too late are his type. Who would've thought? I gave him every reason to reject me up front. Then, I felt like maybe in doing that, that I had mind-fucked him into feeling an emotional connection with me. That by laying out my life challenges and mistakes for him, I'd conned him into pitying me. He is an empath after all. Maybe he can't stop himself from caring. Or maybe I'm smarter and more manipulative than I gave myself credit for. Whatever the reason for him being interested in me, I wasn't going to fuck this up. I promised myself I was done fucking things up. Which I was sure was a lie, but it was a little white lie I told myself. And one I desperately needed for inspiration to fuel me.

Between Chances's shift work at the hospital and my nights at the club, we hadn't found time for a second date. Dating seemed too conventional for us anyway. The last thing I wanted to do after a day with The Stooges was go bowling and be subjected to those rental bowling shoes superficially sprayed with disinfectant that I was certain contained at least one strain of fungus and a flesh eating bacteria the CDC hadn't even discovered yet. I didn't want to deal with all the dating hoopla either. Like dressing up in nice clothes, which I didn't even have. Then there's all the dating dilemmas. Like what restaurant should we go to? And do I let him pay for the date or be an ardent feminist and insist that I pay? Or should we go dutch? The word "should" seemed to imply some kind of a threat and always tripped me up a bit. And I wasn't one for social niceties, which I side-stepped, preferring to just get to the point without all the overthinking that these kinds of things seemed to require. Lucky for me Chance's love language was also brutal honesty, although his delivery was so charming it bordered on intoxicating. I know this because we talked on the phone every day for an hour or longer since we'd met for coffee at Perkatory. Our conversations delved into topics ranging from the every day drudgery of doing shift work at the hospital, to my challenges of being a pseudo single parent, to us both commiserating about growing up Catholic, and of course, heated debates over the best music, movies and books. I didn't know it was possible to find someone's addiction to reading and watching science fiction movies endearing. But, maybe that's just because I hadn't been forced to sit through two hours and forty minutes of 2001: A Space Odyssey (one of his favorites) with him yet. And I hadn't subjected him to enduring my epic mood swings and it's accompanying soundtrack that includes The Smiths, Jeff Buckley, Nina Simone and The Clash on repeat. Maybe little things like these would prove to be barriers to us ever becoming a real couple. According to People magazine, celebrity relationships end for stupid, petty reasons all the time. But, what about real people, with real problems living on really small incomes? What about us? How could we find out if we were good for each other if we couldn't even find time to see each other - even though we really wanted to?

The next morning I'd have two kids arriving on my doorstep at 8:00am when Henna's Hands officially opened. The first was Aiden, a 3 year old only child with some separation anxiety. I started to panic wondering what I'd gotten myself into. I'm no expert on child psychology,

I was just going on the instinct that art was therapeutic, at least it seemed to be for The Stooges and me. I met Gina, Aiden's mom at Max's kindergarten concert where the kids stood on stage whacking large plastic tubes with sticks. It wasn't my idea of music, but who was I to judge? Music is just as subjective as art is. Gina only lived two blocks away from me and was going back to work as a bookkeeper at an architecture firm after being a stay-at-home mom since Aiden was born. Her husband Spencer traveled out of town frequently working in some kind of sales, the nature of which I didn't catch. Chance found Audrey through his work. She was a precocious four year old, who was mature beyond her years because she had an older and more worldly sixteen year old sister. Her mom, Denise, was a nurse at Lostport Hospital and she was looking for a day care that would challenge her exceptionally bright, albeit not artistically inclined, daughter. But, also one that was affordable on her modest income. Jack and Casey rounded out my preschool students. I wasn't sure exactly how it was going to work. I only knew that it had to work so I could make enough money to keep the house. Hoping that having a home and working my ass off at a stable job, would somehow be enough to convince a judge that I should keep custody of The Stooges. The kids I not only loved as my own, but thought of as my own too. Not because this is what Lara wanted. But, because this had become not only what we all needed, but also what I wanted.

It was a few exhausting days into having four kids to occupy, feed and challenge for nine hours straight. Audrey had taken to bossing around the boys whom she found inattentive and a bit needy. Granted, she was right about that, but she was the one who was insufferable. Casey had become uncharacteristically quiet since the new preschool kids "stole my house" as she put it. While no one claimed responsibility for clogging the toilet on the third day of preschool, I was sure it was Casey. That she was backsliding a bit with the adjustment of sharing both the house and my attention with other kids. Casey always had a very Freudian way of coping with change by either peeing her pants or trying to withhold her poop, a tactic that usually backfired and resulted in her pooping her pants. As odd of a set up for romance as it was, it was that clogged toilet that lead to me finally getting a second date with Chance. Not the date I imagined, but one befitting of the extremely glamorous lifestyle to which I'd become accustomed. When I was talking to Chance on the phone after Aiden and Audrey got picked up, I mentioned the toilet clog and how I couldn't afford to pay a plumber after hours rates to come out and look at it. He insisted on coming over to see if he could fix it. It seemed way too early in our relationship for him to see my house and meet The Stooges, never mind to look at my toilet. But, since I really didn't have any other plan of how to fix it, the only toilet in the house, I let him come over with a box of tools to see if there was anything he could do.

My suspicions were proven correct. Maybe I had some mother's intuition after all. Chance found a small pair of petal pink panties stuck in the toilet. Casey had attempted to flush the evidence of her accident. I couldn't really blame her and it did seem like a high level cover-up for a three year old; a real sign of intelligence on her part. If she threw them in the trash I was sure to find them immediately because they would've left a foul stench in the bathroom and she would've been discovered. By flushing the evidence of her accident down the toilet she avoided any consequences that might result from the incident. The bonus of Casey's unintended consequences from the mishap being that I finally got to see Chance again. Which was pure genius.

After a long day The Stooges were finally asleep in bed. Chance and I were sitting next to each other on the couch, too tired to laugh at how entirely laughable the evening was. How we looked like a family shopping for a new toilet together with The Stooges in tow at Lowe's. Then the two of us huddled in the bathroom next to each other with a vanilla scented candle flickering. I'd say the candle was to add romance, but it was just to help disguise the foul odor coming from the old toilet while we installed the new American Standard together. And by "together" I mean he installed the toilet while I handed him the tools he asked for while I ogled him like he was the god of home improvement while he did it. There's nothing sexier than a man who knows how to fix things.

We were both reaching for the remote to turn on the TV when his fingers grazed the top of my hand, sending an electric current through the rest of body. Our heads turned away from the TV and towards each other. We studied each other's eyes for what seemed like an eternity. His blue eyes had flecks of olive green and were framed perfectly by his ginger eyelashes. He looked at me intensely with his brows furrowed. I couldn't help myself from staring at his mouth. It was perfectly sensuous with his bottom lip slightly fuller than the top. I wanted him to just fucking kiss me already.

When he leaned in toward me there was a faint smell of pepperoni on his breath from the pizza we had delivered and eaten with The Stooges earlier. Finally he kissed me. His soft lips barely touching mine; kissing me tenderly and innocently. I'd say it felt like the first time I'd ever been kissed, but since it actually was the first time, I had nothing to compare it too. But, I knew I didn't want it to stop. He reached his hands up to cradle the back of my head. I could feel the unshaven scruff on his chiseled cleft chin brush against my cheek. Then he started nibbling and sucking my bottom lip slowly between his. His lips became more insistent and pleading before he slid his tongue inside my mouth. It felt like he was making out with my soul. I sunk deeper into the couch cushions with his body pressing into mine, returning his kisses. I freed my arm that was lodged between his ribs and the decorative pillows, reaching around him to stroke the back of his neck. Running my fingers over the short bristles at the base of his hairline and then down to the sleek skin on his neck. The contrast between smooth and rough was so incredibly sensual, the sensation overwhelmed my fingertips. My attention wandered to his ears. I'd never noticed how perfect they were before. They complemented the structure of his masculine face perfectly; neither too prominent, nor too inconspicuous. I took one of his earlobes between my fingers, caressing it before tracing my fingertips down his neck to the collar of his shirt. I slowly unsnapped the pearl snap buttons of his plaid shirt, moving my hands down his chest as I did. He pulled away from me briefly to take it off and pull the white v neck T-shirt that was underneath it over his head. Revealing his broad shoulders and a patch of ginger hair that stretched across the expanse of his chest, thinning into a trail down his stomach and under his boxer shorts that peeked out over his belted jeans.

Thank god when Chance insisted on coming over, I instinctually changed out of my big baggy sweatshirt and sports bra, swapping it out for my best black push-up bra I bought when I started working at the Booby Trap with a tight fitting black T-shirt over top of it. Because that's when he pulled my T-shirt up slowly over my head, careful not to catch it on my face, before throwing it on the floor. Hungry for more, we pressed up against each other to kiss again, the bare skin of our stomachs touching. His fingers traced the straps of my bra, building the anticipation before he reached behind my back to unclasp it. He looked into my eyes as he cupped my breasts in his hands only to retract them and pull away from kissing me. He started at my neck, kissing his way down to my chest, my back arching when I felt his lips tease my nipple. He kissed it and flicked it with his tongue taking my other breast in his hand pinching the nipple gently between his fingers. His free hand reaching down to search for the button on my jeans. Hastily, he unfastened them and slid them down over my hips and I wriggled myself out of them. He propped himself up on his side with one hand holding his head up to watch me, using his other hand to trace his fingers down my body, across my paunchy stomach until he reached my inner thighs. Before his fingers wandered and he began caressing me over my cotton bikini underwear while his head leaned over my chest, grazing my flesh with the stubble on his chin while he licked and sucked my nipple with his tongue. My heart raced. My body moved in time with his and I couldn't contain my moans. He moved my panties to the side sliding his finger inside me. I couldn't hold back any longer. I was writhing, throbbing and pulsing with more pleasure than I'd ever felt before. After I orgasmed, I started sobbing while he held me.

"You okay, Hennessy?" He looked at the tears streaming down my face.

"Never better." I said looking into his eyes with a shy smile.

Then we made love.

CHAPTER 25

I'd spent weeks consumed with anxiety over the rapidly approaching court date with Dickhead for custody of The Three Stooges. In the short amount of time since I got served with court papers, I'd finally gotten my life straightened out. Not that being twenty-two years old is late for finding a direction in life, even if it turns out to be the wrong direction. In fact, it's painfully young to have so much responsibility thrust upon you. I'd taken in three young kids when most people my age were graduating from college. Excited to start their careers only to be disappointed when they find out that their college education only gets them a cubical and a bare basics medical plan without dental, if that. Whereas I skipped college altogether and got schooled by life instead. Rule 1: Life is completely unfair. Rule 2: Suck it up. I thought I was sucking it up all along. But, when I was confronted with the possibility of losing The Stooges I realized that I'd mistaken giving up for sucking it up. Passively letting life happen to you is giving up. While sucking it up implies you're actively fighting for the life you want. Rule 3: Fix your fuck ups. I finally stopped making excuses for myself: I stopped drinking, changed careers and reconciled with my dad. And it was all so much simpler than I imagined it would be. The extra added bonus of my newfound clean living was falling in love with Chance in the process. I finally felt that I deserved it, all of it.

It'd been nine months since Lara died and I became the guardian of The Stooges, the same duration as a pregnancy. But, I didn't have months to anticipate or prepare for the arrival of kids the way most mothers do. It was instantaneous. It was sink or swim from the beginning. And now it was all over. I was sitting in my kitchen in an outdated navy blue pant suit I'd bought at the thrift store because I thought it made me look older and wise enough not to be concerned with what's trendy and fashionable. But most importantly, it was cheap and I was being fiscally responsible because I was only going to be wearing it one day out of my life. Which also happened to be the biggest most important day of my life. One long, excruciating day spent at the court house where a complete stranger had complete control over the fate of my sister's kids. I slumped over the kitchen table sitting in one of the four unmatched wooden kitchen chairs: the one with a short leg that wobbles when you shift your weight. My dad sat next to me rubbing my head at the scalp like he did the day my mom passed away. And again on the day my sister died leaving me to care for her kids.

"Tell me how this happened." I begged my dad for answers.

"I've already told you," my dad replied.

"I want to hear it again." I said childishly.

"Ok then, I'll tell you again. Do you want to move to the couch where it's more comfortable? Or change your clothes first maybe?" He urged me.

"No. I don't want to be comfortable, I need to hear how this happened."

"I think you need to hear it from someone else who can explain it better than I can."

He picked up his cell phone, excused himself to the living room and made a call while I sat mortified thinking about all the disparaging things my father had heard about me at court. The worst part being, they were all true.

I thought when I deleted the photos from my phone and the thread from my Twitter account that they were gone forever. But, in the digital age, nothing is ever erased completely. Especially nude photos. Especially when the recipient, @AverageGuy, turned out to be anything but an average guy. I found out in the courtroom it was Dickhead; looking for a way to discredit me as a suitable guardian of his kids. I don't know how he found my Twitter account in the first place or why I sent him the incriminating nudes he was after. Other than the fact that I was drunk and desperately seeking validation. That's why he brought the photos to court. He was using them to try to get custody back from me, not because he wanted to raise, love and nurture his own kids. He was fighting for custody because he didn't want me to have them. Because that would mean he lost the battle for control he'd been waging against Lara and then after she died, it got passed down to me. And given the chance, he'd do the same to his own kids. Exerting control over them in an attempt to feel more secure about himself. That's what abusers do. I never considered why he became an abusive dickhead before.

It never mattered to me which played a bigger role in his childhood; nature or nurture. Until he mentioned his parents at court that day.

Dickhead explained to Judge Hannigan that his plan to care for his kids included his mother who would "help him out with the kids from time to time". Which translated from Dickheadese into English as "I'm gonna dump these kids on my mom for her to raise". I prayed that the judge was also fluent in Dickheadese. Don't abusive parents learn how to be that way by being abused as kids? Isn't it a vicious cycle of violence that repeats itself? I admit I didn't know anything about Dickhead's childhood or his parents and I didn't have any sympathy for whatever he went through that made him into the monster he was. All I knew was that The Stooges were better off with me than being raised by him or his parents.

Dickhead could put on a good act of being a concerned dad under the right conditions, for a limited amount of time, when there weren't any kids around that needed him to actually parent them. I learned that the day he showed up at Haven Hills Elementary for the conference about Max. The key was shutting his mouth and keeping quiet so he didn't incriminate himself. Something he couldn't afford to do at court since he was representing himself, just like I was. At least we were on a level playing field in that respect. Forcing him to muster up all the charm he had to put on his best performance for the judge. My dad hung up the phone and handed me an address written in pencil on a torn brown paper lunch bag I'd bought at a craft supplies store for my daycare.

"What's this?" I asked grabbing it and giving it a perfunctory glance. "128 Locust Street." I read baffled.

"This is where you're going to go to get the answers you need." He said.

"If you're too exhausted and need to go home you could just tell me and we could call it a night. You don't have to pawn me off to someone else." I said defensively.

"I'm not pawning you off. It's just that I haven't told you the whole story and I think you need to hear it from her."

"Her? Who's her?"

"Amitty."

"Amitty? My old boss from The Sweat Shop at the mall?"

"Do you know anyone else named Amitty?"

"What does a woman I haven't spoken to in years, have to do with any of this?" I asked, confused.

"Just drive to that address, it's not far from here. She's waiting for you. I'll be here holding down the fort when you get back. Although I might be asleep on the couch. Today was a draining day for an old man with a weak heart."

I waited for what seemed like an eternity standing under a dim porch light at the front door of an unfamiliar house. Inspecting the wreath made of twigs and dried flowers that was affixed to the door by a piece of twine tied around a nail hanging directly in my line of sight. The slender ribbon interwoven in the branches read 'You belong among the wildflowers' in a sleepy, free-flowing, black, cursive script. This was all the confirmation I needed that I'd arrived at the right doorstep. Amitty always had a very hippyish vibe about her.

When she answered the door, she still had the same long gray hair, but had gained about thirty pounds since I'd seen her last. Which was nearly five years earlier when I quit working for her to move to Niagara Falls and work at Doodles art supply store.

"Hennessy," she said in a familiar, but more breathy voice than I'd remembered while gesturing for me to come in.

"I know you've had an emotional day. And I can't hear so well anymore even with my hearing aid in. So, let's skip the chit chat and whatnot and get right to it shall we?"

I nodded in agreement. She eased herself down to sit in an arm chair and I took a spot on the floral patterned couch directly across from her.

"I made a mistake that I needed to correct." She told me. "Let me start at the beginning." That's when she told me her story.

Starting with when she gave her child up for adoption all those years ago. And how a part of her died when she saw her daughter for the last time at the hospital before her adoptive family took her home and she became their daughter. Instead of going back home and finishing high school, she met a man named Ray and got married. When she changed her last name to her husband's she also changed her first name from Sandra to Amitty, trying to make a clean break from her parents who'd shamed her into giving her baby up for adoption. With her new name and new husband, she started a new life for herself hoping it would extinguish the guilt that she'd harbored for allowing anyone to force her into giving up her daughter. Of course she was glad her daughter was in a good home. Or she assumed she was in a good home anyway. Because no one ever asked what she wanted for her child. Furthermore, she didn't have a say in selecting the adoptive parents because even though she was the biological mother, she was also still a minor. Her guilt and resentment about giving up her daughter only grew over the years when she didn't have any other children of her own. When she first saw me that day in the mall, a sullen girl with chip on her shoulder, she was reminded of herself at that age; lost and angsty. Since she couldn't go back and change her path, she thought maybe in some small way she could help guide me on mine. That's why she offered me a job.

When she deduced that my best friend Tonya was pregnant, it triggered all those old bitter feelings of not having a choice about what happened to her body or her baby. She wanted to give Tonya the choice that she never had, which is why she arranged and paid for her abortion. She thought of it as an act of kindness and compassion. Until a couple of years ago.

That's when she got a message from a stranger on Facebook. A woman in her forties, informing Amitty that she was a grandmother. That woman was her daughter, Felicity. She'd been searching adoption forums for years trying to find her birth mom. Amitty changing her name so many years ago had complicated the paper trail. They messaged each other back and forth for weeks before they were both ready to meet in person. When Amitty arrived at the restaurant for lunch, she recognized her daughter as soon as she walked in. Felicity was sitting at a table alone, nervously bouncing her leg under the table. She had clear bright blue eyes and thick wavy dirty blonde hair cut into a long bob mirroring the features of Amitty as a younger woman. Felicity must've seen an older version of herself in Amitty because she rose from her seat to embrace her before Amitty even arrived at the table. Their conversation flowed as naturally as did their tears of joy. She had found the daughter she thought she had lost forever. In an instant everything changed. The forty something year lapse in time since she'd last seen her daughter seemed transitory and unimportant. All that mattered was that they had each other now.

It was a compelling story and I was happy for her, but I didn't see how any of it had to do with me.

It was about a month earlier that Amitty had a chance meeting with my dad while he was exercising his injured knee, walking laps in the mall when he bumped into her stocking T-shirts at The Sweat Shop. When they started talking she mentioned she was trying to find Tonya and me. She didn't tell him the reason, but she told me it was to help relieve the recent guilt she'd had over not trying to talk Tonya out of having an abortion. It was during her conversation with my dad in the middle of the mall where he told her that my sister had died and that I was going to court for a custody battle to keep her children.

After talking to my dad, she figured that with the stress of the impending court case on my shoulders, it wasn't a good time to contact me in order to explain everything and apologize for what she perceived as her negligence in not counseling Tonya or suggesting other options for her situation. Instead she called the court clerk's office to see who the judge assigned to my case was. It was nothing really, she said. She didn't interfere with fate. She just did some research and flagged some records pertinent to the case. She submitted what she found to the clerk's office and ensured that the judge would see them. She'd found several old domestic violence reports that Lara had filed. And two recent ones filed by two different women I'd assumed were girlfriends of his at some point. Who knows how many others there were who didn't call the police or file a report the way I'd neglected to the first time Dickhead assaulted me. In retrospect, it seemed so absolutely stupid and irresponsible. What was I thinking? I was just helping him maintain his cover as a stand up guy, so he could keep on abusing other women. The fact that he'd abused other women wasn't a surprise to me. But, finding out through Amitty's detective work that he'd served time for running a meth lab out of a rental property owned by his parents was. That's why he didn't fight me to get custody of the kids when Lara died, because he couldn't do that from prison. Which might have something to do with why his parents hadn't pursued custody of the kids either, because they wanted to keep the fact that they'd owned a meth lab and had a son who was incarcerated buried. And those took priority over having a relationship with their grandkids.

I was in court to hear Judge Hannigan address each and every one of Rick's offenses in detail, in person. And I still don't know exactly what it was that made Dickhead decide to sign papers terminating his parental rights, right there in the middle of the courtroom with plenty of witnesses looking on in disbelief. And I can't claim that I care what motivated him to do it. Because it was finally over. The Three Stooges were staying with me. Before I left the court that day, I filed a petition to adopt my niece and nephews. The hearing to finalize the adoption was set for the following month, in front of the Family Court judge who also happened to be Amitty's daughter, Felicity Hannigan.

EPILOUGE

It's been ten years since I adopted The Three Stooges. Max and Jack are annoying, know-it-all teenagers (the way all teenagers are) now. And Casey is a beautiful, self-conscious tween who spends too much time on her phone and re-evaluates her personal brand daily. We had some rough years to get where we are now. Going to therapy helped, especially Jack who it turns out did suffer from an attachment disorder. And putting Max on medication for his ADHD also made a big difference. As for Casey, after the adoption was finalized, she was finally completely potty trained and never had another accident.

Between work, the kid's sports and me being the official chauffeur of my kids' social lives, our house is constantly in a state of semi-functional chaos. Although, we do make a point to get together and have a family dinner at my dad's house every Tuesday. A house he's shared with Amitty for almost a decade now. Not as a couple, but as unlikely best friends and life companions. I never expected my conventional, traditional father to find a deep and meaningful friendship with a woman who's free spirited and unrestrained, but somehow it works. It was Amitty who was able to help my dad to give up drinking for good. I'd always worried that it interfered with his heart medication. I'm not sure that it's the reason he was more energetic and engaged these days or because Amitty had a way of coaxing his emotions out of him. He in turn, gave Amitty a quiet sense of stability and strength that she needed. And sharing a mortgage on their fixed incomes was mutually beneficial too. We even saw Felicity from time to time too, usually on holidays, birthdays or other special occasions.

It was Chance who encouraged me to follow my dream and go back to school to get my degree in Art Therapy. Likewise, I supported him when he told me he wanted to get his doctorate in nursing at a university in Florida. I knew the distance would be a heavy hit to our relationship, but I encouraged him to go do it anyway. I didn't want to hold him back from his aspirations. We were both committed to making our long distance relationship work. We FaceTimed and bridged the gap from being apart from each other with short visits back and forth to try to keep our connection strong. We held on for another year that way before we ultimately accepted that we both needed to move on. If I hadn't loved him so much, I wouldn't have been able to let him go. And in some ways I never did let go. I've held on to the kindness and the love he gave me. He believed in me before I believed in myself. In a weird way I think it was Chance led me to find my husband.

I was at a seminar on therapy treatments for trauma survivors held in the conference room of the Lostport Hospital where Chance used to work. The guest speaker was the renowned Buffalo psychologist, Matt Stone. After he spoke, I went up and introduced myself. I'd been working as an art therapist for over a year at the time and I knew I needed to network to expand my client base. Our relationship started out professional, with him sending me articles and job leads. But, things quickly turned personal. Though he was ten years older than me, his mostly gray hair made our age difference look more pronounced than it was. But, on closer inspection, his boyish good looks and fit body made him appear to be in his mid-thirties the same as me. Matt's soft spoken, but hardworking nature reminded me so much of Chance, which is probably why I fell for him so hard so fast. Except Matt wasn't going anywhere and neither was I. We were married six months after we met. There was only one condition to our marriage: The Stooges and I would keep our last name Greypath, in honor of Lara.

ACKNOWLEDGMENTS

Writing a book can seem like an extraordinary waste of time while you're doing it. Even more so when you're avoiding writing altogether because it's such an excruciatingly painful process. Finishing is it's own reward. But even after the writing is finished, there's still more work to be done. In some ways, it's just beginning. Because now you need to start the process of editing, publishing and getting it out there for people to read. Thankfully, I had help.

Annie Lane, who volunteered to read and edit the very rough first draft. Thank you for encouraging and supporting me. Victoria Young, for proofreading my manuscript. Thank you for making me look far more polished than I actually am. Lisa Perzentka, who took an idea from my head and created a brilliant cover design that captures the essence of the book. I cherish my friendships with all three of you. I'd also like to thank my faithful blog readers and social media followers for staying with me through it all. And of course, my family, who has no choice but to stick with me because they're stuck with me forever.

ABOUT THE AUTHOR

Marie Loerzel is a Certified Grief Recovery Specialist. She lives in Colorado with her husband and four children. *Greypath* is her first novel. She's also the author of *Rock the Kasbah: A Memoir of Misadventure.*

www.ingramcontent.com/pod-product-compliance
Lightning Source LLC
Chambersburg PA
CBHW072257130726
47910CB00012B/2053